"Top-no... WITHDRAWN

"Sweazy writes the most realistic and exciting accounts of the Rangers, bar none . . . The reader feels as if he is right there, fighting the dust, heat, flies, and fear, riding into the thick of battle . . . gut-wrenching . . . completely true to life."
—*Roundup Magazine*

"Josiah Wolfe is a complex and interesting character."
—*Buddies in the Saddle*

"Sweazy fills his action-packed book with moral issues [and] sketches out fully dimensional characters and vivid descriptions."
—*Nuvo*

THE COYOTE TRACKER

"A masterful page-turner full of suspense and surprises. It demonstrates the skill that has won Sweazy an appreciative following and numerous awards and recognition."
—*Buddies in the Saddle*

"A great entry in what has become one of the more solid Westerns still coming out. This harkens back to the old writers of the Old West . . . It's the Western that Erle Stanley Gardner never wrote."
—*Bookgasm*

continued . . .

THE COUGAR'S PREY

"[A] gem among gems. Sweazy is a superb storyteller, and this quick-moving yarn is cut from tightly woven cloth. He breathes life into the frontier, and readers are immersed in the sights, sounds, and ever-present threat of death lurking at every corner."　　　　　　—Phil Dunlap, author of *Cotton's Inferno*

"Larry D. Sweazy once again spins a fine historical adventure full of compelling characters and gritty action."
　　　　　　　　　　　　　　　　　　—James Reasoner

THE BADGER'S REVENGE

"A richly layered story that offers twists and turns that dare the reader to speculate who is guilty and why."
　　　　　　—Matthew P. Mayo, author of *Speaking Ill of the Dead*

"[A] fine entry to a great Western series . . . Wherever he goes, I'm on board, through thick and thin."　　—*Bookgasm*

THE SCORPION TRAIL

"Larry D. Sweazy's Josiah Wolfe books promise to stand among the great Western series. Think *The Rifleman* in the deft hands of a Larry McMurtry or a Cormac McCarthy."
　　　　　　—Loren D. Estleman, Spur Award–winning author of
　　　　　　　　　　　　　　　　　The Confessons of Al Capone

"Larry D. Sweazy takes you on a fierce ride with his memorable Texas Ranger Josiah Wolfe. This crisp, well-written story returns you to the West as it really was—and you'll like being there."

　　　　　　—Cotton Smith, author of *Sons of Thunder* and
　　　　　　　　　　　　　past president of Western Writers of America

VENGEANCE AT SUNDOWN

A Lucas Fume Western

LARRY D. SWEAZY

B

BERKLEY BOOKS, NEW YORK

THE BERKLEY PUBLISHING GROUP
Published by the Penguin Group
Penguin Group (USA) LLC
375 Hudson Street, New York, New York 10014

USA • Canada • UK • Ireland • Australia • New Zealand • India • South Africa • China

penguin.com

A Penguin Random House Company

VENGEANCE AT SUNDOWN

A Berkley Book / published by arrangement with the author

For information, address: The Berkley Publishing Group,
a division of Penguin Group (USA) LLC,
375 Hudson Street, New York, New York 10014.

ISBN: 978-0-425-26932-9

PUBLISHING HISTORY
Berkley mass-market edition / August 2014

PRINTED IN THE UNITED STATES OF AMERICA

10 9 8 7 6 5 4 3 2 1

Cover illustration by Bruce Emmett.
Cover design by Diana Kolsky.
Interior text design by Kelly Lipovich.

For Robert J. Conley

ACKNOWLEDGMENTS

I am lucky to have a lot of people in my life who enjoy stories. Special thanks go to Liz and Chris Hatton, who listen to my stories and offer encouragement along the way. It was in a discussion with them that the name Bojack Wu came up. I was immediately fascinated with the name and was happy to have permission to use it. Thank you. My Bojack Wu is a made-up character and is not based on anyone living or dead.

Thanks also go to my agent, Cherry Weiner, for continuing to keep the flames lit to my dream. You are tireless, relentless, and some days you make me laugh when I need it the most.

I feel really fortunate to get to continue to work with the same editor, Faith Black, that I have worked with on my previous books. My books are better because of your work. Thank you.

And finally, thank you to Rose—my wife, my best friend, my first reader, my champion. We had greater personal challenges during the writing of this book than any that I can remember. We survived like we always survive: by hanging on and refusing to give in, or give up. I couldn't do what I do without you.

PART I

Desperation at Sunrise

Nothing can bring you peace but yourself. Nothing can bring you peace but
the triumph of principles.

—RALPH WALDO EMERSON, FROM *SELF-
RELIANCE* (ESSAYS: FIRST SERIES)

ONE

LUCAS FUME DREW BACK JUST IN TIME, ducking a hard punch. The only weapons he had to defend himself with were his wits and his fists; everything else had been stolen from him longer ago than he wanted to admit. There was no time to ask his attacker about the offense made, or to reason his way out of it. Like so many times before, this attack had come out of nowhere.

Every second of every day in the Tennessee State Prison was a matter of life and death. There was no such thing as being safe. Not in prison, not locked away behind cold iron bars, or out in the open in the cavernous mess hall, where he had been standing minding his own business.

Fighting on an empty stomach was as natural as breathing to Lucas, and he was happy to oblige the attacker no matter the cause. He was accustomed to attempts on his life—at least this fighter had come straight on, instead of from behind like so many of the other failures. It did nothing but fuel his fire.

Lucas had been enraged since the first day he'd been dragged, kicking and screaming, inside the filthy prison, and that rage had only grown the longer he'd been forced to remain locked up for a crime that he most certainly did not commit.

Every man in prison claimed innocence, but in his case, it was the truth. He had been falsely accused of murder, railroaded by powers beyond his own reach, and tossed in a cell, with the key thrown away forever.

"Get 'im, Fume!" someone shouted from behind him.

"Kill the bastard," another man yelled. "I never liked that surly son of a bitch in the first place."

It only took Lucas a second to size up his opponent. He was tall as a ladder, bony as a sturgeon, and uglier than a pale white nag horse—but strong and light on his feet, that much was obvious. The attacker's name was unknown to him, but his reputation as a troublemaker, a leader of sorts to a gang of his own ilk, had not gone unnoticed by Lucas in the days past. He had been wary of the man from the first sighting.

This fight was not for honor. Most likely, it was a show of power and nothing more. Lucas had a reputation as a hard fighter, a tough opponent to beat. A victory over him would be a feather in the stranger's cap, garner him even more respect.

The pale man looked surprised at his missed punch. He spit at the floor in disgust, barely missing Lucas's foot with his foulness, then turned up his lip for another round, and a surer aim. He cocked his fists upward as if the fight had been preordained at a set time and place.

Whispers of wagers started to make the rounds, passing from man to man. The bet-taker, a sheepish man dressed in tattered gray rags, and a known prevaricator, offered unknown currency to the victors.

The prizes ranged from extra food at evening meals to protection in the depths of the night, or whenever needed, from the legion of maniacal and, often, sadistic guards. There were a hundred different types of money in prison.

Lucas stepped back, nearly bumping into the wall of men that had suddenly surrounded the two pugilists like a living, breathing boxing ring.

Entertainment was not expected, it was demanded. The moment a line was crossed, a punch thrown, or curses exchanged inside the walls of the prison, the prospect of a fight brought sudden joy to the mundane drudgery of every day.

Chants rose to the roof like the opening chorus of a cathedral hymn; only there would be no salvation at the end of this fight, just an accession to the top of the ranks of toughness—if it came to that.

Lucas quickly gathered his thoughts and calculated his next move.

Big men had reach and power, but they were usually clumsy on their feet, slower than they thought they were. On the other hand, Lucas was of medium height, solidly built, and quick on his feet, like a good fighter should be. He'd spent his lonely hours in his cell keeping as fit as possible, by walking in circles, squatting repetitively, lifting himself up and down prone to the floor, passing the time as positively as he could, preparing for whatever the future threw at him. Given the gruel and poor diet he was forced to accept, some days the only protein he ate were the roaches floating belly-up in his soup. All things considered, he was in pretty good physical shape.

Lucas was confident in his skills and ability, as confident as he could be with the key to his freedom tossed to the wind, but he knew little of his opponent, his past or his training. Something had propelled the pale man to challenge him, and Lucas had no earthly idea what that something was outside of the organizer taking bets. It didn't matter. The fight was started, and an end to it was a pleasure to face. Passing up a fight rarely occurred to Lucas, and losing a match of this type was rarer.

Lucas's reaction to the realization of his perceived advantage against the pale man was instant.

Instinct drove him straight at his leering opponent, on the inside, ducking low, sliding straight up the man's body like a squirrel skittering to the top of a tree. He landed a hard, perfectly placed blow to the man's jaw before the attacker could even think about launching a follow-up to his original punch.

The echo of the hit reverberated throughout the hall like the loud smash of a cymbal in a marching band, announcing something more to come.

The pale man spit again. A pair of rotted teeth exploded outward from his mouth, quickly followed by a stream of warm blood.

Dead men smelled better, but Lucas wasn't about to step away; he was in close enough to do some real damage and end the fight before it got out of hand. Be done with it, eat breakfast, and return to his cell alone, a victor left to his spoils, another notch on his belt, and a silent hope that he would have a day left alone to himself.

If it was a show of power the man wanted, then by God, that's what he'd get. Lucas had no posse or gang to impress, just the population of the prison as a whole. The last thing he could afford to do was show any weakness at all. Predators of all types waited in the shadows.

Lucas followed up the first punch with a quick left jab to the man's sternum, knocking the wind out of his fragile chest, sending him flailing backward into the crowd so deep that he nearly disappeared.

The chants transformed to cheers and more yells. It was a real fight now—gladiators surrounded by a bored and hungry crowd. The smell of blood was in the air, and the crowd continued to grow in size and volume. But all Lucas could hear was his own heartbeat. His focus was on the fight and nowhere else. Finish it, end it, beat the man to within an inch of his life, but leave him living as an example. No matter the right of self-defense, there was no just cause to see the pale man to his death—at least at the moment, under the current circumstances. Though he would kill him if he had to, there was no question about that.

The blood in Lucas's own veins ran fast. He felt nothing in the heat of battle but hot adrenaline, a sweet drug he'd learned to crave a long time ago. His rage transformed into the desire to survive, to live—not to see another day, those far hopes had been vanquished—but to see the next minute, the next second, because that's all there was. Dreams. Prosperity. Hope. Those words had ceased to exist in his mind, in his heart, from the first moment the cell door had locked behind him, and his prison nightmare had become an unending reality.

Lucas rushed in toward the man, but stopped just short of his reach. His opponent had produced a shiv, a thin piece of wood sharpened and honed over time, and out of the sight of the guards, to resemble a real knife. The crude weapon could be just as deadly as a knife forged of the finest metal if it was used properly and thrust into the right part of the body.

Sweat dripped down Lucas's forehead and crossed his lips; the taste of his own saltiness was pungent, but it reminded him that he was still very much alive. His hair, solid black and shoulder-length, was soaked wet, like he had suddenly stepped out into a thunderous rainstorm. It felt heavy, like a helmet, but offered no protection, nor did his beard. It was thick and unkempt; formal mirrors and razors were unheard of here. He looked like a backwoodsman or a fellow countryman, fresh off the boat from Scotland. Pride in his appearance had been one of the first things to go.

The air inside the hall had suddenly turned hot, and the light dimmed, turned to a diffused gray. It was more like early evening instead of morning inside the fortified limestone walls of the prison.

Tension between the prisoners had been thick for the past

few days, unsettled as if a storm was coming—except there was no horizon on which to see it looming. The prison's windows were sparse, up high, glazed with the sooty grime of years of neglect.

Maybe this fight had been brewing longer than he knew, and Lucas had just not noticed, but he doubted that. He tried to constantly be aware of his surroundings. It was his training, his way, to notice everything, and everyone, to calculate his own survival, his own safety. It was rare that he would miss an event like this one. He was a planner, a plotter, a thinker—or he had been once upon a time. Maybe the time in prison had dulled his senses more than he thought. It was the only explanation for his current situation that made any sense at all.

The pale man stepped back out of the wall of men, his shoulders squared, a slightly dazed look in his eyes, the shiv held tightly at his waist.

"You think that weapon scares me?" Lucas said. "Looks like your little pecker is sticking out. Which ain't too far, if you ask me. I'd be embarrassed to show it in public if I was you."

The crowd laughed and hee-hawed.

The pale man glanced quickly at the knife, then back to Lucas. "Ain't no pecker."

Lucas thought about making his move then, but he waited. The man had shown he could be distracted, and that was all Lucas needed to know.

His attacker wiped bloody drool from the corner of his mouth with the back of his hand, ignored the laughs, and scowled. His face was as serious as an undertaker's. "You're a little pecker is what you are, Lucas Fume. Won't be the first one I cut off, neither."

"Oh, a competition? Do you dance, too?" Lucas swayed right and left, drawing a few more chuckles from the crowd. It was a show now. He needed as many fans as he could get if things turned out differently than he thought.

"I've kilt more'n one of you black-haired, black-eyed, heartless traitors, and I'll be happy to do it again." The pale man's face was no longer white but blushed red from the base of his throat upward.

"Traitor is a serious thing to call a man." Lucas's tone grew stern. He gripped his fists tighter.

"Scores still need settling no matter what the words on paper say, no matter what the lyin' politicians and lawyers say about the end of things. Any man who thinks the war is over is a fool. You wore the blue uniform and the gray. Which was you? I say you was a Federal all along."

"I don't have to defend my service to you. I wore whatever uniform, or getup, served the cause."

"So was you a spy? Or a profiteer?"

"Call it what you want."

"Some say you betrayed us at the second Bull Run, held back on what you knew. There's blood on your hands, Fume. Maybe my own kin. I had people die in that battle."

Lucas shrugged; he'd heard that charge before. "Those would be children's tales to get you through the night."

"Don't disrespect me or my dead, or I'll just string out your sufferin' longer. The rebel flag still flies in the hearts of men stronger, and smarter, than you. Deeds still need answering for. Justice will be sought after the last breath of the oldest soldier has been taken. I am the deliverer of said justice. I am here for you, Lucas Fume."

"So you are," Lucas answered. There was an intentional hint of Scottish brogue on the tip of his last words, an exaggerated roll of the tongue offering a reflection of his father's home country more than proof of being an immigrant himself, which he wasn't; he had been born on American soil before the country split in two. "And so you are."

He'd had to answer for his deeds in the war more than enough since the end of it. The past was the past, and it couldn't be undone. Not that he would've changed any of his actions if he could have.

Without any further warning, Lucas dove toward the ground headfirst, tucked into a tight roll, and extended his right leg as he came up, shoving his boot, with full force, directly into the man's groin.

The move shocked the pale man again, giving him no time to get out of the way. He buckled in pain and gasped loudly. The painful sound was like the desperate screech of a rat as its head slammed hard against a wall. The shiv fell to the floor, landing inches from Lucas's hand.

"A man who fights with his feet ain't no man at all," someone shouted in protest.

Lucas ignored the slight. He was still alive. That's all that mattered. This wasn't entertainment; it was life or death. Gentlemen's rules had gone out the window as soon as the pale man produced the weapon.

Lucas grabbed the shiv and jumped up, ready to end the fight. But something had happened when he had been on the ground and faced away, something so unexpected that it nearly took his breath away.

Instead of the pale man coming face-to-face with him, there stood in his place, ready to continue the fight, one of the biggest, angriest looking Negroes Lucas had ever seen—with a real knife in his hands.

TWO

THE TRAIN SPED INTO THE NIGHT, BARRELING out of St. Louis for Kansas City with such fury that Joe Straut feared the wheels would jump the track. He could barely maintain his balance as he made his way from one railcar to the next. There was no explanation for the sudden departure at such a late hour. There never was. But this one felt different, especially coupled with the unexpected demand of his presence from the Boss.

The last passenger car was private, an example of new luxury, like the poorest of the poor could never imagine. The world had changed once the railroad in the West had opened up fast travel. The time from New York to San Francisco had been whittled down to a week or so, instead of the arduous months it once took, not so long ago. And in finer accommodations, too.

This railcar had smooth, rich mahogany wood lining the walls comfortably and covering the curved ceiling in perfect sheets, as if the trees had been made for just that purpose.

It was like walking into an oversized, very expensive pipe. The car glistened with an expensive sheen, and the wood still smelled fresh cut.

The floor was covered with hand-made Oriental wool carpet, red and gold in odd, unidentifiable symmetric patterns that must have meant something to their creator, but not to Straut. The carpet, like a lot of the decorations that adorned the railcar, had been shipped from places that Joe Straut had never heard of, and most likely would never see. It was so soft and pliable that he could barely hear his own footfall.

Dimly lit brass sconces lined the outside wall of the railroad car, offering visible passage to the last set of doors, at the end of the passageway, at any time of day or night. Oddly, there was not a hint of coal oil in the air, and the flames barely flickered with effort to stay lit.

The double doors at the end of the passage were ornately carved with a peacock in each front panel. Behind them was an even more luxurious room, the quarters of the owner of the railcar, and Straut's boss, a man known as Lanford Grips, rarely seen in the light of day, or away from his desk as far as that went.

Straut knew the man's name was a fake, but it didn't matter to him, he just called Lanford Grips the Boss, and tucked the gold coins that were paid to him on the first of every month into his pocket—and left it at that.

The money was a good amount for the deeds that he did, or was expected to do—better than what any other man had ever offered to pay Straut for his services before. He was indebted to the Boss, forever at his beck and call.

The food and comforts in Lanford Grips's midst were better, too, regardless of what the Boss's name really was, or where he got his money from. Hired hands had no business knowing such details, and no one knew that better than Joe Straut. The less you knew, the better off you were.

West of the Mississippi, names didn't seem to matter

much these days. A man could leave the past behind him and start anew with little worry of any questions being asked. Especially if a man had as much money as the Boss had.

The train swayed and rocked furiously, but his time on trains had been long, so Straut was able to steady his balance pretty quickly. All that mattered, at the moment, was that he'd been hailed by the Boss, and answering, sooner rather than later, was in his best interest. Lanford Grips didn't like to be left waiting.

Joe Straut had been a loyal sergeant in the war, seen more years in battle than he liked to admit. He hadn't served with the Boss, but there was no doubt that the Boss had a fighting background, had fought in the War of Northern Aggression. But like almost everything else about him, the specifics of the Boss's duty were unknown. There was no question, judging by his accent, by his manners and likes, that he was a rebel, a man of the South. Gray not blue. The loss had been hard for them all to swallow. Straut could see that in the Boss, too, even though it was never spoken of, or shown in action or material possessions.

Order, discipline, and leadership were rare qualities among common men. Training never wore off. You could see it in how men stood, how they quietly commanded the men around them to do their bidding, and how they reacted when orders went off the rails. Straut had seen the Boss in all of those situations, and the Boss had mirrored Straut's captains' and other officers' actions during the war. There was no question that the Boss had had formal training. Could've been West Point for all Straut knew.

Straut passed smaller berths in the railcar that were reserved for esteemed guests and appointed people within the organization. All of the blinds were closed, the doors locked tight as a bank drawer. With no sounds coming from inside any of the berths, there was no clue to the reason for his call.

The last railcar was silent except for the persistent and urgent rumble of the iron wheels underneath and the huff and puff of the steam locomotive behind Straut. It was long after midnight. Time enough when most decent people should be asleep—as Straut had been before the demanding alarm had roused him. That would explain the silence, but there was a feeling of emptiness in the railcar that had not existed hours before when a group of well-moneyed men and women had been shepherded onto the train and shown to their quarters. These quarters. These silent sleeping quarters.

Two men stood outside the peacock doors that led into Lanford Grips's domain, their eyes focused solely on Straut.

The men were shorter than normal in stature, arms crossed behind their backs, their round, yellow-skinned faces stiff and emotionless as statues'. They were dressed in black tunics and baggy linen pants, their feet in open shoes, flat on the bottom, strapped between the toes.

The men were Chinese, castoffs left with little work now that the railroad had been mostly completed. At least these two had found employment. If they possessed any weapons—knives, guns, or otherwise—Joe Straut had never seen them, but he did not doubt their existence hidden deep somewhere in the foreign clothing.

The Boss would not entrust his security, and safety, to unarmed men. There were rumors that they were hand-and-feet fighters, could kill a man with the quick flick of their palms and nothing more. Straut had never seen such a thing, and didn't want to provoke them to action to see for himself if the gossip was true or not. Rumor and the Boss's choice of their presence outside his door were enough of an endorsement for him.

Both men stiffened and squared their shoulders, like lean guard dogs on the alert, rising out of the shadows, as Straut approached. He half expected them to growl.

Straut stopped before them with a grimace, and tried to remember the latest password. The Boss changed it daily. At times it felt odd. These same two men had allowed him to enter the room multiple times, but they always demanded the password regardless of recognition.

There was, Joe Straut figured, reason to be protective of wealth and physical existence in troubled times, and in dangerous, unknown lands. Outlaws and Indians were out and about on the railroad line, striking anytime they wanted. The advent of trains had brought gold and guns to a desolate and isolated world—there was no one for miles to come to a person's aid. But this depth of security still unsettled Straut, though he didn't protest. He knew better. One day, though, he hoped to gain the Boss's trust so he wouldn't have to remember new passwords. He constantly worried about proving himself.

"Red," Straut finally stuttered to neither man in particular, mostly to the door. He didn't like looking the Chinese in the eyes.

Neither guard moved, or implied that the word was correct. A bead of sweat swelled to existence on Straut's upper lip, and his trigger finger flinched unwittingly. He carried a Colt .45 Open Top, but the holster was buttoned up. If the rumors about the Chinese were true, there wouldn't be enough time to defend himself. Sleepiness had made him sloppy, forgetful.

The guard on the right nodded after taking a long breath, then tapped three times softly in the middle of the door and stood back and waited.

Straut relaxed. Yesterday the password had been "greenhorn," and he had been a little confused about what day it was. Yesterday or today?

Tomorrow was Monday, and he expected the password to be "horn blue one," if he was correct in his thinking. He'd tuck that thought in his memory to see if he was right.

The process to open the door was always the same, too, with the exception of the number of taps and the placement of them. A small brass bell was mounted over the door, and it would tinkle when it was clear to open it.

The train bounded around a curve, and Straut failed to anticipate the sway, to shift his weight properly, and stumbled hard to the left, nearly bumping into the second guard. For some reason, the engineer blew the horn. Must have been antelope or deer on the track.

The Chinese man, who was a good head and a half shorter than Straut, sneered, but didn't lose his footing. The Chinese always smelled of salt and starch to Straut, and this guard was no exception. Straut had never smelled opium smoke on any of the guards, but he knew that smell well enough from his time in San Francisco. He doubted if the Boss would tolerate such behavior from his security force.

The Chinese were mysterious, with their odd language and even odder ways of eating and living. Among the men Straut commanded there were more grumblings about having to deal with the Chinese than about the Irish that the Boss used as muscle when he needed it. The Chinese made Straut's men nervous. The Irish just pissed them off.

The bell finally tinkled, and the door opened, almost magically, just as Straut regained his balance. Both guards stood aside, expressionless, waiting for Straut to enter the Boss's quarters.

It was at that moment that a strong, cold shiver trembled up Straut's spine, and for a reason he didn't know, he felt like he was a dead man walking in to face his Maker.

THREE

LUCAS WAS MORE SURPRISED BY THE SIGHT of the Negro than he was by the knife. Negroes were segregated, kept in another, unseen wing of the prison. Their existence was known of within the prison walls, but they were never seen walking free among white men in any capacity. Especially not armed with a knife in their hand.

The tense, warm air that Lucas had noticed earlier grew even warmer, and was followed by a rise of volume in the chorus of yells that had suddenly turned to screams of fear instead of antagonism and vented rage. Panic had replaced chants for blood as the smell of smoke became apparent to every man in the hall.

A quick glance to the distant wall told Lucas all he needed to know.

The Negro wing had been breached; they had busted out of their cells, or mess hall, and a fire had started in the melee. Gangs of Negroes spilled through a normally locked door, more of them than Lucas could count, looking for a fight—and knowing they would find one. The boxing match had lost its entertainment value. In the blink of an eye the fight erupted into a full-fledged riot.

Elbows and fists started swinging, and the circle of men around Lucas broke apart, becoming a mass of ants fighting for survival. Black man against white, pent-up rage unleashed, punches thrown and revenge taken for crimes committed in the past and present, or punches thrown for no reason at all, other than pure, unadulterated hate.

There were no guards in sight, but it would be only a matter of time before an army of them would show up to quell the fight—if that was possible. The only advantage held by prison guards was their access to guns. Lucas expected a brigade of them, fully armed, with orders to shoot to kill, no matter the color of skin that fell into their sights.

"Behind you!" someone shouted, directing Lucas's attention back to the pale man who had initially faced him down.

At first, Lucas didn't understand. It was the Negro who had yelled. But that's all he had time to think about. Something hard slammed into the back of his head, sending him flying forward to the floor.

Lucas slid face-first into the fighting crowd. It was like being thrown to the ground in the middle of a cattle stampede. He froze and cowled his head with his forearms, doing his best to protect himself from being stepped on or kicked.

He realized then that the Negro had tried to warn him, but there was no time to consider the wonder of such a thing— someone grabbed both of his feet and started dragging him through the crowd, toward the fire beyond the open door.

Lucas twisted around to find it was the pale man who was dragging him.

There was madness and rage in the man's eyes. Eyes that were full of murder and battle, even though the cause for the attack had never been given. It didn't matter. All Lucas could do was fight for his life. Screaming for help would do him no good. He had no compatriot, no savior, to offer rescue or redemption. Building a fellowship among killers and thieves was fraught with more peril than it seemed worth, but suddenly it looked like a mistake not to have aligned himself with a gang of some kind so he would have allies in a fight. As it was, Lucas was lost in a sea of men just like him, trying to stay alive.

The heat inside the mess hall had grown as intense as a smokehouse, even on the floor.

Fear of fire was spreading as quickly as the flames. Before long there would be nowhere to run. They'd all be trapped like rats on a sinking ship. This wing of the prison was built of nothing but wood and iron on top of the old limestone foundation from the previous prison. It had burned down, too. Men locked in their cells faced certain death if help didn't come soon.

Alarms sounded—bells inside the prison and out. Somewhere in the distance, a gunshot rang out, followed by another and another. But none of this mattered. The pale man had plans for Lucas and kept dragging him away from the crowd, toward the burning Negro wing of the prison.

Lucas grabbed the doorjamb as they passed through the entrance, throwing the pale man off balance. The sudden hitch gave Lucas an opportunity to swing his feet back and forth, successfully breaking the man's tight hold.

He jumped to his knees and dove forward, leading with the shiv.

The point of the wood weapon caught the pale man just under the chin, not quite in the curve of his soft throat. The shiv pierced the man's skin easily. The force of it sliced upward into his tongue. No scream came out of the pale man's mouth as Lucas withdrew the shiv, just a gasp and a gurgle. The pale man's eyes brewed black with rushing blood and pain, and if he had smelled like a dead man on the first strike, then Lucas was about to make that smell a certainty now.

In close, Lucas drew back and jammed the shiv into the man's chest, pulling the weapon in and out as quickly as he

could, stabbing him multiple times. The attacker withered
to the ground without a peep, falling against a wall that was
already warm, ready to give itself to the fire at any second.

The gunfire came closer, had arrived inside the mess hall.
But so had the fire. Flames leapt upward to the ceiling, while
smoke swarmed to the floor, gobbling up men like venomous
snakes, stinging their eyes, and looking for entry into their
lungs any way it could find.

Smoke was more lethal than the fire itself. If Lucas had
had a choice in his death, he would have chosen to burn up
instead of being strangled by formless smoke.

"I know about a way out."

The voice came from behind Lucas. He glanced quickly
down at the pale man to make sure that he was dead, that
he wouldn't rise up and attack again, and Lucas didn't turn
around until he was satisfied that that was, in fact, the truth.

The Negro with the knife, which was now nowhere in
sight, stood before Lucas. "Why in the hell should I trust you?"

"'Cause your only choice is stay to here and die or to be
free."

"Not much of a choice."

"No, suh, it's not."

Lucas shrank back and studied the Negro for a long second. The man was taller than him, broader and more muscular, dressed in prison rags like the rest of them, and most
assuredly could have just attacked him from the broadside
if he had wanted to kill him.

There was a simple way about the Negro, but that
could've been an act. Lucas had learned a long time ago that
Negroes were masters of manipulation. They would behave
one way in front of whites and another, more honest way
when they were among themselves. Life in prison and on a
plantation weren't that different.

"How do you know about this way out?" Lucas asked.

"I worked in the kitchen many a day," the Negro said.
"And . . . I's the one that set the fire ablaze."

FOUR

LUCAS FOLLOWED THE NEGRO AWAY FROM the mess hall, toward the fire, and just as suddenly as he had appeared, he disappeared.

The Negro ducked into an open arched door that Lucas hadn't known existed. The flames followed after them, rushing down an interior wood wall on their right. A lock dangled open. It was either a curious stroke of luck, or there was more to what was happening than Lucas knew. It unsettled him, put every ounce of his being on alert, more than it already was.

With a deep breath, Lucas trailed the Negro into the darkness, ready for anything.

The internal passageways of the prison were a mystery to Lucas. Only his well-worn path of daily travails was known to him. Dim limestone blocks stacked in strong patterns, cell bars themselves, had numbed his mind with routine and sameness. In truth, he knew little of the prison in its entirety. There had never been reason to care about more than what was right in front of him. At the moment, that attitude appeared to have been another mistake on his part. He didn't know where he was, or where he was going.

Smoke wrapped around Lucas's ankles, trying to pull him down, trying to poison his lungs. He pulled his shirt up and breathed through it as shallowly as possible.

The hall was dark in front of him, his way lit only slightly by the angry and glowing orange flames behind him.

The exterior wall of the passageway was made of carved stone, carefully stacked, ages ago, long before Lucas had been born, let alone thought of doing anything wrong, or doing anything worthwhile for that matter, which was closer to the truth. If he had ever planned an escape, this would not have been the way he would have thought to go about it.

Lucas stopped and stood with his back to the wall. It was moist and cool to the touch, offering him a moment of relief and comfort.

It was almost like he had jumped inside a deep well, the path to nowhere, horizontal instead of vertical. There was no end to the darkness, no clue where the next door was or what lay in wait before him. All of his instincts told him to turn around and go back. Common sense finally prevailed over the desire to flee.

"Wait, why should I follow you any farther?" Lucas's voice echoed off the walls, louder than he'd expected it to. Fear of giving himself away revealed itself. Another surprise.

The Negro stopped ahead of him, nothing more than a shadow, though the whites of his eyes shone like small moons, orbs of distant light reflecting a certainty back to Lucas that was unsettling, and comforting at the same time.

Behind them, screams, yells, and gunshots continued to rise above the crackle of the hungry fire. The riot echoed so loudly that the force of the fighting threatened to collapse the roof, adding more to the disaster than was already present.

The sounds of battle were familiar, buried deep in

Lucas's memory, put in a place he'd like to have forgotten—but that was not possible, and he knew it. This was a different time, and a different war, one that he didn't volunteer for or have a choice in. It was his own personal freedom that was at hand, not a nation's. A personal war set on him by forces out of his control.

It was either a miracle or a trap, he wasn't sure which, but his current predicament was one that he would have never imagined when he opened his eyes that morning.

"You ain't got no reason to trust any man inside these walls, suh, but I's about to take you outside of this dark place if that be your wish. Troubles will follow, that be true, but my aim is to bring you—and myself—outside to the free world."

"Troubles are a constant companion of mine. That's not my concern."

"You be a fugitive. You ready for that?"

"Are you?"

"Who says I'm escapin' from anything?"

"I 'spect no one is. I just assumed you were a prisoner. Where's your knife?"

"Got took from me."

"Lucky it didn't end up in your chest like that shiv."

"Don't matter, ain't no escape for a man like me, inside or out. That knife wouldn't have done me no good here." The Negro's words were a whisper, loud enough to hear but not clear enough to end any confusion held at the forefront of Lucas's mind.

"What is your name? Why are you here? Who are you?"

There was a long moment of silence from the Negro, followed by a couple of deep, thoughtful, breaths. "None of us knows our real names, just what folks calls us where we are, ya knows what I mean? I been called Zeke all my life. The long of it is Ezekiel Micah Jones Henry, but I's just Zeke, mostly, to those who wants to call me by my name. Mistuh Henry gave me his name when I was born. Mostly, it's just a scar more'n a name."

"Zeke, then."

"Yes, suh. And you be Lucas. Lucas Fume. Master of the Seven Oaks plantation, honorable war hero and known spy, a keen businessman throughout the states and territories, and convicted murderer of John Barlow, the bestus friend a man could ever have—or so it once was told that way. I knows who you is, I sure do."

"I didn't kill John Barlow. I got into an argument with him about the state of our finances, which were rigged to look like I had stolen from our company. In other words, I was the last person to see him alive, and I had the motive and means, according to the lawyers, to kill him."

"Ain't my business what you did or didn't do, now is it?"

"It is if I say I'm innocent."

"I ain't the law."

Lucas recoiled. "How do you know *my* name?"

"I knows a lot more than that, but now's not the time to trade on more stories than we need to. That's just proof that I ain't no foe, and this here ain't no accident. I come for you, Mistuh Fume. That has to be good enough for now. We stand here much longer, we die from the smoke, or by the gun of a guard lookin' to make a name for hisself. Way out is this way. You wants to stay, that's all right with me, but it'd be a sad end to be sure.

"Won't be no mercy for this mess. Turned out to be far more than it was supposed to be, the way it is. I's in no mood to hang, no, suh, not on this day, Lucas Fume. Not on this day. Not for the likes of you or no one else. Now, let's get, before we can't get no more."

"So I should trust you, that you're going to see the both of us out of here? And that's that?"

"Yes, suh, that is so. And once we're out on free ground, you're on your own in the world. My duty'd be done then, and the same for me, true as a ringing bell. If they catch either of us, we die for sure. More dead men at my hand than yours once the ashes settle to the ground and the smoke disappears. Hear those screams? White men be murdered from the flame set by a black hand. Negroes just gone, but soon replaced, but the white men, they be counted and judgment set forth. Breathin' is just cause to anger free men. You knows that. I lit the flame, and white men died. What you think they gonna do to me if they catches me? I won't make it past the nearest tree, much less get me no fair trial. I didn't mean no one to die. Do that make me innocent, too?"

There was nothing Lucas could say. Innocence was his last concern at the moment. The thought of freedom was a strong drug. He nodded with recognition.

The defeat of the South had been hard to take. A way of life for everyone had been changed, taken, or lost, even from him. Whether it was right or good—time would tell—but the cause of it no longer mattered, or wasn't supposed to. Just because there were signatures on paper, like the pale man had said, and the proclamation of peace and emancipation had been inflicted on the populace, it didn't truly mean the fighting was over. The struggle between white men and slavery would live on. Any man of intelligence knew that to be true, no matter the color of his skin.

Before Lucas could utter another word, a silhouette formed on the wall to his right. It was of a man in the midst of raising a rifle.

A single shot exploded inside the passageway. It reverberated so loudly in the tight, dark space that Lucas thought his eardrums would shatter.

The bullet ricocheted off the floor, inches from his boot. The muzzle flash lingered for a long second, like a candle struggling to stay lit, then disappeared, offering the familiar taste of gunpowder along with the smoke. It was a recipe for death.

"Run or die. Them's your choices, Mistuh Lucas," Zeke said, then turned and disappeared completely into the darkness.

The guard started shouting, ordered them to stop and

surrender. He fired several more rounds from a Spencer repeating rifle, but he was shooting senselessly into the darkness, missing them because of luck and the blessing of darkness.

The bullets sparked off the stone, thudded into the ground, barely missing Lucas as he hugged the cold wall as tight as he could and ran after Zeke Henry with every ounce of strength he could muster. If he had anything to do with it, today would not be his day to die.

FIVE

THE DOOR CLOSED BEHIND JOE STRAUT WITH
a heavy thud. It was as cold as a tomb inside Lanford Grips's
quarters. Straut stopped just inside as the peacock doors
closed him in. He shivered again and took in the room, tried
to gather his thoughts, his fears, and his strength, all into
one place.

Never tremble in front of an angry dog, that's what
Straut's old pa used to say, but that was before he stepped
into a snake hole and broke his leg because he wasn't watching where he was going.

Both were valuable lessons when it came to dealing with
a man like the Boss, and Straut had already failed at one
lesson before he got started. He just hoped the Boss hadn't
noticed the outward show of fear.

Straut had been in the Boss's railcar quarters several
times before, but the grandness of them never ceased to
amaze him. He'd never seen anything so beautiful on
wheels—or off, for that for matter. Not that he'd ever stepped

foot in the fine hotels in St. Louis, the opera house in Kansas City, or the nicer homes in Abilene to know the difference. Saloons, flophouses, and cathouses were more his style, more his bailiwick. He'd never rubbed shoulders with the hoity-toity too much. Joe Straut had always been on the outside looking in, at least until the Boss had recruited him, had brought him into the organization and realized that Straut was better at being a sergeant than most men could ever hope to be.

Men followed Straut with ease, that was for sure, did for him what he wanted them to without question—which had always been a surprise to Straut. It had been that way all his life mostly, and something he'd been able to use to his advantage from an early age.

Being in charge had been a gift and a curse at times, but he'd discovered his true talent in the war. As with most fellas, though, it was what came after the war that was the hard part, living in the world of Reconstruction and within the federal union. There weren't many places for a man like him to go. No home to return to, no easy future at hand, no fortune to cash in. The only currency he carried was experience with a weapon in hand, drumming men up into a killing rage or talking them through a defeat, a loss on a bloody battlefield, where they most likely had learned, or lost, something of themselves they hadn't known they had in the first place.

Luckily, he'd found the Boss, or the Boss had found him, after the last rebel shot had been fired.

Straut couldn't really remember how it all came about. It just did. One day he was whiling away time in a saloon, and the next he was standing in front of a group of ragtag men in an abandoned hell-on-wheels town, getting them in shape for something that the Boss considered useful. Laws were less worrisome west of the Big Muddy.

It was a new land, a new start, albeit in old boots. The promise of employment, of a place to belong, had seemed like a godsend then. At the moment, Straut's position felt like a curse.

He couldn't quell his fear, couldn't help but believe that something was wrong, that he was in deep trouble with the Boss—which never turned out good for anybody. The Boss had no tolerance for errors or ignorance.

Straut stood at attention, took a military position, even though his shirt was half-tucked-in, and one pant leg sat atop his boot, while the other, ragged at the cuff, had fallen to the floor. The Boss never expected him to be precise, or dressed in a uniformed way, but the Boss liked things neat, accountable, put together so as not to draw any attention. Dirty outlaws were offensive.

There was no sound inside the quarters, just the roar of the train, the loud and constant heartbeat of the locomotive pushing hard into the deep night.

To say the room was opulent was an understatement. The walls were covered with the same mahogany wood as the rest of the railcar, but the carpet was different. More plush. Straut's boots sunk down half an inch when he stepped into the room. The carpet was red. Blood-red, sculpted with patterns that seemed to rise and fall perfectly. And like the patterns in the outer car, these didn't make any sense to Joe Straut, either.

If the designs on the floor meant something, then the meaning was lost on him. He never was good at design or culture, barely knew the difference between a sideboard and a cupboard—but he knew the difference between a Spencer and a Henry rifle just by the sound of it, by seeing from a good distance how it was loaded and fired.

All he really knew about the railcar was that the furnishings and draperies were expensive, most likely shipped over from England or China, and that unless he was told to, Joe Straut wasn't going to sit anywhere or on anything anytime soon.

Lanford Grips sat at the rear of the room, behind an

ornately carved writing desk. "It took you long enough." He motioned with a jerk of his head for Straut to come forward, to stand before him. Like a good soldier, he obeyed.

The Boss was a small man in stature, even smaller when he was sitting behind a large desk, his arms held tight to his side, hands out of sight. A fleck of solid white hair pierced his temple like a streak of unspoiled snow sitting atop the darkest, blackest soil any man had ever seen. His nose was thin, hooked upward slightly, and he had the eyes of a wolf, so blue that in the dim light they looked as black as his hair. The Boss wasn't an old man, but he wasn't young, either. In regular daylight, he looked, and dressed, like a banker. A respectable businessman, deciding whether or not to give a loan to some desperate rancher.

"I was asleep," Joe Straut said. "The rock of the train puts me out easy, Boss, once I settle in. Sorry, I wasn't expectin' any trouble."

"You should always expect trouble." Lanford Grips didn't show any emotion, and he commanded Straut's full attention. But there was no mistaking another man standing in the shadows, just behind the Boss, to the right of him, as always, an ever-present valet known as Bojack Wu—another, more worrisome, Chinese in the Boss's employ.

Like the two door guards, Wu was dressed all in black, loose-fitting clothes. His face was hard and his eyes tight, as if he were a snake always on the ready to strike. If you blinked in Bojack Wu's presence, you could find yourself dead before you knew what hit you.

Straut's throat was dry as an Arizona gulch. He'd seen what Bojack Wu was capable of more than once in recent months. Fact was, the Chink scared him more than the Boss did. Recognizing again that the strap was still on, he figured the Colt Open Top on his side wouldn't do him any good, even though it was loaded and ready to go. He felt like an idiot. "Sleeping's no excuse, Boss. No, sir. It was just late, and we'd pulled out of the station. Deets is on shift. He's a good man to keep an eye out for any troubles. I trust him."

Grips leaned his head forward. "What's the word on Fume?"

Straut stopped in front of the desk. "No word since we pulled out of St. Louis, Boss. Didn't figure there'd be any until we could stop and tap into the wire, see if there's any message that the act is complete."

"He's still alive?"

"As far as I know, Boss. But I put the best men on it I had. Gettin' inside that prison wasn't going to be easy."

"He better be dead by the time we reach Kansas City. I've waited long enough, and suffered through more than one fool attempt, to finish him off. Goddamn it, it ought to be as simple as shooting a carp in a whiskey barrel full of rainwater. I've paid good money to see him to his end, and it's not done yet." A normal man would have smashed his fists on the desk, but Grips's arms didn't flinch; he just set his jaw tighter, and his eyes drew together with intensity.

"Fume's a skillful man, Boss."

"I know all about his goddamn skills!"

"I can't make something happen from a thousand miles away, Boss. I can only hire the men I think are capable of the job."

"You listen to me, and you listen close, Straut. My patience has run out. I want good news, and I want it now—and if I don't get it, then you're the one that's going to pay the price. Do you understand what I'm saying, Straut?"

"Yes, sir, Boss. I think I do."

The train whistled then, and Straut just about pissed his pants. His heart skipped a beat, and the cold shiver returned.

There was no use arguing with the Boss, no sense making things worse for himself than they already were.

Joe Straut began to back away slowly to the door, hoping like hell he made it out of the room before Bojack Wu jumped over the desk and put a quick end to a problem he didn't know how to fix.

"One more thing, Straut," Grips said.

He stopped, his back to the door, his hands stiff at his sides. "Yes, Boss?"

"You and Deets need to clean out the passenger berths before sunrise. Make sure there's not a trace to be found or one speck of dust to be seen by new eyes. We wouldn't want the guests to think we're untidy, now would we?"

"No, Boss, no, we sure don't."

Bojack Wu stood as still as a statue, staring so hard at Straut he thought holes were going to burn through his forehead. He knew better than to ask the questions that were bubbling on the base of his tongue, so he clamped his lips together tightly.

"Just remember," Grips said, "there's a constant inferno raging in the firebox. All sorts of things disappear there. Forever. Understand, Straut?"

"I do, Boss, I sure do."

SIX

IT SOUNDED LIKE A SCREAM. A LONG, PAINFUL
scream, strung out in the darkness like an intentional act of
torture. Pain inflicted without the result of death—for the
sport of it, or a desire to coax something of importance from
someone, or a need demanding fulfillment but then denied
with outraged force, hate, and unrestrained violence. It was
a horrible scream. Distant, unreachable, lost in infinite
blackness, the reality of it frightening, like nothing Charlotte
Brogan had ever heard before.

She sat up in her bed with a start, her hand pressed hard
over her heart just to make sure she was still alive, awake,
not in the middle of some bad dream. She could feel the
pitter-patter of the organ inside her chest, and the touch of
her own skin assured her that she was, in fact, awake—and
alive.

The room was dark, the draperies of the berth pulled so
tight it was hard to say for sure what time of day or night it
really was. It was only the familiar and regular rock of the

entire room that gave notice to the fact that she was inside a railcar, in the middle of God knew where. She feared Indians. Robbers. Heathens of all types. Reasons for fear lurked in every corner beyond the door to her quarters. Some women kept laudanum hidden in perfume bottles for such moments of panic, but Charlotte had never been fond of the use of such things to calm herself. There was a price to pay, a constant need, a demand to feed that, unlike the stomach, could never be sated. She had seen the consequences, seen the addiction wear a beautiful woman down into a withering witch, and chosen to be free of those chains.

Thank goodness she was in her bed, in the same place where she had fallen asleep, safe and sound.

The locomotive chugged forward, gaining speed, and the railcar lurched and drew back, trying to keep up, even though it had no choice.

The whistle blew a short blast, then tooted a long one, giving Charlotte cause to relax. It hadn't been a bad dream at all. It had only been the train, offering a warning, a good-bye to a water tower, or a signal to clear the track of an unseen herd of beasts, real or imagined.

Nothing was the matter. Nothing at all. She was just being silly. Charlotte chided herself, scolded her fearful imagination, then drew in a deep breath and tried to relax into the moment she had awoken to. But she remained upward in the huge bed, denying the inclination to lie back down and cover her head. She pushed her hands down into the soft feather bed to anchor herself, to maintain her balance, almost in spite of herself. This was no nightmare. But there *was* something lingering in her mind . . . a vision from her sleep, a dream of some kind that hovered in her memory, begging her to revisit it, to come to it.

Shadows and shapes churned with an old, almost forgotten, emotion. There was no music, but a pattern of sound, a constant, consistent beat. Precipitation, maybe. A storm, drawing closer. Rain falling on a tin roof, matching the rhythm of her regulated heart. It could have been the train, but she didn't think so.

Charlotte closed her eyes as tight she could and tried to conjure the vision, tried to order it back to the forefront of her mind with every ounce of authority that she could muster.

It only took a minute or two of focused desire for that to happen.

In a fleeting moment, the vision rushed back to her consciousness—ghostly images from the dream: A familiar door opened to an empty room, inside a house she knew well, with her standing at the threshold, her toes daring to step inside.

It was a memory as much as it was a dream, and it seemed to her like a different life, a different time, a different person. Pages on the calendar had flipped by faster than she could have ever imagined, allowing wounds to become scars—but the horror of what had happened in *that* room remained with her, fresh, like it had just happened two seconds ago.

Charlotte was reminded of that moment, of that day, with every breath she took, no matter how far away, or long ago, it was. She had lost herself. Or changed from the woman she was then to the woman she was now.

There were shelves full of books on every wall of the room, the pages wet with blowing rain. The touch of the water to her skin was cold, but not cold enough to freeze. Close. Almost. It never got that cold in that house—but that night it did. Her breath crystallized into puffs, distorting her view even more than it already was. It was winter and all of the windows were open.

The room was full of the most expensive furniture that could be bought, and even finer carpets and draperies covered the floors and windows, rivaling the finest castles in Italy and beyond. The house was grand, as was all of the land that surrounded it.

Every lamp in the room was ablaze, lighting every corner, every inch. Charlotte knew the room like she knew an aunt or an uncle; it was part of her past, part of her future. She had laughed there, cried there . . . loved there—and been loved there.

The pictures that hung on the walls were burned into her memory. Triumphant men on white stallions, celebrating the victory of wars, of battles hard fought. Others with sporting dogs, clad in formal wear—red coats, black knee boots—offering a view of the hunt, not for the necessity of killing for food, but for pleasure. Pure pleasure. The paintings were markers in time; a lineage of heroes and warriors looked down on her, just as wealth surrounded her in the dream—just as it did in the present.

The feel of the fabric on the sofa, the way the floor would creak, just before the desk, were as familiar to her as the back of her hand. She had spent a lot of time in that room. But this memory was of the last time she had ever stepped foot in that room—or that house, for that matter.

Coal oil smoke mixed with other, foreign smells that had never touched her nose before. The awake, future Charlotte wanted to turn and run, pull herself out of the memory, with all of her will—with the same intense command that she'd used to re-create the dream in her mind in the first place.

She wanted to make it all vanish.

She didn't want to look into the room.

She didn't want to see it again.

But she couldn't help herself.

She stepped inside, and walked to the desk.

It was there that she stopped. The vision was a complete mirror of the reality that had changed everything, that had propelled her from her comfortable, respectable life into the fearful, uneasy life that she lived now.

The desk was covered in blood. Not in drips, but in a thick crimson pool that ran over the edges, splashing to the floor, marring the carpets forever, leaving a stain and stench that could never be scrubbed away, no matter the effort. It smelled sweet, and the tip of her tongue tasted of metal and madness.

Blood covered all of the papers, all of the pens and inkwells, the books and the open ledger, and was splattered on the wall, spoiling the horsehair wallpaper just as it had the carpets.

Whatever had happened had come in an explosion of rage, with the swift swing of a sharp, sharp blade. There was no mistaking, even to a woman without battlefield experience, what had happened. It was the why of it all that lingered, that kept itself secret, unknown, at least to her.

Who would do such a thing?

Charlotte blinked her eyes and tried to clear them, girding herself for what was to come next. This memory was old. She had made this walk a thousand times or more. There were no more surprises.

Positioned squarely in the middle of the desk were a pair of hands. Hands that had been severed. Hands that had been burned in the war and unmistakably, along with the gold signet ring on the right hand, identified the body and human face to which they belonged. They were John Barlow's hands. She knew them as surely as she knew that the sun rose in the east and set in the west.

John, John, dear John, what have you gone and got yourself into this time?

Just like the first time, the seed of a scream quickly germinated at the base of her throat and grew quickly, until it blossomed and exploded fully from her mouth.

The scream was matched by the train's whistle, and it was then that Charlotte Brogan realized that she had woken herself up in the first place, alone, as always, in the dark, reliving the past, hoping upon hope that it had truly been a nightmare and not a reality. But that was never to be.

There was no body to be found in the room, only the hands.

SEVEN

LUCAS INCHED ALONG THE PASSAGEWAY IN
the dark, where he quickly found an alcove, a deep indentation in the wall that he could duck into.

The scuffle of Zeke Henry's feet echoed away from him, continuing on. There was no time to signal to the Negro, to hatch a plan, to see them out of the darkness—all Lucas knew to do was follow, which was a position he didn't like being in and had never been comfortable with.

The guard was close. Too close. And besides, Lucas wasn't entirely trusting of anything Zeke had said. He had no reason to believe the story he'd been told, that the Negro was there to see him out of the prison, help him escape, then go off on his own—the act its own reward for a dangerous mission. *A mission from whom? Why now?* A lot of questions swirled inside Lucas's mind, but in the end he had no choice but to do as he was told, "run or die," even with the guard closing in.

But Lucas didn't run. He stopped, hugged the wall inside the alcove, and waited.

The passageway smelled of smoke, and fire still threatened beyond the door they'd escaped through. Alarms clanged on, and the yells of rage had transformed into screams for rescue and survival. Burning men sounded a lot different than angry men. The orange glow was more intense. Flames flicked down the hallway, biting at the darkness, threatening to bring more light and danger with every second that passed.

Lucas had little time to accomplish his intention—to give himself, and Zeke for that matter, more time to get away.

The guard stopped two feet outside of the alcove and fired his rifle again. The shot was fired directly into the darkness, toward the scuffle of feet that gave away Zeke's trail. It would have been a matter of luck if it had hit the Negro.

The muzzle flash was all Lucas needed—it was what he'd been waiting for, hoping to see. He jumped out of the alcove and grabbed the rifle just at the base of the barrel. The swiftness of his movement surprised the guard, and the man stumbled back with a sudden gasp.

Lucas couldn't see the man's face, didn't know if he recognized him or not. It didn't matter; all of the guards were bad eggs in one way or another. Torturous bastards. Drunk with power over men who were trapped behind four walls because of their own actions—or not, like Lucas, who to his peril proclaimed his innocence every day, at any opportunity he was given to speak. Which was rare.

Regardless, none of the guards deserved fairness or consideration. They deserved the same kind of pain and suffering they inflicted every chance they had. The miserable bastards had no compassion and whiled away their time by making life inside the Tennessee State Prison a living hell for all of the prisoners, save the ones they used as snitches or spies.

Lucas flipped the rifle up into his hand, swinging it so the butt was pointing straight into the air, then jammed the hardwood butt straight into the guard's chin as hard as he could.

Cracking bone echoed throughout the passageway, bringing Zeke's shuffling feet to a stop.

"What the hell are you doing, Mistuh Fume?" Zeke hollered out.

Lucas ignored him, recoiled, and swung the rifle, catching the guard across the face as the unknown man fell to the floor with a heavy thud. There was a softness to this hit, sinew and muscle exploding into the darkness. The blood looked like black water, and it sounded like he had stepped on a giant cockroach in the middle of the night.

Rage exploded inside Lucas's body. Retribution. Payback. It didn't matter what it was called. He wanted it. Killing another man didn't matter. If he was going to be a fugitive with the cause of murder on his head, then by God, that's what it could really be. This guard might never have violated him in any way, but he was a guard, and judging from Lucas's experience, surely he had inflicted pain and ugliness on some man that didn't deserve it.

Lucas flipped the rifle around, settling the butt square against his shoulder, his finger finding the trigger with ease. The gun felt good, like an old lover sliding back into his lonely arms, the time lost not apparent to either one of them. Some things just aren't easily forgotten, no matter the amount of time that has passed.

Before Lucas could pull the trigger, finish what he had started, Zeke grabbed the rifle away from him.

"Stop it, Mistuh Fume. Just stop it, before you goes and does somethin' stupid. Somethin' that you'll come to regret."

Lucas was surprised by the boldness of the Negro's action. "Give me back the goddamned gun."

Zeke pulled it away and looked up the passageway—toward the door they'd escaped from. Lucas followed his gaze. More guards were coming, but the one on the floor wasn't a concern at the moment. They had attracted more attention than they needed.

"They can't hang you for somethin' you didn't do. If you's innocent like you claim, then you won't be anymore, you go and do this thing—if you kill this man. Guards are mean for sure, but they ain't worth dyin' for."

It was like being slapped upside the head. "I'm here for a crime I didn't commit, and I killed that man inside," Lucas said.

"Self-defense."

"You sound like a lawyer, not a Negro on the run."

"That don't mean I'm stupid, do it?"

A shot exploded from the gun of one of the oncoming guards, missing them both.

Zeke stared directly at Lucas, his moon-white eyes penetrating the darkness, and said, "I ain't comin' back for you again. I'll be free with—or without—you. Money or time be damned, I ain't dyin' for you." And with that, he turned and ran in the opposite direction, disappearing into the pitch-black tunnel faster than Lucas could have ever imagined.

EIGHT

LUCAS RAN AS FAST AS HE COULD AFTER
Zeke. It only took him a minute to catch up with the Negro. The darkness felt like a trap. He couldn't see how far he'd come, how far he had to go, or where he was going, for that matter. It was like running in a dream, lost in a giant solitary hole—or falling down a well, the bottom uncertain, the way out unthinkable, impossible.

Shouts to stop, followed by a barrage of uncertain gunshots, rang out behind them.

A glance over his shoulder told Lucas that there were at least three guards behind them in hot pursuit.

Bullets pinged off the stone floor and the walls, barely missing him. Chunks of stone peppered his face. They stung like bees swarming to save the queen. Sparks in the darkness issued warnings, leading up to an impending explosion, a battery of rifle shots that would find their target sooner rather than later at the rate they were firing.

Zeke returned fire with the rifle he had taken from Lucas,

keeping the guards farther at bay than they might have been if he hadn't taken up the gun.

Still, Lucas knew each breath could be his last. He could taste doom and gunpowder in his mouth, smell them in his nose, feel them all over his body. As awful as it was, the sour flavor told him that he was still alive, still capable of attaining freedom. He ran with all his might, like his entire being depended on it . . . because it did. He'd been in a lot of close scrapes in his life, but this one topped the list.

Zeke's breath was regulated, about five yards ahead of Lucas. "That you, Mistuh Fume?" His voice was unsure, the first crack in his confidence, mixed with heaviness, a sign that he was wearing down.

"If it wasn't for you I'd be dead already," Lucas said.

A shot whizzed by Lucas's leg, close enough to rip his pants, but not nick his skin. He felt the heat of the metal against his flesh. Too close. Too, too close. He grimaced, yelped as softly as he could, then ran a little faster, coming shoulder to shoulder with Zeke.

Zeke fired back, slowing again, forcing the guards into the shadows. He might have hit one; it was hard to say with all of the noise from the fire and riot echoing down into the passageway.

"I think that might've been the last bullet," Zeke said. "Won't know for sure till we step outside this darkness. No tellin' how many shots that guard got off 'fore we took away his rifle."

"They don't know that."

"True. You all right?" Zeke said.

"I hope you got a plan."

Zeke didn't answer right away. A flurry of gunfire erupted again. It sounded like there were more than three guards. Zeke and Lucas clung to the wall like bats.

It was more like a posse had fled the burning prison in search of them and were just about to accomplish their goal to kill or capture. The exchange of gunfire might've drawn attention, done Zeke and Lucas more harm than good.

"Door at the end here supposed to be unlocked, if all's gone the way it should have. The way I was told it would. So far, so good, exceptin' the walls were like tinder, dry as straw. I done run farther than I think I should have. I might have missed it in this here darkness—but I can't think likes that, or we're dead mens."

"And if it's not unlocked? If you *did* run right past it?"

"We this far, ain't we?"

The man had a point. "An unlocked door in a prison is another thing."

"Then you best be ready to face your death, meet your Maker, or whatever it is that you believes in. 'Cause they ain't gonna take us back to no cells. Not if I shot one of them. They gonna kill us for even tryin' to run. Probably hang us from the rafters as an example to the rest of the mens here. No buzzards to pick our bones, but rats can climb."

"That would be a favor to us both."

Light suddenly blazed next to Lucas, startling him, blinding him momentarily. Zeke smiled. He was holding a lit match in his hand. A door stood waiting ten feet to their left. They were almost there.

"What the hell?" Lucas said, cowering as he ducked into the shadows.

More shots from the guards followed, coming close, hitting all around them. From what Lucas could tell, the guards were about thirty yards up the passageway.

"Lucifers," Zeke said with a grin. "This is the only weapon besides the knife I was gived, but we evened up the score a bit with this here Spencer." A lock dangled open on the latch of the door. Zeke rushed over and pulled the lock off, then pushed open the door. He stepped through without hesitation. "Come on now, it's time to go."

Soft morning light cracked into the darkness, shattering it like it was a mirror. There was no hiding now. Lucas glanced up the hall, saw the guards coming, then tore after Zeke.

It was just like the Negro had said it would be. Planned and purposeful. Lucas didn't hesitate to leave the prison, but that didn't mean he didn't have questions.

Once Lucas was outside, the Negro slammed the door shut, threw the lock on the outside latch, and clicked it shut as tight as he could. The guards' yells were muffled, and they shot at the door, but it would take a while to shoot through it.

The two of them, Lucas and Zeke, were free, their feet on the ground, the sky over their heads, walls behind them, and nothing to hold them back.

Lucas drew in a deep breath, surprised at how relieved he felt, swallowing the morning air in thick gulps, like it was made of honey.

The sun had already crested the horizon and was in the process of burning off a thin haze of gray mist that lingered over the mountains. It was a sight to behold—one he had never thought he'd live to see, especially with the help of a Negro. There was no question that it was spring. The air was full of flavor, and dogwoods bloomed—shining like porcelain in the soft sunlight, dappled with dew and new-ness. Tender leaves were bright green, and the canopy of the nearby forest had yet to completely fill in. The sight nearly brought tears to Lucas's eyes.

The only thing marring the sight was the thick black smoke rising from the middle of the prison, blowing in the opposite direction, like a storm cloud drifting from the west instead of the east. Alarms clanged. Gunshots fired. And there were muffled screams—men dying, burning to death—the sweetness of the dogwoods tinged with the odd, uncomfortable smell of burning flesh.

Before Lucas could draw in another breath and enjoy the moment of freedom, Zeke said, "Don't think you be out of trouble yet, Mistuh Fume." There was dread in his voice.

The Negro nodded forward, north toward the main gate of the prison.

Lucas followed his gaze and saw another group of guards heading toward them, skirting the outside prison wall cautiously, their rifles raised, prepared to shoot.

NINE

JOE STRAUT NEVER KNEW WHAT TO EXPECT
when he walked into the one of the passenger berths. Sometimes they were empty, just in need of sprucing up—
sweeping out, and putting back to order. Other times, it was
more complicated, as with this one. There were still dead
bodies to deal with, left behind to be disposed of quietly in
the middle of the night.

"What is it?" Finney Deets asked. He was straight on
Straut's heels, had nearly bumped into him, being as Straut
had stopped cold in the doorway.

"Looks like a damn shame to me, is what it is," Straut
said in a low voice. He took a deep breath and shivered. He
tried to hide his reaction from Deets. There were some
things a man never got used to no matter what he'd done, or
seen, in the past. Death was hard to swallow these days.

Deets didn't say anything right away. He was a rangy
man who'd tired of punching cattle from San Antonio to
Abilene. He preferred the comforts of life under the employ

of someone else, rather than riding drag in all kinds of weather for money that never seemed to stay in his pocket. The type of work never mattered much to a man like Deets as long as it didn't land him in jail. He wasn't a bright man, but he had skills—the right kind of skills to rise up in the organization and become trusted by Joe Straut.

The good thing about a man like Deets was his strong stomach, and his ability to keep his mouth shut. He never asked questions in the wrong company or spilled beans at the wrong time. The Boss's assignments were never easy, and rarely were they within the normal laws of the land, or man, for that matter. The Boss operated by his own rules, there was no question about that.

"What're we gonna do with 'em, Sarge?" Everybody called Joe Straut "Sarge," a sign of respect for his time spent in the war and his long-held position with Lanford Grips. He barely noticed, and he answered to it readily and comfortably. It felt like his name, and he liked it. Made him feel powerful, especially in difficult moments, like this one, when power was hard to come by—or an unwanted garment that was impossible to toss off.

"Take care of it. What else is there to do?" Straut shook his head as he stepped into the small berth and surveyed what had been left to him.

Deets didn't answer, just shrugged compliantly and followed Straut inside.

There were three people occupying the berth. It was a simple space—two benches, a window, and shelves overhead that held luggage and overcoats.

At first glance, the passengers looked like they were asleep—but they were pasty white, their sleep was obviously permanent. Death had come recently, since they had left the station but long enough ago for the effects of it to stiffen them.

Straut had to satisfy himself and find out for sure. He reached down and touched the hand of the closest body, a man Straut had never seen before. The hand was cold as ice, and the fingers lacked any kind of pliability; they were as unyielding as one of the Boss's starched shirts.

"Dead as a doornail, ain't they?" Deets said.

"Long enough to seize up."

"They look like the normal players."

"The Boss has a keen eye."

"Knows one of his own when he sees one."

Straut flinched. "You best be careful with that kind of surmising."

"Sorry, Sarge, I was just makin' conversation 'tween you and me. I wasn't sayin' nothin' contrary about the Boss. I wouldn't say such a thing. Boss's been good to me since I rode in. I like bein' on this here train, though there's moments that are tough to take at times." Deets looked at the bodies before him and recoiled slightly.

"Just be mindful of what comes out of your mouth, that's all I'm saying."

Deets looked over his shoulder, down to the end of the railcar.

Straut stepped back to the door, next to his sidekick, and followed Deets's gaze. He saw standing outside the peacock doors the same two Chinese guards that had been there earlier. He cringed slightly, then turned his attention back to the task at hand. The sooner they got this mess cleaned up, the better.

"We best get on with this," Straut said. He stepped back inside the berth, and Deets followed.

"Them Chinks got big ears, as big as their mouths."

"Mind yourself, now."

"All right, all right. But I got Bessie here to protect myself." Deets tapped the 1860 Colt Army he wore holstered on his side. "She looked out for my pa at Shiloh. Got good luck boiled into her barrel."

"You need to get rid of that old cap-and-ball revolver. Gonna get us both killed one of these days."

Deets shook his head no. "You'll have to pry her from

my own dead hands. Those newfangled Colts don't feel right. Never can find the balance."

Straut exhaled loudly. "Just watch my back."

"I always do."

There were two men and one woman in the berth. On one side, a man and woman sat next to each other, slumped together as if one had fallen asleep on the other. They were older, the man just graying in the beard, and wrinkles just coming in at the corners of the woman's eyes—which were wide open, fixed on the ceiling. Fear had frozen on her face, which looked to have held at one time a high amount of beauty.

The other man, the one Straut had checked for life, lay across the seat, facedown. He was younger than the other two, but not young enough to be a son or a nephew. Straut knew nothing of their relations, whether by blood or money, but something, bad luck or otherwise, had settled their fates. The lone man was of the same stature in life, there was no mistaking that, but just as foolish and just as greedy as the pair he had sat facing.

The blinds on the large lookout window were closed, and the room was cool, almost cold. It smelled bad, like one or more of them had fouled themselves. Straut had smelled the smell before, in situations similar to this one. It always embarrassed him.

All three of the passengers were dressed to the nines, the men in fancy suits, top hats, gold Waltham pocket watches still strung out of their pockets by gold chains. Their clothes looked remarkably similar, like they had come from the same tailor.

The lady wore a gray serge traveling dress, a collapsed parasol at her feet. Her kid-and-cloth shoes looked brand-new, like they were bought just for the trip. The heels weren't worn and didn't bear any mud. She was as perfect as a picture in a mail-order catalog, except, of course, she was dead.

There was no way the lady could have known she would

die in those shoes or that dress when she bought them—and Straut found that tragic, though he didn't let himself linger too long on such thoughts.

There was no blood, no outward sign of struggle. It was almost like they had drunk poison, or died from some unseen insect or snakebite. But Straut knew that was not the case. He knew how they had died.

Upon taking a closer look, and knowing what to look for, Straut found a slight bruise under the first man's Adam's apple. The woman bore the same mark in the same place. There was no use checking for the third. The method had been the same to kill all three of them.

These people had been boxed in, then attacked with a set of powerful hands, hands that knew how to kill as well as any gun. Straut guessed that the killer, the assassin, was Bojack Wu, but it could have been any of the Chinese that served Lanford Grips. A silent blow, a chop, had been the cause of death—so at least there wasn't any blood to contend with. The only time that happened was when one of the marks fought back.

These upstanding folks hadn't known what hit them, save the last one, the single man, it looked like. He must have known that his own death was at hand, that they all had been lured away from their homes and their businesses with lies and false promises of wealth and guaranteed success, only to face a trap where there was no way out.

It never failed to astound Straut the lies that some men would buy into to have more than they already had, the greed that would pull them away from their routines and comforts. Especially when he was left to clean up the mess.

If he had been dealt a different hand, had known what wealth really was instead of being a common man of common means, then there would have been no way in hell he would have given that up. Not for anyone, including a silver-tongued devil like the Boss.

"What're we gonna do with 'em?" Deets asked.

"Boss made reference to the firebox on the locomotive."

A curious look crossed Deets's face. "They ain't gonna fit all in one piece are they, Sarge?"

Straut shrugged. "I suppose not."

"We ain't never had to do that before." Deets grimaced, and Straut couldn't blame him. Butchering a man like he was a cow and feeding the limbs into a blazing firebox to dispose of them was one thing, but doing such a thing to a fine lady, even a dead fine lady, well that was another thing. It was a morbid consideration, and one that Straut had to figure a way out of.

"I'll think of something," he said. "Let's just get 'em bundled up and out of here first. Those slanty eyes down at the door make me nervous."

"Me, too," Deets said. "Me, too."

TEN

ZEKE HENRY AIMED THE SPENCER RIFLE AT the oncoming guards and pulled the trigger. The shot echoed loudly, just as did the empty click of the next pull on the trigger. He had fired the last shot. The rifle was useless unless he intended to use it as a club.

Zeke looked calm. Even in the face of certain death, he didn't have one bead of sweat, or any indication of worry, on his brow. Either the man had a grand plan or he wasn't afraid to die. Both choices gave Lucas a little bit of confidence, but he wasn't sure that he could see a way out of the predicament that they'd found themselves in.

Upon seeing that the two of them were armed, the cadre of guards—there were at least three of them—dove for cover, then pressed up against the wall of the prison so tightly that they were barely visible. Only their shadows gave them away.

Lucas drew in another breath, burned another second in consideration of what was next. And then the guards started shooting, adding to the sounds of chaos that continued to surround them. The wind had shifted, and black smoke roiled overhead. Beyond the smoke, the perfect blue morning sky stretched out over distant hills like a picture or a dream. The smell of the smoke was less irritable outside the passageway. It was like a big campfire had gotten out of hand.

Screams, alarms, and gunshots echoed from over the high prison walls. The unlucky would die, but Lucas was sure that the riot would end soon, and normalcy would be reinstituted with vigor. The warden had little use for chaos— and even less patience for escapees. But this was a big event, bigger than any Lucas could ever recall. The hell that would be paid would be doled out generously and viciously.

The guards' shots pinged off the walls and thudded into the ground inches from Lucas's and Zeke's feet. The prison wall jutted out into a thin grove of oak trees, making it difficult, at the distance the guards were at, to get a clear shot. They were shooting from an odd angle and at quick intervals. Luckily, they hadn't figured out yet that Zeke's Spencer was empty, and that he had no more ammunition to carry on the fight.

"Come on, then, don't just be standin' there waitin' for the angels." There was a hint of annoyance in Zeke's voice. He stared at Lucas like he was an insolent child, one that had been reprimanded more than once already.

Lucas had little time to consider his options. Whether he liked it or not, his fate was in Zeke's hands.

Oddly enough, it wasn't the first time in his life that he'd had to rely on a Negro to see him out of trouble. When he was a boy on the plantation, he'd been saved from troubles more than once by the old mammy, Miss Mattie Pol, or one of the house boys who were her minions and, most times, his only friends. Being an only child, the heir to all that lay before him, he had no brothers or sisters, and no cousins nearby, either.

That was a different time, though. Friendships were not out of the question—there was the social circle that his family operated in, bringing him in touch with like-minded boys like John Barlow, and in his early teen years, girls like Charlotte Brogan, of the same stature, came into the circle. But it seemed, for the most part, that he had found himself alone, relying on his own wits.

Later, when he grew up and left the plantation in search of his own fortunes, before the war and then during, Lucas had been in the company of Negroes who had been at hand to see him to safety, or to help him accomplish his most risky spy missions.

Those situations were rare, given that his allegiance was to the Confederacy, but just as there was an Underground Railroad that saw runaway slaves safely to the North, there was a network of Negroes that collected information from the North and brought it back south, serving masters or their own interests, it was hard to tell. The information that the Negroes provided had, at times, proven to be extremely valuable to the cause. They were as invisible in the North as they were in the South.

So his reliance on Zeke was not as unheard of as most of the other prisoners might have thought, if they would have seen, or been privy to, what was happening.

The prospect of spring, of the surroundings, was lost on Lucas, and the past was only relevant in considering his hesitation to trust a Negro, or anyone for that matter. His only aim was to keep up with Zeke, or at least keep him in his sights. Zeke was a fast runner.

Shots continued to fire at them, behind them, but Lucas was able to keep the Negro within sight, catching up to him slowly.

Ten yards turned into twenty, then twenty into thirty. Lucas's heartbeat raced and his eyes grew wide at the revelation that lay in front of him.

The land sloped downward, aiding in his speed, and the

oaks became fewer. The ground grew softer, and clouds of insects hung in the air in the distance, like smoke clouds breaking apart then re-forming. The sounds rising from the prison grew distant, like the mumble of a faraway crowd, and the smell of smoke faded away, replaced with the fresh smell of a rolling, spring rain–filled river.

Just at the Cockrill Bend of the Cumberland River, on a barren bank crumbling from erosion and time, two horses stood still as statues, saddled and ready to go. They were tied to a towering sycamore, white bark cracked with age, that bent toward the river, its roots thick as a man's leg, showing at the base, digging deep to hold it upright.

Zeke looked over his shoulder. "The promised land ain't far now, Mistuh Fume. No suh, not far now."

The words, and the hope, were answered with the crack of a rifle shot, catching Zeke in the back of the shoulder, sending him tumbling forward, falling out of control like he was an insect, smacked down by a giant, invisible hand. He bounced off the ground as a fountain of blood exploded upward.

The horses jumped and nayed, spooked by the shot. Lucas didn't look over his shoulder. He swerved past Zeke and kept running. He ran toward the horses, toward freedom, certain that he was about to take his last breath, too, that a shot would catch him from behind. He was determined to reach the horses. He was so close to escaping he could taste it.

"Go, Mistuh Fume, you just keep goin' on now," Zeke called out painfully but directly, like he was a captain giving an order. "Just go!"

ELEVEN

CHARLOTTE BROGAN STOOD STIFFLY BEFORE
the mirror as she buttoned the top button of her princess-
seamed gown, without the train—the Watteau back—
attached. The gown was proper for breakfast or tea, and in
accordance with common manners, it had a high-necked
mandarin collar.

The tightness of the buttoned collar pinched Charlotte's
throat, a reminder to breathe as evenly as possible. It was a
persistent annoyance to her to dress so completely in the
middle of the night, or any other time when the need came
to leave her berth, but for her own peace of mind, she needed
out of the room, as far away from her dreams and nightmares as possible. She most certainly wouldn't want to show
herself in a bad, undignified light, to any of the upstanding
passengers riding the train, by dressing in a manner that
was unseemly or inappropriate.

The gown had been laid out for the next day, and there
were plenty more to choose from once this one was soiled.

Her feet were steady as she headed to the door, her balance completely adjusted to the rock and sway of the train. Walking about on the train was second nature to her now, after spending so much time on the move instead of in one place. She felt no regret, no loss of days past, at least not that she would confront alone in the dark.

Charlotte opened the door of her berth and peeked up and down the long aisle of the railcar. She saw no one and heard nothing but the constant rumble of the wheels clattering along the iron rails below her. It was a comforting sound, much like the waves of the ocean constantly beating against the shore. Sometimes softly, sometimes with rage—it depended on the speed of the train, how much it reminded her of the water. Those times, those visits to the ocean, were in the distant past, but seeded deep within her mind and soul. Some days, she could barely remember being a little girl.

Certain that the way was clear, she stepped out of the berth. Charlotte squared her shoulders and pushed her freshly combed hair, red as a rose, over her shoulder. It was a habit that she thought little of, but one never knew what one would encounter with strangers coming and going as they did on the train.

There was no question of her destination.

The living quarters at the back of the train held pitchers of drink, most likely water at this time of night, and other refreshments, and a collection of books that she had only made her way halfway through.

She wished there was more Austen, but alas there were only so many of those books left to the world, and she had conquered all of dear Miss Jane's novels more than once. She was still working her way through the Brontë sisters' works, but she was in no mood to slip into *The Tenant of Wildfell Hall* on this night.

The story of a woman living under an assumed name, who had fled a terrible life only to find, potentially, a man who longed to know the truth of her, was intriguing, if not instructive. The book offered a bit of rebellion, scandalous as it was in its nature, breaking English law and the social expectations of those involved. Of course, she had to know how it all turned out, but this night, after the powerful vision she had suffered at the edge of sleep, called for something less combative, something more comforting. Perhaps poetry and a warm sip of milk, if that was possible, would suit her.

Charlotte made her way toward the peacock doors, unconcerned about the presence of the two Chinese guards who stood in wait for anyone who approached.

Without a flinch, or utterance of one word, both of the guards opened the doors for Charlotte in unison. It was as if she were truly a princess or a queen, her passage into the room undeniable, unquestioned. And just as they did not acknowledge her personally, Charlotte did not acknowledge them. Their presence was expected, counted on, a large piece of her continuing comfort. The offer of protection and safety was never far away.

Beyond the train, and sometimes on the train, savages lurked, outlaws raided, and bad men sought to do bad things. She had hidden means to protect herself, but she knew she would be an easy target for Indians if they ever overtook the train. Her red scalp would fetch a great deal of notice for the brave who brought it home. But there was no question that the Chinese guards would give their lives in defense of hers. It was their job.

Once she was over the threshold and inside the room, the doors closed behind her. The locks slipped back into place, echoing with certainty and comfort behind her. She would have to signal her departure, the process and procedure as sure to her as the steps she took into the room.

The compartment at the end of the train was much like a parlor in a grand house, the furniture lush and expensive but comfortable to lounge on. The windows were hidden behind heavy velvet drapes that fell to the floor, closed tight against the darkness and unknown landscape outside them.

The sconces burned low on the walls, offering enough light to navigate anywhere in the room.

Shadows flickered easily about Charlotte as the small flames reacted to her presence, to her passing. The room smelled of freshly cleaned fabric—a daily chore for the porters—a dash of coal oil from the flames, and another smell that Charlotte couldn't directly identify, a food with a sweet spice.

She smiled slightly as she made her way to a long buffet against the far wall. Next to a hurricane lamp with a slight flame sat a pitcher of milk and a glass plate that held half a cake.

"I get hungry in the night."

The voice startled her. She hadn't seen him, though she should have expected him to be in the room. He always was.

Charlotte didn't acknowledge his presence; she knew he was sitting in the darkness that surrounded his desk. It was his island, his safe place, from which he directed, and worried over, his empire. "I am less hungry than thirsty. I am glad to see the milk," she said.

"Sleep is a distant mistress," he said.

"And there is nothing to tease away the day's worries? I am sure there are ladies on board that would be glad to offer you a bit of their tonic."

"What? And cloud my judgment? Become dependent on the need of opiates? I am no fiend. Nor do I wish to lurch about numbed to the demands I face. My pain is a constant reminder of what once was, that is all. I have learned to live with it. You must know that by now."

"I am sorry," Charlotte said, "I didn't mean to cause you any discomfort."

"There is never any pain in your presence."

That had not always been true, and she wasn't sure that it was now. Lucas Fume and John Barlow had vied for her affections as teenagers, but in her mind, in her heart, there had never been any competition. Lucas had had her heart from the first moment she saw him, and in the end, she had broken John Barlow's heart—but business, a shared greed, and desire for what they could not have had forged a forgiveness—and a partnership that required more of Charlotte than she had ever thought it would.

Charlotte poured herself a small glass of milk, eyed the cake, then decided to avoid it. She still had not turned to face him. She sought to maintain her comfort for as long as she could, her back to him. Regardless of the length of their relationship, and the nature of it, being astutely aware of her own intentions and words was extremely important.

She ignored the compliment and whatever meaning had been underlying the statement. "I had thought that milk and poetry would see me safely back to slumber."

"But you encountered me instead?"

"A delightful surprise."

"Are you uncomfortable?"

"I beg your pardon?"

"In the berth, I mean, on the train, since we have left St. Louis?"

Charlotte took a sip of the milk. It tasted fresh, luke-warm, the way she liked it. "No, no, why would you think such a thing? I am completely comfortable. Everything is as it always is."

"But yet, you cannot sleep."

"An affliction of old. I wake up sometimes and it is difficult to return to sleep. That has nothing to do with my accommodations, or the state of my life. I have no worries at all. All of my needs are cared for. You have seen to that, John."

Cold silence answered Charlotte, followed by the hard scoot of a chair, tumbling backward. She turned suddenly, as if bidden, to see him rising, standing up, still hidden in the shadows, just a silhouette of himself, really, the anger on his face unmistakable.

"You can't call me that," he said through clenched teeth.

"I'm sorry, I thought we were alone."

"It doesn't matter. You must never, never call me that again. Do you understand?" He stepped out from behind the desk, but stopped at the corner of it, almost as if he was afraid to continue on any farther.

"I'm sorry," Charlotte said.

"Lanford. Say it. I'm sorry, Lanford."

A cold chill ran down Charlotte's spine. A hint of fear followed, reaching all the way to her toes. She shivered.

Just as she was about to do as she was told, the screech of the train's brakes and the unexpected lurch of the slowing car forced the words back into her throat. She took a second to reconsider, to regain her balance. "Why are we stopping?"

He stared at her for a long second, still glaring. "I have business to tend to. A wire to send. We won't be stopped for long."

Charlotte nodded, acknowledging her position—and his. There was no need to question his ways or his business. She had ceased doing that a long time ago. She walked over to him slowly then, never looking away from his deep, penetrating eyes that always seemed black no matter the time of day or position of the sun. He did not move, did not yield to her approach. He did nothing but stand there as she cupped his face in her hands. She smiled for a brief moment, calming the air between them.

Without saying another word, Charlotte Brogan leaned in, kissed him gently on the cheek, and said, "I'm sorry, Lanford. It won't happen again. I promise."

TWELVE

LUCAS MADE IT TO THE FIRST HORSE, A BAY gelding that seemed unaffected by the gunfire or any of the chaos arising from the prison. He used the horse as a shield for a brief second, long enough to recognize that there was a rifle in the scabbard. Without hesitation, he grabbed the weapon, pulled it out, and brought the first guard he could see into his sights.

The rifle was loaded and ready to go. He emptied the chamber with vigor and accurate aim. It was another Spencer. There were ten shots, enough to let his pursuers know that he was well armed and capable of answering back. It was a battle now, not a matter of shooting sitting ducks.

The problem was, no matter how much ammunition was stored in the bay's saddlebags, Lucas was outmatched. There would be more guards, especially once the word got out that there had been an escape, that two prisoners had made it outside the walls.

Lucas reloaded the Spencer quickly and threw himself

up on the bay gelding's saddle. He hunkered down as low he as could, making himself as small a target as possible.

The guards had stopped shooting for a long moment, maybe regrouping, reloading, or waiting for reinforcements. There was no way for Lucas to know whether his aim had found its target or not. He could only take the silence of rifles as a good sign. He couldn't see any shadows to tell how many guards stood to shoot.

Zeke was still on the ground, struggling to stand. Blood soaked though the big Negro's shirt, and his eyes looked weak, but he seemed determined to make it to the other horse. He pulled himself up on his knees. It looked like he was pulling a cartload of boulders instead of trying to regain his footing.

"Go on now, get out of here!" Zeke yelled as he stood weakly, one leg at a time. The pain of the act showed with twists of his face. His forehead glistened with sweat and determination, but there was no mistaking the bullet wound. If it was left untreated, there was no question that the Negro would die.

The horse Lucas had found himself on was already pulling on the bit, ready to make a run for it. The gunfire might not have bothered the gelding, but once a rider climbed onto the saddle it was set to go.

Lucas had known horses like this one before, runners, always ready to flee or run a race. Someone had known what they were doing, depositing the getaway rides here, and the right kind, too. It made him even more curious about the events that had played out since the fight with the pale man started, but there was no time to question anything at the moment. His life was still at stake. And he had to decide whether to give the horse its head or hold it back.

A quick glance over his shoulder told him that he was close to the river.

The waterway would be the safest exit. If the water was low enough, he could ride out from the banks, leaving little or no trace of hoofprints. Once he was far enough downriver, it would be impossible to track him. It was a fault in the placement of the prison, and an advantage that Lucas had thought about more than once.

Every prisoner dreamed of his escape, plotted it in the middle of the night—but few saw that dream become a reality. Lucas would have been confident and assured if he had been privy to the planning of his escape, had had a say in the timing and direction. As it was, he knew nothing and was left, again, to survive on his own wits.

The question that faced him in that brief second was simple: Run now or circle around and make sure the Negro came with him?

It would be simpler to travel alone, without Zeke. Traveling alone was always easier. But all things considered, no matter the color of the man's skin, Lucas couldn't leave him there to die. The decision was that quick, and that simple. But it came just as the guards either regained their courage, reloaded, or added to their ranks. They started shooting.

The ground behind Zeke exploded in multiple clouds of dust.

Lucas answered back just as quickly, shooting in return, as he reined the horse loosely and guided it to the far side of Zeke.

He was too late.

One of the shots hit the other horse, a darker gelding that had seemed more nervous at the onset of the gun battle, in the hindquarters.

The horse brayed with pain and skittered sideways. It was tied to the sycamore, and there was no way it could pull itself free. Another shot hit the horse in the neck, and the force of the bullet knocked the animal sideways, then to its knees screaming.

In a quick, calculated motion, Lucas reared his horse back, and yelled to Zeke, "Come on, with me. I'm not leaving here without you." He stretched his hand out, signaling Zeke the best he could what his intentions were.

Zeke nodded, drew on what remaining strength he could muster, and stood fully erect.

No more words had to be spoken. Death was in the air, the

smell of blood and black powder as common as ragweed in the fall. Pain stood carved in Zeke's face, the anticipation of Lucas's rolling intention as certain as the next breath—which was hardly guaranteed if one of the guards got lucky with a shot.

Lucas pushed the gelding, broke it into a run, and circled as close to Zeke as he could get. He leaned down, his arm extended fully on a running pass. He grabbed the Negro's good forearm. The bloody arm was limp and useless.

Zeke leapt into the air, jumped with all his might, as gunshots peppered the ground—close enough to create a wall of dust that was detrimental to the guards' aim and surety of success. The Negro groaned with pain, but it dissipated into the air unacknowledged by Lucas.

There was nothing Lucas could do at the moment to help Zeke other than to flee. "Giddyup! Go!" The horse's spirit carried it forward, happily giving into Lucas's command as he pointed it toward the river and gave it its head.

A barrage of gunshots from the prison guards followed, hitting the trees and ground around them. It sounded as if a storm were chasing them, but that didn't stop Lucas from turning around.

He could make out movement in the shadows along the prison wall, more guards firing while taking cover. But they were not his concern. He felt confident that the mount he was on would see them out of range quickly. Most likely, in a matter of minutes, there would be a larger posse of guards hot on their trail.

But Lucas could not abide unnecessary suffering of any kind. With as much accuracy as he could attain, he turned in the opposite direction, on a jostling horse, with a bleeding Negro at his back, barely holding on, and sighted on the wounded horse. He breathed in, then out, calming his trigger finger, before he pulled it.

The shot hit the dark gelding just above the eye, sending it the rest of the way to the ground in a cloud of dust and a quick death.

Lucas shoved the rifle at Zeke, who took it right away, and then Lucas focused his attention on the land before them.

"You gonna die on me?" he asked.

"I hopes not," Zeke answered. "Be a shame to die now, wouldn't it?"

"Any more surprises I should expect?"

"None that I knows of."

"You're sure about that?"

Lucas could feel the man shake his head behind him. It was a good enough answer for him, as the wind washed down his throat and wiped the sweat from his forehead.

"Ride to the river," Zeke said.

"I was planning on that."

"Ride away from Nashville," Zeke said. There was a weakness in his voice, the confidence gone, drained from the jump onto the horse.

"Been silly to go the other way," Lucas said, expecting an answer. But none came, not as quick as the others.

He looked over his shoulder, and saw that Zeke's eyes were starting to ride up into his head. His grip on the rifle fell away, and Lucas was able to grab it just before it fell to the ground.

He had no choice but to slide the Spencer into the open scabbard. That done, he grabbed Zeke's arm as quickly as he could, before the Negro toppled sideways off the horse.

Lucas wasn't sure whether Zeke had passed out from the pain or just died on him. He wasn't about to stop and find out.

Lucas urged the gelding on with another hard flip of the reins, a solid press from both legs, and as harsh a "giddyup" as he could force out of his dry mouth.

The gelding answered with a kick and a leap forward, pushing them farther away from the prison and farther into the depths of freedom than Lucas had thought, at least at the beginning of the day, was never going to be possible.

THIRTEEN

LUCAS KNEW LITTLE OF THE LAND EAST OF
Nashville. He was more familiar with the city itself, having
traveled the streets from time to time ever since he was a
little boy. He pushed away those memories as quickly as
they came—foggy images of his mother and father at the
height of their health and wealth. That life of privilege was
gone, and no matter what he did, it couldn't be brought back.
He ached for it though, but more so in the depths of a dark
prison cell than now, on the run.

Since he had no knowledge of his whereabouts, Lucas
had only his instincts to rely on. He drove the horse as hard
as it would run, away from the burning prison, pushing it
in the most open direction there was. At the same time, he
held on to Zeke as tightly as he could with one hand, trap-
ping the Negro's big arm between his arm and belly. It
seemed an impossible task, but one that was fueled by fear,
adrenaline, and the overwhelming desire to be as far away
from the prison's walls as possible.

Zeke had collapsed forward and remained unresponsive. Lucas worried about how far they could go, and how fast, but there was no stopping—unless the Negro fell off. Then Lucas would be forced to figure out another solution for their escape.

The bend of the Cumberland River cut through a flat part of low-level hills that rose up slowly beyond the Tennessee State Prison. Mountains were to the south, farther than Lucas's family home, which was a shame—hiding in the heavily forested ridges would have been easier than finding cover in the hills. As it was, the rise offered a clear ride. A visible trail cut through the thick forest that led away from the prison, and from Nashville itself.

Not far off, sycamores, cottonwoods, and a hearty selection of hardwoods towered along the banks of the river, which, much to Lucas's disappointment, was not going to be as easy to navigate as he had originally hoped.

Spring rains had swollen the waterway, forcing floodwaters over the banks and into the natural plains that were normally dry and sandy.

The trail was about to end in a rush of swirling water, brown and muddy, full of debris. Anything man-made, or otherwise, that had tumbled into the river zipped by at great speed. An opossum huddled on an uprooted tree, worry and fear pinned in its beady eyes, as the tree swerved and tumbled from side to side with the speed of a great ship, making its way downriver to an unknown port.

There was no way that a horse with two men on it, one of no use, could navigate such powerful water with ease. They'd come too far to die drowning.

There had been no posse showing up behind them. At least, not yet. Any shots being fired were distant echoes, if they could be called that. There was no mistaking the continuing gunfire at the prison. The sound of the riot, the smell of the fire, the burning of human flesh, the results of the action to see him out of prison—all settled deeply in Lucas's soul.

Warfare and violence flowed through his veins far more prominently than gentler actions, though he could account for those if he had to. Fighting for his life, one way or another, had been required of him since the onset of manhood, and actually before. He'd always been quick to raise his fists to a fight. Too quick, his father always said—mostly with admonishment and shame. But innocent death unseated him, mattered to him, probably more than ever now that he had truly experienced the hopelessness and depression of prison life.

Just ahead, the trail ended abruptly as the river cut into new territory, rushing through the floodplain, conquering every ounce of dirt and undergrowth in its path.

The river was loud. It roared like unfettered and unorganized music in an opera house. The intense volume of it nearly drowned out the riot at the prison.

Lucas was lost and left with the unenviable consideration of possibly going back the way he had come. The flood was a line of invisible infantrymen, bayonets at the ready, driving him in a direction he did not want to go. Ghosts of Shiloh and Chickamauga taunted him, reminded him that in the end they had all failed in those battles, regardless of what the record books said, and he might face the same fate now. If his future mirrored the end result of the Confederacy, then he might as well swim the horse straight into the river and give himself over to the raging current.

It was then that he felt Zeke's heartbeat against his back. The Negro stirred, and Lucas looked over his shoulder.

"I thought you were dead," Lucas said.

"If this be heaven, then I have come to it on an ugly day."

"More likely hell than heaven."

"That would explain the smell," Zeke said, his voice deadpan, void of emotion.

"I'm afraid there's no going forward."

"Where is we?"

"Down the trail, east of the prison. I know the way south

to Franklin and beyond, but I don't know much of the roads east, toward Mount Juliet or Lebanon."

"Roads lead to surrender or death," Zeke said. His breathing was shallow, but he pulled back, sat up, and took his arm from Lucas's grip. "They be lookin' for us in all the 'spected places. You knows that."

"What was the plan?"

Zeke hesitated, then spoke even softer. "I don't know as much as you think I does. I told you, I was to see you free, then I was on my own to go where I needed to. They was supposed to be plans in the saddlebag beyond my know-how."

"And where would you go?"

"Ain't no home no more. Nowhere that there are arms to run to. This ain't the end of war. If they was a place waitin' for me, then I'd just lead more of my trouble there. Ain't gonna do that no more. I was gonna run, that's all. Make a new life. But now, with the burn and bloody hole in my shoulder, I 'spect I'll see the grave sooner than I'll have a chance at livin'."

"Why you?"

"Pardon?"

"Why was it you that helped me to escape?"

"'Cause I was the only one that'd do it, I s'pose."

"Someone came to you?" Lucas could feel Zeke nod yes. "Who? Who was it that came to you, and why?"

"Don't know. It was dark, in the middle of the night, no flames burning, dark as the inside of my eyelids. Might have been a guard, but I never heard the voice before. Just a man with an offer and a plan."

"For what?"

"I'm free, ain't I? No, suh, there was only one answer— and it had nothin' to do with you."

Lucas nodded unconsciously. "Neither of us is free, and you know it. A posse and a pack of dogs'll be on us before we can blink, and our faces'll be plastered on every sheriff's wall in the state. That ain't free. It's not a life, always looking over your shoulder to see what's coming after you. You know that, too. Surely you saw what happened when a Negro slave made a run for it and was caught? It'll be as bad, or worse, for us."

"They was supposed to be instructions with the horse," Zeke said. "That's all I know."

"Well," Lucas said, "I hope they were with this horse, because the other one's dead."

Silence settled between the two men. Lucas considered the possibility that they might be on their own, that there weren't redundant instructions on each horse. It would be a failure of process if that was the case—but he had no idea who was behind the plan, so he didn't know anything of their plotting skills. But, so far, the escape had been impressive in its undertaking and planning.

Lucas was just about to hop off the horse and search the saddlebags, when a shot rang out close by, garnering his attention.

"You know how to swim?" Lucas asked Zeke.

"Not too good, but I figures you gonna head straight into that water whethers I say yes or not."

"You figured right," Lucas said, spurring the hesitant bay gelding forward into the raging, flooded Cumberland River.

FOURTEEN

JOE STRAUT STARED AT THE GOLD POCKET watch with dry admiration. It dangled from his hand, swinging softly like the pendulum of a fancy grandfather clock. The cover was closed, the picture hidden inside of a man and woman, the same two in the berth, on the day of their wedding. He'd peeked at it out of curiosity, opened the watch and closed it quickly upon realizing that the picture had captured the couple on a happier day.

An inscription on the back of the watch read: *To my wonderful husband on the occasion of our marriage. 07/04/1871. JLW.*

The watch would have to be disposed of, too, just like the bodies. Trinkets were not what the Boss was after. Straut liked this one, and thought it a shame to destroy it, but that's what would have to be done. He didn't want to know the whys or wherefores. It made him less accountable, less apt to make a mistake of the tongue in the wrong place, or at the wrong time. Not knowing the motive was safe. Just the way Joe Straut liked it.

The task at hand was very simple: Leave no trace that these three people ever existed, that they had ever set foot on the train, that they had ever had any kind of connection with Lanford Grips at all.

The Boss had made that clear the first time Straut was assigned the task of disposing of ill-fated patrons. Most of those times had been on land, so a deep well or a fire set to a house had served the purpose of leaving no trace. But this time, well, it seemed different; rushed, less thought out by the Boss, desperate somehow. It had come sooner than the others. These three didn't even have a nice dinner before they were shoved off the earth and into the heavens—or wherever their dear, departed souls had ended up. Joe Straut had lost his belief in anything good or heavenly in the broad daylight at Shiloh.

"This looks like the last bit of tidying up," Straut said to Finney Deets.

Deets rubbed his right hand through his oily hair, a stoic but concerned look on his ratty face. "What we gonna do with 'em, Sarge? You thought about that much?"

Straut shook his head no. He hated to show Deets a shred of doubt, but he just had, and there was no taking it back.

Just as he was about to prove to his underling that he was still in charge, the train lurched forward, coming to a sudden and unexpected stop. The iron wheels skidded on the rails underneath their feet, and both men bobbled sideways.

Straut wasn't prepared for the stop, and he lost his balance. He crashed into the closed door and dropped the watch. It bounced on the floor and under the bench seat, out of sight.

Deets was unprepared, as well, and swayed in the opposite direction, ending up on the floor next to the window, square on his butt. "What the hell?" he gasped, jumping up as quickly as he could, dusting himself off, a look of embarrassment on his face replacing any other emotion. Without any regard to Straut, Deets peeked out the side of the drapes to see what was happening.

"You see anything?" Straut asked.

"Darkness is all. Just black nothingness for as far as I can see. No water tower, no town—nothin' but stars and the unknown. You'd think there'd be a band of outlaws hootin' and hollerin', but I don't hear nothin', either. Just the rumble of the engine. Sounds like a mad bull to me, restrained and still rarin' to go. Odd time to stop. Not planned, is it?"

"I don't think so. It's odd." Straut sighed, and shook his head. "You sure there's nothing out there?"

"Sure as it's nighttime and I'm standin' right here talkin' to you."

"All right." Straut gathered himself, stepped back, opened the door to the berth, and looked up and down the passageway.

The sconces were dim, the flames almost nonexistent, and even odder, the two Chinese guards outside the peacock doors were gone.

"Something's up," Straut said, pulling his head back inside the berth.

He thought about what he'd seen and looked out again to make sure he was seeing things right. He was. The guards were gone. There was no sign of any living human being in the railcar. It looked eerie—like the inside of a tomb, and it felt just as chilly as one, too.

An exit door sat almost directly across from the berth. Straut eyed it carefully, and hadn't considered it until that moment. "I got an idea about getting rid of these three," he said to Deets, "but I'm not sure if it's a good one."

"Whatcha thinkin'?"

"I'll be right back. You stay here. I need to figure out why we're stopped first."

Deets shrugged. "All right, Sarge, whatever you say. But hurry up, these dead folks are makin' me a tad uncomfortable."

Straut ignored the comment and ducked out of the berth, all of his senses alive, just waiting for one of the black-garbed Chinamen to jump out and attack him. His draw strap was open, and his hand rested firmly on the grip of his six-shooter. As fast as those feet-fighters were, he knew he'd never get a shot off if he was attacked, or stopped, but as he made his way to the door, it helped calm his nerves a bit to know that he could reach for his gun if he had to. He always figured he'd die fighting for his life one way or the other.

He unlatched the door as quietly as he could, then slid it open with as much silence and ease as he could apply.

Darkness pervaded every inch of his sight. There were no mountains, no towns, no light but the silver pinprick stars overhead—just like Deets had said.

The moon had risen or fallen; Straut had no idea of the orb's course in the sky, because he had been stuck inside the train, and not on the trail, for a while. It had always been a comfort to him, knowing how things moved in the sky, and what to expect next.

The only sound he could hear was the ongoing rumble of the locomotive as it stood still, waiting to move on.

It was obvious that they were not stopped for the night, but Straut had no idea what had precipitated the current lack of movement toward Kansas City. Like the quickness of the kill, this, too, was outside of the Boss's normal set of behaviors.

He looked over his shoulder and made sure the passage-way was still clear. It was, so he climbed down the outer ladder cautiously, listening for anything out of the ordinary, and planted his feet squarely on the ground—but ready to retreat at a moment's notice.

A cloud of steam was exhaled from underneath the loco-motive, an unexpected belch in the night that brought a jump to Straut's heart.

There was nothing to worry about, he told himself. He had every right to investigate the stop, every right to use it as an excuse for his actions, if he needed one. But he *was* nervous, because the truth was, he wasn't looking for the cause of the stop—he was looking for a place to dump three bodies.

Straut eased along the side of the train in the shadows, careful with every step. His vision adjusted to darkness quickly. It didn't take him long to find a spot he thought would be perfect.

A creek ventured under the tracks about twenty-five yards north of the train. A small trestle had been erected over the waterway, which from the look of it was nothing more than a trickle at the moment—hard to say what it was when the seasonal rains came, but the trestle had been built for a reason, there was no doubt about that. Timber was scarce in these parts, ties hard to come by. Nothing was built that didn't need to be. Despite all the things that Straut didn't know about Lanford Grips, he did know that part of the man's fortune was steeped in the timber business. Railroads would always need lumber, either for repair, new lines, or spurs. The railroad that now stretched across the country was just the beginning, not the end.

The bridge stood about ten feet tall, and from the look of the lay of the land, there was nothing but flat, uninhabited plains beyond it. Though it was difficult to tell since the night was so dark. Spring frogs jingled in the distance, offering evidence of a body of water, maybe a pond, a lake, or even a river, close by. It was hard to tell which. Straut had no idea where in the world he was, but he sighed with relief at the discovery of the bridge.

If he hurried, they'd be able to tuck away the bodies before the train departed. It would save him from dismembering them and tossing the remains, piece by piece, into the firebox. That was a task he wanted to avoid at all costs. It was the most sure way of making the bodies disappear completely from this earth—but not from his mind. He didn't want that memory, plain and simple.

Straut's plan to deposit the bodies under the trestle relied on nature, coyote and the like, to do away with the ill-fated passengers. The thought worried him that they might somehow be found, but there would be no way to identify them if that were the case. He hoped there would only be bones left, and those surely could tell no tales. The land west of the Mississippi was littered with bones and lost stories. Straut was sure of it, counted on it, with every gambling breath he took.

FIFTEEN

CHARLOTTE BROGAN SAT STARING AT THE struggling flame of the small hurricane lamp, her mind focused on what was before her, and little else.

The distant roar of the train's hungry steam engine vibrated under her feet, idling in wait for the command to move on into the darkness. They were stopped miles from Kansas City.

The rumble was a little louder than normal, since the railcar's window was open. Sounds of the night were drowned out, but the chill of it was apparent, as was the smell. There was water nearby, she was sure of it. A breeze wafted in, carrying the aroma of dead fish. It was a smell she could hardly abide, but she knew better than to protest against the open window.

"Is there any answer?" Lanford Grips demanded.

He sat behind his desk stiffly, eyeing the telegraph operator with expectation. A wire was strung through the window, attached to a simple brass Morse code telegraph key sitting on the desk. They had stopped to communicate, to tap into a wire, for some reason or another. It must have been for something important, but Charlotte was not privy to such information. At least not directly.

The operator, Ernest Hanesly, a mousy little man Charlotte had seen from time to time on the train, was sweating profusely as he stared at the little machine, waiting for an answer. He looked all a muss, like he'd been roused from his bed for this very exercise. Charlotte found the current situation all very curious, but she said nothing. It was only a matter of luck and timing that she had been in the room when the train came to a stop.

The key started tapping. Charlotte ignored it, at least physically—but in her mind she put together the long taps and short taps, dots and dashes, on paper and began deciphering the message silently in her mind. Word from a distant, unknown messenger came fast and very simply: *Still alive. Maybe.*

Charlotte did not move, but watched Lanford closely out of the corner of her eye. She kept that name close in her mind so she wouldn't make another mistake, though it was difficult. Her secret-keeping skills had always been extremely well honed, but they had not been thoroughly tested of late.

Hanesly wrote each letter out, stared at the paper once the key had gone silent, and slid it across the desk directly in front of Lanford Grips.

As always, Bojack Wu stood behind Lanford, always within reach, a shadow with a mind of his own, duty forever etched on his emotionless, yellow-skinned face. There was no sign that the guard was even breathing.

As she watched, Charlotte realized she knew little of Bojack Wu—how he had come into the employ of Lanford Grips, where he came from, what his life was like before he came to this country, if that was, in truth, his reality. For all she knew, he had been born here. There was no way to tell.

Charlotte could only surmise that he was once a worker for the Central Pacific, one of the many Celestials brought across the sea by the promise of riches, only to find toil and hard work that reflected back to the recent battles of slavery. Something told Charlotte that bondage wouldn't have suited Bojack Wu well. Somehow, he had found his way to where he stood, a man whole in body and mind, with invisible skills that at once offered fear and respect. Lanford trusted the man with his life, but Bojack Wu was much more than just a guard or a valet; he was like an extra appendage, a gun always cocked, a cannon with a fuse constantly lit, a fist always pulled tight, ready to protect, ready to defend, ready to serve at any moment for any cause. The manner of compensation was unknown, and it, too, could only be surmised. There had to be something more than money involved. Perhaps it was just employment for its own sake and nothing more. Some men, no matter their color, needed something to devote themselves to.

Bojack Wu made Lanford Grips what he was . . . now. Charlotte had known Lanford long enough to see the difference that the valet had made in his life.

"Still alive." It was a whisper from Lanford Grips's hard, pursed lips, as he read aloud from the paper Hanesly had slid over to him. "And what the hell does 'maybe' mean?" He tensed up even more. If his face had been made of stone, it would have shattered, and as always, his arms were ticked tight to his sides, disappearing under the desk. "What the hell does 'maybe' mean?" he repeated, this time louder, his voice rising in pitch to almost a yell.

Charlotte glanced over to Lanford, then looked away quickly. She had seen a similar rage settle in his eyes before. She knew that an eruption, emotional or violently physical, would most likely follow this outburst. It was difficult not to feel sorry for Ernest Hanesly. The poor man's teeth chattered with fear.

"I can't make it say anything other than what it does,

Boss," the wire operator said. Sweat dipped off his nose and splashed onto the desk.

Lanford noticed the little man's fear, and stared at the wet mark for a long second. The tips of Grips's ears burned red. "Well, ask them what it means, goddamn it. Ask them what it means!" The volume of his voice was high now, operatic, the primal scream of a sullen toddler, demanding and petulant.

Charlotte saw Bojack Wu's chest heave slightly, showing a deep breath, but the emotion on his face did not change. Nothing did—on the outside.

In a quick flurry, Lanford pulled his hands out from under the desk and slammed them on it. But they were not hands. Not real hands. It was not the slap of flesh against wood that exploded inside the luxurious compartment, garnering everyone's attention. It was metal against wood.

Lanford Grips had no hands. Hooks had taken their place. Cold, engineered metal hooks that lacked feeling, dexterity, and the ability to create anything—anything but pain and terror. The exposure of the hooks to the world beyond Charlotte and Bojack Wu was a rarity, an occurrence akin to a white buffalo being seen from the window of the train. Or a live brown one, these days.

Ernest Hanesly began tapping the key furiously, as Lanford raked his hooks across the desk, gouging a deep scratch with each one. The scraping sent chills up and down Charlotte's spine—but she didn't move.

Lanford Grips stood up abruptly as he pulled the hooks off the damaged wood. "Why is it that he always seems to escape my reach? I should go there and just kill him myself, and be done with it. That was my gravest error. One I have come to regret in more ways than one. I should have just killed the bastard." He stepped out from behind the desk and began pacing back and forth in front of Charlotte.

"You know that's impossible," Charlotte said. Her voice

was calm. She remained sitting, doing her best to avoid Lanford's wrath.

"Impossible? Is he a roach? You stomp on them, and they live on. I am at my wit's end with this charade. I can turn this train around and go back to Tennessee anytime I wish."

"And then you will cease being Lanford Grips, and John Barlow returns from the grave," Charlotte said. "A dead man walking on the earth to settle a score. You will be recognized, and so will the need to free Lucas from his imprisonment. He will be set free, his claim of being framed for your murder proven true, and you will be put in his place. You know that."

Lanford stopped. "I told you to never say that name again. Now look what you've done, Charlotte. Now look what you've gone and made me do." He glanced quickly over to Ernest Hanesly.

"Oh, dear." The blood drained from Charlotte's face. Her toes felt the chill and reality of her error. She stood up. "Really, Lanford, you mustn't."

Grips put up his right hook in protest. "Wait," he demanded.

Charlotte exhaled, and a tear seeped out of the corner of her eye. She followed his gaze over to Hanesly, who was busy scribbling down the taps that were coming across the wire more furiously than ever.

"There's more bad news, I'm afraid," he said. "The maybe is now a certainty. He *is* alive."

"Pray tell," Lanford answered. "Why am I not surprised?" He had not allowed the hook to fall to his side. It hung in the air, the center of attention. The flames of all the lamps in the room flickered off the silver, making the metal glow orange, like it had just been forged. Grips's voice was calmer now, like he had taken a deep breath and was sane again.

But Charlotte knew that wasn't it at all. Lanford Grips was not sane. He was anticipating what was to come next.

"Yes," Hanesly said. "There's been a riot at the prison. It is on fire."

"And that's bad news?" Lanford asked.

"It is," the mousy little wire operator said, setting down his pen and looking fearfully into Grips's cold eyes. "It seems that Lucas Fume has escaped." He drew back unconsciously, the words weak, breaking out of his mouth like shattered glass.

All of the air seemed to disappear from the room. The lamp flames jiggled, offering a Greek chorus of shadows struggling on the wall to retreat. Any sound that was apparent was drowned out by the screaming inside of Charlotte's mind. She was frozen in place, her feet stuck to the floor, like the words, the screams, buried in her throat, blocked by a sense of dread and responsibility for her lack of discipline.

Lanford Grips did not react vocally, did not yell out again. He flinched, and subtly, ever so subtly, nodded to his left. It was more of a tick than a flinch.

Charlotte saw it—and so did Bojack Wu. It was the only command he needed. Before Charlotte could blink, before she could allow one of her bubbling screams to be free of her mouth, Bojack Wu stepped back, produced a machete out of nowhere, but presumably from inside his black garb or from behind him, and swung the weapon with such surety and force that it completely cut off Ernest Hanesly's left ear before he could squeak out a word of protest.

The man's ear toppled to the floor, and Lanford Grips began to laugh, as it plopped to his feet and presented itself to him like a bloody gift to a long forgotten king. He picked the ear up with his hook and brought it to Hanesly's face, so he was staring directly into the dead man's eyes.

"You should have lied to me, Mr. Hanesly," Grips said to his face. "Not that it would've done you any good. Poor man. Look what you've gone and done, again, Charlotte. Really, you'd think you'd learn."

In a swift, seamless move, Bojack Wu cut off the other

ear. Like the first, it fell to the floor, but this one was quickly followed by the collapse of the mousy telegraph operator's body. Blood spouted from both wounds, draining the color from Hanesly's surprised face.

Charlotte Brogan drew in a deep breath, tasted nothing but bile, fear, and repulsion, and proceeded to do what any proper lady would do under such circumstances: She fainted.

SIXTEEN

THE MILES HAD PASSED BY UNBIDDEN, UN- restrained, without the two of them being accosted by any man, good or bad. There was no telling how long they'd been in the water, but judging by the sight of the afternoon sun, it was ticking toward midday. Any sight of the prison, guards, or a posse of any kind had long since been left behind. The rage of the flood had slowed, but only slightly. Navigating it any farther, with a tired horse, was asking for more trouble.

"You got any idea where we are?" Lucas asked.

"No, suh, I has no idea where we is." Zeke's voice was a little weaker than it had been.

"You all right?"

"Told you I was a good healer. But I thinks the lead is still lodged inside a me. It's gonna have to come out soon. You ever done that?"

Lucas shook his head no. "I'm no doctor."

"You was in the war, wasn't you?"

"You could say that." Lucas eyed the shore ahead and spotted a stretch in the bank that sloped down, free of brush, offering an exit from the river. Thick woods bounded the bank, and there was no sign of any houses or a town. The land looked isolated, far enough from Nashville to provide a feel of the country—and the ability to hide from curious eyes.

"You musta seen fightin', and the results of it."

"Some," Lucas said, "but I spent a fair amount of my time in Richmond and Washington, and parts in between."

"You was a bizinus man?"

"Something like that. There was more to the war than just shooting back and forth, one side set on killing the other. I wondered sometimes what I would have done if I had been born and raised a Yankee, what would have held my allegiances." Lucas stared at Zeke blankly. The question brought up old memories, old pains. His days of duty in the war had ended, and his mistake, it now seemed, had been to toss off his own ambitions and return home after the war, and acquiesce to his father's wishes, demands really, that he learn the family business.

The building of the railroads demanded timber. Lots of timber. But the wood-filled highlands of Tennessee were too far, the shipments too difficult, to offer serious trade in the transcontinental effort.

Land in Minnesota was bought, thousands and thousands of acres, for the trees bound to be ties, and to fill other needs, and they could be floated down the Mississippi. That business eventually required a partner, a trusted companion to help traverse the land between distant offices, and that alliance fell to a boy Lucas had known from childhood and served in the war with as a fellow spy. A boy who had grown into a man that Lucas called friend, that he considered to be as close as a brother, if that were possible. But he was sure that John Barlow had betrayed him, set him up for a murder he didn't commit, and everything had been lost—the family home, the business, the love of his life, everything . . .

"Lots of mens asked that question. But it don't matter no more, now, does it?" Zeke said.

"No, it doesn't."

"You don't have to tell me about that bizinus. Buyin' and sellin' things didn't stop no man from searchin' out his fortune during those times. Men mades money and got blood on they hands in more ways than one."

"That's not what I was after. Goods and services came and went, but they had to get where they were going safe and sound. Information was currency. Most of that wasn't found on the battlefield. The battlefield was the result of it, for better or worse, depending on who knew more or what was true."

"You was a spy, then?"

"Something like that. I was whatever I needed to be to serve the cause. The man that picked a fight with me before you showed up called me out on that. Now that I think of it, I wonder how he would have known such a thing. It's not like I go around talking about the war. I never talk about it, or what I did, if I can avoid it."

"Was you famous for anythin'?"

"Hardly. There are only a handful of folks who know the truth of my service."

"Somebody knows."

"Yes, it's curious."

"You got friends left that would want to see you free of prison? That might 'splain why we be sittin' here right now. You was important to someone, that's for sure. I knowed there had to be somethin' special about you, that you wasn't just no common man."

"Those friends have done left me, Zeke," Lucas said. "There's no money to be made on my freedom—just spent on ending it, the way I see it. I have no idea who would want to see me free. I'm as much in the dark as you. Maybe more so, if I'm being honest. My freedom means one thing to me. It's an opportunity to set things right. I know what I did, and what I didn't do. There's nobody that that means more to than me."

"If you says so."

"I do."

"Damn it," Lucas said under his breath, tightening the reins in his grip, pressing harder in the saddle, like he had before.

"What's the matter?"

"Horse can't break the current."

"Load's too heavy, and it's too tired to fight no more."

"We can't toss nothing off."

"Sure we can," Zeke said. Without another word, and without any warning at all, he released his hold on Lucas, leaned over to the side, and promptly fell straight into the roiling river.

The release of his grip and the splash from Zeke took Lucas by surprise. "What the hell are you doing?" he yelled over his shoulder, eyeing the Negro floating out of reach quicker than he might have ever considered.

"Go on now, I'll be fine."

There was no fear on Zeke's face, nor was he struggling, just floating upward, watching out for debris, bobbing in the water like a piece of old wood.

The lack of weight agreed with the gelding. It broke for the shore on its own, not waiting for Lucas to command it. He was still struggling with the surprise that Zeke had given him, but it quickly occurred to him that the best thing he could do was get to shore, then find a spot where he could pull the Negro out. Hopefully there was a spot in the river where it funneled down in width somewhere ahead. It was a thin hope, but it was the only one Lucas had at the moment.

There was no question that he could have left Zeke Henry right then and there to fend for himself—but Lucas didn't have it in him to do such a thing. Negro or not, the man had risked his life to see Lucas out of prison, taken a bullet for him, without any obvious compensation other than his own freedom—which would be marred, much like Lucas's own.

He pushed the horse toward the shore, and with both of

their efforts, they made it to land quickly. There was no sign of the permanent bank; it had been covered over by the flood, but the water ended right before a line of young nettles and wild raspberry thickets just popping their white blooms, giving Lucas room to maneuver and dismount. He quickly tied the gelding to a nearby tree. It was a prudent action, even though the horse didn't look like it had the energy to bolt. But he didn't know the horse well enough to trust it with its freedom, and the last thing he wanted to do was lose everything that had been left for him with the animal.

Lucas easily spied Zeke, still in the middle of the river, caught in the strong current, his head upright, an odd look of contentment on his face.

"Hang on," Lucas shouted, as he ran along the edge of the water, searching for a way to rescue the Negro.

Zeke didn't offer a word, a cry for help, nothing. He looked like he had already surrendered to his fate, like he was ready to become part of the river, ready to die.

SEVENTEEN

LUCAS RAN ALONG THE RIVER, TRYING HIS best not to lose sight of Zeke, all the while keeping an eye out for a spot where he could rescue the man. He'd pulled the rope off the horse, carrying it with him in hopes of tossing it to Zeke. It was all he knew to do.

Lucas hadn't been raised to be so coldhearted as to let a human being die needlessly, without offering the effort to save him, no matter what Lucas had had done to him. Time in prison had hardened him, given him deeper cause to hate, but at the moment those emotions were not riding on the surface of his skin.

Time for hate would come as surely as the sun would rise tomorrow, and most likely just as fast. But that hate would be directed at those who had betrayed him, locked him away, left him for dead, and stolen everything from him that he'd once loved. Or had thought he loved. He wasn't so sure of that anymore. But with Zeke's life at stake, Lucas recognized his own heart, his own being, and faced the truth of his blood; he was still a Fume, and that had meant something not so long ago in certain respectable circles of society, and within the confines of his own home. Especially when his mother had been alive. She didn't subscribe to the mistreatment of any living creature, man or beast. A life was a life, a value given by a Maker greater than any human being willing to pass judgment, with or without cause. She would have loved him even if he had chased the dream of being on the stage. He knew that now.

The war, and the events that came after, had long since destroyed any belief that Lucas might have held in the existence of such a Maker. Surely his mother would have been disappointed in him for that, but she had already left this earth, and appeasing a ghost, or the past, was not Lucas's concern at the moment. Zeke needed his help. That's all that mattered. What came next was out of his hands.

The river roiled with angry floodwater at every glance, a brown, gurgling soup that offered no hint of forgiveness, or an easy way out. It didn't winnow down into a stream of helpful size for as far as Lucas could see—it was as wide as the mouth, like the confluence of three different rivers, except there was only one.

Zeke Henry didn't call out, he didn't struggle—he just floated quickly south, disappearing under the water, then rising up again, sopping wet, without a gasp for breath, with alarming frequency.

Lucas dared not call out for fear of giving himself away. He ran harder than he had run in months, maybe longer, he couldn't remember. He still found it difficult to believe that his feet were slapping the soft, warm earth instead of the cold, hard prison floors.

He zigged, then zagged, jumping over freshly deposited brush piles, with a quick glance to the ground, insuring a secure landing, all the while trying to keep the Negro in sight.

Let him go, a voice deep within his mind called out. *Just*

*let him go. No one will miss him, and the world will be free
of one more Negro. Traveling alone will be easier . . .*

It was an old voice, and Lucas wasn't entirely sure that
it was his own. It may have been his father's, or a friend lost
to the past. He could barely broach the name of his betrayer,
the one whom he was accused, tried, and imprisoned for
murdering. It could have been *his* voice—the dead man's
voice, John Barlow's voice, clear as day, as if he were still
alive, taunting him, reminding him of his old ways, his old
prejudices, his old hate. Only, Lucas knew that it wouldn't
be his betrayer's voice, or he thought it wasn't likely. He was
dead. *Maybe.* They had only found his hands, severed and
left behind, unmistakable in their identity, the scars of war
apparent to any who had known him. If the entire body had
been found, they would have hung Lucas right then and
there. The trial would have been the end of his life. Simple
as that.

Lucas struggled through a thicket of wild raspberries,
pushing it away gingerly, not with enough force to matter,
trying his best not to get entangled in the wiry branches any
more than he was in the voices of the past.

The raspberries only slowed him slightly. He finally
pushed through, drawing on all of the strength and desire
he could muster. He'd lost sight of Zeke again, and the pit
of his stomach ached because of it. He'd failed, he was sure
of it.

Sweat streamed down Lucas's forehead, the saltiness of
it burning his eyes, adding to his growing discomfort. The
sun was transforming from an awe-inspiring orb into an
enemy determined to defeat him.

The act of running had drained what little strength he
had stored away, and the warmth of the day left him no time
to restore any of his lost energy. He hadn't eaten a meal since
the night before, and then it had been gruel, the bits of meat
in it butchered from a rat for all he knew.

At a certain point, he might not have a choice when it

came to rescuing Zeke. Matters might resolve themselves. It might not be possible for either man to offer up the effort and desire needed for such a heroic deed. What was done was done. He had tried. Lucas would have to live with that if this was truly the end.

Bent on trying until the matter was completely settled, Lucas broke onto free ground with one last thrust, the rope still in his hand. He ran again, this time on clearer, drier land that did not try to hold him back with every step he took forward.

For a long moment, he couldn't see a thing, just more logs, more debris, all bobbing and rolling in the muddy river. Then finally, he spied the Negro, his head facing south, the whites of his eyes full, showing no fear, or life for that matter.

Lucas tied the rope as quickly as he could with a lasso at the end, an old skill conjured without hardly any thought at all, then broke into a full-out run. He quickly passed by Zeke, who saw him now. There were no words needed; the Negro seemed innately to understand the restraint required to keep from drawing attention to their plight. Either that or he was just too weak to speak. The shot to the shoulder had not been treated or even looked at; the bleeding had not slowed or stopped. There simply had not been an opportunity to tend to the wound.

The lay of the land finally cooperated—to a point. Ahead there was a mass of trees and debris, including what looked like the roof of a house all caught up at a narrow bend in the river. It wasn't quite a dam; the raging water still had passage through a ten-yard opening, and over and under the blockage.

If Lucas managed his footing properly, he could climb out onto the fallen trees, and maybe the roof, then toss the rope. From the looks of Zeke, and the state of the river beyond, it was going to be his last chance at being rescued.

Lucas wasn't deterred. He made his way to the makeshift dam and walked out as far as he could go, balancing his weight as best he could. Zeke was coming at him fast, but was still out of reach of the rope. A practice toss was necessary. Lucas Fume was no cowboy, but he had many skills, especially when it came to coordinating his hands with his eyes.

The rope slapped the water about twenty yards from the Negro. Zeke raised his hands, reaching out, giving Lucas a better target. If he was lucky, he'd have more than one chance.

Lucas reeled in the rope as fast as he could, bit his lip, ignored as best he could the flies swarming around his face and the unsteadiness of the logs under his feet. He focused straight on Zeke, concentrated as hard as he could only on the task at hand, visualized the success of the capture in his mind, then threw the rope with as much certainty and force as he could.

The rope fell short of Zeke—but he lunged forward at just the right time and was able to grab hold of it securely enough to insure that he wasn't going to lose his grip. The tug felt to Lucas like he'd just hooked a whopper of a catfish. There was no fight, just the pull in, aided by Zeke's willing paddle with his good arm.

With determination, and some exasperated effort, Zeke crawled up out of the water, remaining prone on the logs. "Thank ya, Mistuh Fume, thank ya very much."

"Falling off that horse on purpose was a foolish move. You could've drowned."

"I'da died a free man. Not freed. But free. There's somethin' to be said for that."

"So I should've let you die?"

"Didn't say that. Glad you didn't, but I ain't afraid. Is you?" Zeke said. He took a deep breath, wiped his face, and tried to stand. His knees were a little wobbly. Lucas offered his hand, but Zeke hesitated. "You sure about that?"

"I didn't let you float on down the river did I?"

"No, suh, no you didn't." Zeke grabbed Lucas's arm just above the wrist, and in unison, they hoisted him to his feet. "We free now, Mistuh Fume," Zeke said, relieved.

Before Lucas could agree, or say anything, another voice chimed in, startling him.

"Well, looky what we have here, boys . . ."

"What you think, Hilly, is them here those escapees we heared about?"

"Could be, Milo, could be."

"Well, hot damn, and sell me some lemonade, they's a reward out for these two, ain't there, Carl?"

"Turn around slowly there, boy," the first man who'd spoken said. "And nobody's gonna get hurt. They want you alive."

Lucas and Zeke did as they were told and found themselves standing before three men sitting on horseback, with shotguns leveled at them, all with smiles on their faces and greed and opportunity in their eyes.

PART II

Consequences at Noon

While the world of gain and appearance and mirth goes on, So soon what is over forgotten . . .

—WALT WHITMAN,
FROM "THE WOUND DRESSER"

EIGHTEEN

CHARLOTTE BROGAN COULDN'T BRING HER-
self to eat the food that had been placed in front of her. The
plate of steak and wilted spring greens sat cold and untouched on a tray next to the small unmade bed in the berth.
Food of any kind did not interest her. She could barely bring
herself to sit up from the bed and stop crying. But she had
no choice but to get dressed. The train had stopped. They
had reached their destination, and all she wanted to do was
flee.

The blinds were still drawn, but Kansas City loomed
outside. *It's fitting*, Charlotte thought, *that we should end
up in Bleeding Kansas*. The term referred to the proxy war
between Northerners and Southerners over the once free
state's battle with itself, and its population, over whether the
state should accept slavery. Popular sovereignty was a con-
cept long settled with the outcome of the War of Northern
Aggression, but the idea of it was not lost on Charlotte.
There was still oppression and slavery. It just came in

different forms. In some circumstances, and a lot of minds, the war was not over. For her part, she felt as if she were still in the middle of it, subjected to the violence of bloody battles and the unrelenting loss that always accompanied any struggle for freedom. She could not get out of her mind the telegraph operator's earless body crumpling to the floor.

She had been taken to her quarters, and she presumed that Hanesly was dead. Discarded. Done away with because of her foolish error.

A knock came at the door, startling Charlotte out of her thoughts. "Yes?"

"Mr. Grips would like you to join him in the carriage ride to the hotel."

It was Bojack Wu. His English was perfectly understandable, but there was no mistaking the thick, foreign accent. The others—guards, cooks, laundrymen—never spoke, never looked anyone in the eye. They muttered an acquiescence, usually with a bow, in pidgin, a positive response to any question or demand raised, but it was hardly understandable, or meant to engage in a casual conversation of any kind. The Celestials in Lanford's employ were present to serve, and nothing else. There was no mistake about that— to them or anyone else on the train.

Bojack Wu was different. There seemed to be an understanding between the two men, a silent language that had somehow been forged since "the incident" that had left Lanford in his current circumstances—unable to do much for himself, even scratch his nose, if truth be told. It was spooky how well the two men could communicate with each other without saying a word. Almost magical, even more so than some old married couples, or like twins born of the same blood and at nearly the same time. Charlotte had known John Barlow—Lanford Grips—since he was a boy. It was the power of that age-old bond, as well as a few other reasons, known and unknown, that kept her at his side.

"I am unprepared to leave, Mr. Wu. Tell him that. Tell

Mr. Grips that I am distressed and would rather ride to the hotel alone, if he would please allow himself to understand." She walked to the door and pressed herself against it, knowing full well that Bojack Wu, no matter how small she perceived his physical stature, could power his way through it if he so chose.

"Are you dressed, miss?"

"Of course I am dressed."

"Then you must accompany Mr. Grips. It is his wish not to make the ride alone. He informed me that I mustn't take no for an answer. And I will not disappoint Mr. Grips."

"I still have to pack."

"It will be done for you."

"I would rather do it myself."

"That is unacceptable, miss."

Charlotte drew in a deep breath. Her stomach gurgled. No matter her mood, or reaction to the telegraph operator's demise, food was still an apparent need. Her body was still hungry, but her heart wept for the action she had caused by uttering Lanford Grips's real name aloud in the presence of a man who did not know it.

It was a dire mistake that she vowed never to make again. She would train her mind to forget that the name John Barlow had ever existed. She would delete him from her memory, from her life, in her present and past. She would believe, like everyone else in the world, that John Barlow was dead—his body buried in some secret place. She would have to grieve all over again. "I have no choice in the matter, then?" she said, resigned to the truth of her position.

"No, miss, you do not."

It was nighttime. The entire world was covered in a solid sheet of lukewarm blackness. There was little noise outside of the carriage. The blinds were drawn nearly to the bottom, offering only a small amount of gray passing light to filter inside.

Charlotte sat across from Lanford, his profile barely visible. Bojack Wu sat outside, next to the driver, always on the lookout for any threat that might present itself to the safety of his charge.

"I must apologize, Charlotte."

"Whatever for, Lanford?"

"Bojack Wu's swift solution to our earlier problem. It was a grave mistake, Charlotte. One that we have discussed many times before. You were once considered the best of the best when it came to maintaining an image, a persona, and ultimately, a secret."

"I faltered. I apologize. I don't know what came over me. The time away from home has made me melancholy, and I have grown weak. It won't happen again. I promise."

"No, I don't imagine it will. But I worry for you."

"I must be getting rusty. My employment of the past has been put aside for so long that I have forgotten half of what I knew to do in such circumstances. The war is over, and I have lived a life of luxury since."

"So everyone is quick to remind me, but I do not believe that for a second, do you? That the war is really over?"

"No, I suppose it is not. I had only hoped it was."

"With a different outcome, of course."

"Of course. I will always honor those who perished, or lost a limb"—Charlotte paused, and stared directly at Lanford, even though he could not see her expression clearly—"or their mind, for the cause. The war was difficult."

"The past is littered with fallen heroes. May they all rest in peace."

"Yes, may they all rest in peace."

"You once were one of the best spies, taught by one of the best spies. Have you forgotten what your mentor, the dear Mrs. Greenhow, taught you?" Lanford Grips asked.

There was a sudden change in Lanford's tone. A coldness that Charlotte recognized as imminently dangerous. She wished they would arrive at the hotel. She would like to be done with the conversation. She wanted free of his company. Promptly.

"I will never forget Mrs. Greenhow, but I hope not to repeat her errors," Charlotte said.

"Ah, yes, one the most productive spies in Washington, imprisoned and still effective, released and toured Europe raising money for the Confederacy, only to drown on her return with a bag of gold hung around her neck. Pity that greed took her so forthrightly, isn't it? I think I would rather hang in the public square than to die so tragically, and openly clinging to all that I owned, wouldn't you?"

"I think she thought herself immune to death, or to the punishment of mere mortals. We all have our weaknesses, I suppose. Men swarmed to her like moths to a flame. Men who should have known better. It was a trick I never seemed to master, nor did I want to, at least to the extent of her vanity."

"She was a charming woman, Charlotte. And skilled, from what I understand."

"You were in her company privately then?" Charlotte asked.

Silence fell between them, and as luck would have it, the carriage came to a stop. Charlotte was glad for the reprieve. The discussion about Rose O'Neal Greenhow brought back a flood of memories, both good and bad. She had dearly loved the woman, but if the truth were to be known, she had never trusted Mrs. Greenhow entirely. How could she? The woman was loyal to no one, only to her desire for more wealth and power.

The rustle of feet from above and outside the door told Charlotte that they had arrived at their destination.

"Yes, well, poor Mrs. Greenhow—may she rest in peace, too, and may we not forget the lessons of her avarice," Lanford Grips said.

"Yes, a hero in her own right. Living or dead," Charlotte answered, anticipating her freedom from the darkness—if that were possible.

NINETEEN

LUCAS STARED AT THE MAN THEY CALLED
Carl. He recognized him immediately as a prison guard who
usually worked the halls on the overnight shift. Everybody
called him Carl the Hammer because that tool was the man's
weapon of choice. One constantly dangled from his belt, ready
to use, ready to intimidate, or inflict pain or death, if it came
to that.

Lucas didn't know Carl the Hammer's last name. He had
never cared to learn. It was that way with most of the guards.
They didn't deserve the time of day, much less the respect of
learning their name. This one, though, was easily recognizable.
He liked power, wielded it like most of the guards, who thought
it was some God-given right—when it really was nothing more
than a lowly position offering only a small amount of coin from
the state treasury. The guards could bully penned-up men and
feel good about themselves. They were louts, really, simple-
minded, unfulfilled men whose lives were most likely as miserable outside the prison walls as they were inside them.

"You say they want us alive?" Lucas said to Carl.

The man nodded. His skin was dirty, jaundiced, and he smelled of smoke and gunpowder. Out of habit, Lucas glanced to Carl the Hammer's scruffy boots. During the war, if a man portrayed himself as a Confederate, a quick look to his shoes might betray him. Northern and Southern shoes were different: pegged or sewn, constructed in different factories, with different processes. Likewise, plug tobacco would betray a Southern purchase, while short-cut tobacco would give away a Northerner's true allegiance. It was the simple things that spoke of identity. One false move, and a spy could see the end of a rope without so much as a protest from any commander, near or far.

Old habits were hard to break for Lucas, especially now that he was in an outside environment where everything, and everyone, was suspect. Though, in the end, it didn't matter, since there were no "sides" in this war; Carl the Hammer was fully garbed in Tennessee prison guard clothes. He was exactly what he was supposed to be.

Carl smirked at Lucas's question, then nodded, offering a direction with his chin. His right hand was never an inch away from the hammer. "You come down easy, and ain't nothin' gonna happen to you right now. I ain't no fool. Orders is orders. Money is money. I'd say they gonna make an example out of you, if I was a figurin' man. Parade you through the city and courts, just to hang you in the square. Shoulda probably been done long ago from the tales I hear about you, but I ain't no judge or jury. Not today."

It was obvious that Carl and the two other men were the first posse out of the prison gates. The fact that they had caught up with them so quickly surprised Lucas. He thought they'd had a good lead, that the water and mud had filled in their tracks, giving them a little time to escape, to get lost in the flooded lowlands. Sadly, that was not the case. His strategizing skills were rusty. Or desperate. Errors always came on the heels of desperation.

Lucas glanced over at Zeke before offering anything to Carl the Hammer.

The Negro was breathing heavily but standing squarely on his own two feet. His eyes looked weak, and there was an effort made not to show it. River water drained off Zeke, offering rivulets at his feet, eager to rejoin the nearby flood. Brown muck and blood mixed together, making it impossible to see how bad the bullet wound in the Negro's shoulder really was. The escape had taken a toll on the big black man, but the fact that he stood next to Lucas, firmly upright, spoke highly of the grit that Zeke Henry possessed.

"You up to this?" Lucas asked.

Before Zeke could answer, or nod back, Carl launched the hammer into the air. It thudded into the ground just before Lucas's feet. "You move for that, and I'll kill you straight out. Claim you went for a weapon. Nobody said you could speak to each other, Fume," Carl said.

"The man's wounded," Lucas protested.

"Ain't a man," Carl sneered. The other two men nodded. The three of them sat on their horses, unmoving, just like they had from the moment Lucas realized they were there.

Calculating his odds of survival was as much a habit for Lucas as was checking a man's shoes. At the moment, he didn't see a way out the predicament he found himself in. His fists were useless. The only weapon he had was the rifle stuffed in the scabbard aside the escape horse that had been left for him. But there was no sign of the horse. Once Lucas had broken into a run along the bank trying to rescue Zeke, the horse had been left to its own devices. He didn't know any commands to bring the horse to him. A whistle or a yell might just get him and Zeke shot—and be pointless anyway. He knew that horse as well as he knew the Negro standing at his side, which was hardly at all. There were only his wits and the words that came out of his mouth to rely on. The day had started like that, and it looked like it was going to end that way.

The hammer at his feet offered an opportunity, but it would be risky.

Water surged up around Lucas's ankles, like it was trying to grab him and pull him back in the river. The force of it almost knocked him off the log he was standing on. He knew then what the way out was.

"All right, Carl," Lucas said, "what exactly do you want me to do? I'm in no mood to get turned into a colander on this day. And I don't want to get wet again." He stared straight into Zeke's eyes, hoping the Negro understood the message he was trying to send. It was the only chance they had.

"It would be my pleasure to kill you right here." Carl nudged the shotgun barrel upward. "You know the drill. Hands up, walk easy off them logs onto the solid ground. Then we go back to the prison. That simple. But these here boys, they got itchy trigger fingers, so if you make a silly move, well, what they does is out of my control."

"Might not look so good to the warden. Reward's more if we're alive is my guess."

"You got a brain on you. So what?"

"Shooting us might look poorly on you when you decide you want to be a sergeant or the like, now, wouldn't it?" Lucas kept an eye on the mood of the water, waiting for the right time to make his move.

"That'd be my problem, now, wouldn't it?" Carl flipped the shotgun upward again, more pronounced this time. "You're tryin' my patience, Fume. Come on now, time to face the warden."

"I don't mean to make you uncomfortable, Carl." Lucas obliged and raised his hands into the air.

Zeke eyed Lucas carefully, and followed suit, copying his every move—but neither man took a step forward. Instead, they both dove sideways, and spiraled into the water, splashing almost in unison, like it was a perfectly planned action.

On the way into the water, Lucas reached out and was

able to grab hold of the hammer, taking it with him. He drew as much air as he could into his lungs before he crashed into the rushing floodwater.

Thunder erupted overhead. But he knew it wasn't an approaching storm. It was the blasts from the three shotguns.

Lucas dove as deep into the water as he could, trying to avoid tumbling logs and the barrage of buckshot pelting the river, and hanging on to the hammer like it was gold. It was the only weapon he would have if they survived.

He lost sight of Zeke almost immediately. The brown, murky water drew in around him like the darkness of night. Something hit his ankle, stung like a bee, but he kept on diving. He dodged shadows and limbs. The sting could have been anything.

Lucas finally found the silt-covered bottom of the river. He could barely see six inches in front of him. The water was so stirred up that it looked like gruel, unfit to eat.

There was a constant roar in his ears now, like thunder instead of the *pop-boom* of the shotgun blasts. He was running out of air, and the tips of his fingers were starting to tingle with panic. But he kept on swimming forward the best he could—as quickly away from the bank as possible. Yet the truth of it was that he was rolling over and over, powerless to perform any true navigation. He was caught in the current, being tossed around like a weightless stick.

In a matter of seconds, Lucas didn't know where he was—what direction was up or down, how far down the river he'd gone, or if he was out of range, safe to surface. He was lost, weak, and if he'd had time to admit it, afraid.

It felt like he was drowning, like his life was completely out of his own control—but he had no regrets. His current situation beat returning to the prison and facing the noose. Oddly, he worried about Zeke, and hoped that the Negro survived.

If not, if neither of them survived, at least they would both die free, of their own will. That had been his thought from the moment he'd realized that the escape plan was real.

The desire for freedom didn't go away. It only grew stronger. There was something to be said for that—even though his death would leave him no time to set things straight.

The business of revenge and righteousness would end, too, lost in the swirl of the river, deposited on the bank, used up, his flesh left to the buzzards and any other eater of carrion. *Maybe that's for the best*, he thought.

With his lungs about to explode, Lucas gave up the fight, allowed his natural ballast to take effect, and floated in the current, finally breaking the surface softly, his head rolled back, eyes to the sky, instead of blasting from underneath the surface like a cannonball and exposing himself needlessly to Carl the Hammer and his men.

Lucas could only see pure blue sky, hear nothing but the singing of birds and rolling water. He wasn't sure if he was dead or alive.

TWENTY

JOE STRAUT STOOD ON THE OPPOSITE COR-
ner of Tenth Street and Broadway in Kansas City, staring at
the Coates House Hotel. Just the thought of walking through
the front door of the hotel galled him to no end, even though
he knew had no choice.

The hotel was a grand building, five stories tall and almost a city block deep. It was a marvel if Straut had ever
seen one, built of red brick, standing in the center of Cow
Town as a symbol of pure opulence, offering the well-to-do
a comfortable place to rest along their journey to parts
unknown.

It wasn't the opulence of the hotel, fully situated across
the street from the fancy Coates Opera House, that Straut
found distasteful. He held no grudge against men getting
rich from the opportunities sprouting up west of the Big
Muddy since the war had ended. It seemed the whole world
was moving west in search of adventure and fortune since
the railroads had made travel easier and more comfortable.

Joe Straut served Lanford Grips without question, a man propelled by commerce, motivated by an acceptable amount of greed and the constant pursuit of wealth. The private railcar was proof of wealth beyond most men's wildest dreams. But it was the past, and Kersey Coates's politics and allegiances during the war, that caused Joe Straut to hesitate before entering the building.

Coates was a Federal through and through, a colonel in the Missouri militia. The foundation of the hotel had been laid at just the start of the war, but construction had been halted when things heated up, and the building was used as a stable for Union cavalry horses, among other things. Coates was very much a free-slave man, a great contributor to Bleeding Kansas and the internal battles fought in the state.

Even though the war was long over, it still felt to Joe Straut like he was walking into an enemy camp. It didn't matter to him that he would be surrounded by polished marble and shiny wood paneling instead of mud and dog tents. Kersey Coates's politics, and his business practices since the war, put a sour taste in his mouth. Coates had joined two other businessmen and secured the building of the first bridge over the Missouri River, bringing an economic boom to Kansas City, proof of Coates's powerful connections. His law school teacher had been Thaddeus Stevens, one of the powerhouse congressmen behind the passage of the Emancipation Proclamation.

Just the thought of the man roiled a ball of spit up into the back of Straut's throat. He blew it out of his mouth with great force, but the sour taste remained. Men like Coates had not only survived the war but come away better because of it. Straut found it difficult to understand how Lanford Grips could spend one second under the man's roof—but business and the pursuit of profit knew no boundaries. Or no grudge like the one he held.

Joe Straut drew in a deep breath and tried to settle

himself. He knew he had no choice but to move on, that he had to enter the hotel as if it were just another building in any town. But knowing he had to didn't make it any easier. It just gave him one more thing to despise.

"You gonna go in, Sarge, or wait till the dawn of day? Boss called you in once the train stopped. He ain't gonna be none too happy about havin' to wait on us," Deets said, standing shoulder to shoulder with Straut.

"I got a bad feeling."

It was still night, and the wide street was empty of any traffic. There wasn't another human being in sight. The population of Kansas City was safely tucked in bed, or sat with heads down, staring into a beer at one of the local saloons. Straut wished he was there, too, enjoying the company of a dance hall girl instead of standing next to Finney Deets.

It had obviously rained in the past day or two. The street was wet and muddy. Since it was spring, the throughway probably wouldn't dry out until July, if then. Mud was a common foe, but the smell of it on this night was ripe, like something close by was in the process of dying, or already dead, rotting with flesh falling off the bone.

The air had cooled from the day, and thin wisps of steam rose from the street, hanging a foot or two over the surface, offering an ethereal view of the hotel. It almost looked like a dream, or a nightmare as ghost snakes glided upward into the night sky, their destination unknown.

A few lights were still burning in the hotel. The windows were dotted with light and dark like some kind of child's puzzle, offering a clear solution—even though it was unseen to Straut.

A dog barked in the distance, and it startled Straut. He flinched and drew in a sudden, deeper, breath. It only took a second for him to recognize that the dog posed no threat. There was nothing to do but swallow his fear and face what waited for him sooner rather than later.

"You think he knows we didn't burn those folks up?" Deets asked. His voice cracked with nervousness.

"I don't know what the Boss knows. He's got eyes everywhere."

"We shoulda done what he said."

"Nobody's going to find those bodies. Nobody but coyotes and buzzards." But silently, Joe Straut agreed. If they'd done what the Boss ordered, he wouldn't be pissing his pants every time a dog barked.

"You best hope no one finds them."

"What if they do, Deets?" Straut demanded through clenched teeth. "There's no way anybody'll know who they was, or how they got there, or that we had anything to with what happened to them. Bugs'll eat 'em if nothing else does. I saw enough bodies burn in the war. That was enough for me."

"We didn't kill them. The Chinkies did."

"Don't say that word, you'll get us both killed."

"Ain't nobody around," Deets said.

"Bojack Wu could be standing right behind you."

Deets's eyes grew wide, and he froze like he was trying to disappear into thin air. "He ain't, is he?"

Straut shrugged. "I don't think so."

"That's not funny, Sarge."

"You have to be more careful, Deets. We both do. This ain't normal business we're up to."

Deets nodded. "You're right. You're always right."

"Not always," Straut said, then crossed the street, angling for the entrance to the Coates House Hotel, one slow step after the other.

The two Chinese guards stood outside the hotel room door, just like they had outside the peacock doors on the train; emotionless, void of any recognition or movement. Straut, with Deets a step behind him, walked up to them and said,

"Horn blue one." He hadn't needed to check the password beforehand. He had finally figured out the pattern, which made him comfortable, at least with that part of the Boss's operation.

The guard on the right nodded, acknowledged the correct password had been given, then knocked twice on the door, waited a second, then knocked again, a little louder the second time.

Joe Straut could feel his heart beating inside his chest. Sweat beaded on his lip, but he made no effort to wipe it away. He knew better than to move too quickly, or in any way that was out of the ordinary. One false move could provoke the guards to attack with their hands or their feet, and Straut knew there would be nothing he could do to protect himself. His Colt Open Top would do him no good, even though there was a cartridge sitting in the chamber, waiting to fire. The guards were like wild animals on a leash. Just because they looked tame didn't mean you could trust them.

Deets breathed on the back of his neck, and Straut could still smell the mud from the street, caked on both of their boots.

The door opened from the inside, and Straut walked in, sure of what he would find: Lanford Grips sitting behind a desk, his arms at his sides, his hands, or what once were his hands, out of sight. It was the way it had always been, the way it was from the very beginning, and the way it was now. Grips was a consistent man. That's what worried Straut.

Bojack Wu closed the door behind Straut and Deets, latched the lock, and assumed a position in front of it, giving them no exit, and no mode of escape except jumping through one of the windows—falling five stories to their death—if it came to that.

The room was luxurious, twice as big as the railcar compartment, and every light burned at full wick. The walnut-slated floor was clean, free of carpet. The room was a suite fit for a king, with the bedroom closed off from view. Every fixture was brass, and the furniture looked like it had just arrived from Paris, all curvy and covered in fancy upholstery. There was a clean smell to the room; even the coal oil seemed like it was perfumed, and the smoke drained of its blackness. There was not one smudge of dirt anywhere to be seen.

The only thing out of place or unusual was the woman sitting on a divan off to Grips's right.

Straut knew her to be Charlotte Brogan, and he wasn't sure of the nature of the relationship she held with the Boss. They may have been romantically involved, but there never seemed to be that kind of affection between the two of them. No furtive glances or secret touches. They seemed familiar with each other, though, like they'd known each other a long time. Like business partners, or childhood friends.

Charlotte Brogan didn't acknowledge Straut's entrance. Her gazed was fixed squarely on Lanford Grips.

"You took long enough to get here," Grips said.

Straut stopped a few feet in front of the desk, as was expected of him, as he had done a hundred times before. Once a sergeant, always a sergeant.

Deets followed suit, so they stood shoulder to shoulder, staring at Grips.

"There were things to clean up on the train," Straut said.

"And no one else could have completed the task?" Grips said.

"I wanted to make sure it was done right."

"And was it?"

"Yes, sir. Of course." There was something in the Boss's tone that made Straut even more nervous than he already was.

Lanford Grips stood up, with both of his arms tight to his sides. There were no gloves covering the metal hooks where each hand once dangled.

It was an unusual show of the hooks, and the sight of the prosthetics only added to Straut's since of dread.

"I have bad news, Straut," Grips said. "It seems as if you have failed in your greatest task."

An involuntary tremble careened up Straut's spine. "I'm sorry." It was a weak response. His throat had gone dry.

Grips walked up to Straut and stopped within inches of him. He was a good half a head shorter, causing Straut to look down on his boss as Grips spoke at him. "There are no apologies that will suffice. The future of my business depended on the success of carrying out my orders. We are close to finalizing a deal that will end all of this incessant travel and haggling."

Straut knew the best thing he could do was keep his mouth shut. He didn't know what his failure was, but judging from the sense of dread that permeated the room, it was most obviously a severe offense.

Maybe Deets's fear had been correct. Maybe someone had found those bodies already . . . But Straut most certainly wasn't going to offer the Boss any information without due cause. Joe Straut had managed to stay alive during the war, and in the employ of Lanford Grips for a long time, by shear wits and smart calculations. He wasn't going to alter his methods now.

"I have received word from Tennessee," Grips continued, "that there has been a riot at the prison. Lucas Fume has escaped." He stood on his tiptoes then, so the two men were eye to eye, and pressed the point of his right hook against Straut's temple. "He's still alive, Straut. It was your duty to see him dead. And you have failed. Failed greatly. Do you have anything to say for yourself?"

Straut's eyes glazed over with fear, and he shook his head no. He felt more sweat bead up on his lip, and he tried as hard as he could not to shake, not to show any physical evidence of fear. It was like staring into the eyes of a rabid dog. It was like staring into the eyes of death. He had just been given the opportunity to speak his last words.

"I expected that," Grips said. He pulled the hook back

and stepped away from Straut. "Here's what's going to happen. I could kill you. Both of you. And be done with the mess you have failed to clean up. Hire someone new, start fresh. You have obviously failed to hire the right people to complete the job. And it's a simple job, Straut. Seriously, how difficult can it be to kill a rat in a cage?"

Silence filled the room. Not even a dog in the distance dared to bark. A wall clock ticked, but even it seemed hushed, afraid to tick too loudly.

"How goddamn hard is it to kill a rat in a goddamn cage, Straut?" Grips demanded again, pausing for a brief second, waiting for a response. When he didn't get one, he backhanded Straut with the hard curve his metal hook.

The force of the blow knocked Joe Straut backward three steps. His left canine tooth flew out of his mouth, followed by an unrestrained blast of blood. It rained to the floor before Straut could stop the flow of it by putting his hand over his mouth.

To his credit, Straut didn't scream out in pain. He glanced over to Deets, whose face had gone white with fear, but who stood there waiting for his fate to arrive. There was nowhere to run. That had been clear from the moment they'd walked into the room. Bojack Wu stood at the door, unmoving, a statue dedicated to Lanford Grips and his desire to hold both men captive.

Lanford Grips's face was red with rage and his shoulders trembled, as if he was fighting some interior battle, trying to restrain himself. Finally, he took a deep breath and stepped backward again, away from Straut.

"Here's what you're going to do, Straut. You and Deets are going to take the first train east, and you're going to find Lucas Fume. You understand that? You're going to find him and bring his head back to me as proof that he's dead. And if you don't, if you disappear, or fail in this task, I will hunt you down and kill you myself, one puncture at a time, over days, not hours. You will regret your failure before the reprieve of your death. You will beg me to let you die, and I will refuse you until I am positive that you have suffered enough for your ineptitude."

Straut knew he'd been given a second chance. He cleared his mouth of blood and said, "I understand, Boss. I won't fail you. I promise."

Grips walked over to the desk and put his right hook on a piece paper. "You'll need this, Straut. It's a map of places Fume will most likely go if he remains free."

Straut walked over and picked up the map and studied it, expecting to see cities. Instead, there were roads and markers.

Grips stared at Straut with doubt on his face. "Fume will need money and supplies. These are old drop spots he knows that were used by our network in the war. There may be nothing there, but they're worth checking, a place to start. If you don't find anything in these caches, wire me your location, and I'll put you in contact with a prison official I have a relationship with. He ought to know something of Fume's whereabouts by that time. Do you understand?"

Straut bounced his head up and down cautiously, folded the map, and stuffed it in the breast pocket of the coat he wore.

"Good," Grips said. "Now get the hell out of here before I change my mind."

Joe Straut nodded again and turned away as quickly as he could, never happier to see a door in his life.

"Stop." It was Charlotte Brogan's voice, and it was a command. Straut did as he was told, stumbling once, not sure if she had the power to stop him or not. But she was, after all, a woman, and she had made a request of him. Surely the Boss wouldn't hold that against him. He turned and faced her, still afraid he had done the wrong thing.

"I would like to go with Mr. Straut," Charlotte said, looking directly into Lanford Grips's eyes.

The rage returned to Grips's body and face. "We have not discussed this, Charlotte," he said with a hiss.

"I know," she said, walking to him. "But if Lucas knows that I am still alive, and in St. Louis, he will come to me, I am sure of it, and so are you if you think about it. This would make Mr. Straut's job much easier and the chance for success of his mission much, much greater, don't you think?"

Joe Straut stood silently, trying to disappear, desperate to stay out of the conversation.

Lanford Grips studied Charlotte Brogan, who showed nothing but confidence and certainty in her suggestion. "Lucas could never resist your charms."

"But I could his," Charlotte said.

"So you say."

"Yes, I do say so. Your time is running out, Lanford. Mr. Coates and his associates with the railroad are getting impatient. You don't need me to tell you that, but the fact that I can see it, as can everyone else, makes this situation more urgent. The longer Lucas Fume is alive, the greater the chance that all of your business aspirations will fail. You know what's at stake better than anyone. We must try everything within our power to succeed at ridding ourselves of the barriers that stand in your way. Lucas is the last, and most persistent, impediment to the fortunes that await you."

Lanford Grips winced, cast a quick glance to Straut and Deets, almost as if Charlotte Brogan had told a secret in their presence—or at the very least something they shouldn't have been privy to. But the glance disappeared as quickly as it came. "Very well," he said, drawing in a mouthful of air. "But if this is a trick, Charlotte, you can trust in the fact that I will kill you as happily as I will kill anyone else who has betrayed me."

"Have no fear," Charlotte said, gathering herself, "I am humbly aware of what you're capable of, Lanford. I value our relationship more than anything, and I would never betray you. Never. If you don't know that by now, you never will."

TWENTY-ONE

LUCAS CRAWLED OUT OF THE WATER, UP onto what had only recently become a muddy riverbank. The land was flat, a former floodplain field, planted with corn, making it somewhat easier to navigate. He was desperate to regain his breath, on the brink of collapse. There was no way to tell if he was safe, out of range of Carl the Hammer's posse and their guns, but he couldn't stay in the water any longer. His body ached and hurt all over, like he had been in a fight, pummeled from head to toe by logs, rocks on the bottom of the river, and anything else that had found its way into the raging water. He had simply run out of air and the determination to go on. It was either drown or face the consequences by surfacing. Drowning was out of the question.

Blood speckled Lucas's right ankle, and the wound stung like he'd been bitten by a water moccasin, a wayward craw-dad, or some other hungry, or angry, creature. It was no bite, though; it was buckshot from Carl the Hammer's shotgun, most likely still lodged under his skin.

Even though the ground was flat, there was plenty of debris from the flood scattered about for as far as the eye could see: ripped up sycamore trees, broken window frames, shredded petticoats stuck in limbs, whipping in the breeze like war-torn flags, and a lot of other trash, man-made and nature's own alike.

Mud trapped Lucas's hands with each pull, and he had to fight to move forward. It took everything he had left, and more, but he was desperate to be as far away from the water's grasp as possible.

There was no sign of Carl the Hammer, or anyone else for that matter. The only sign of life was a flock of birds flittering about in the canopy of trees that grew at the edge of the floodplain. It looked like he had landed on the border of a swamp more than a farmer's field butting up to a forest—lucky for him there were no alligators to be worried about; he wasn't in Florida, but he had been during the war. Snakes remained a constant concern.

There was no sign of Zeke, either, and Lucas had to face the possibility that the Negro had lost his life in the swirl of the river, his body most likely gone forever.

After a long crawl, Lucas pulled himself up next to a big tree that had been pushed out of the river haphazardly, far enough from the current and the reach of the water to be stable and offer him some cover while he regained his strength and bearings.

He was covered in mud and muck, his skin almost as brown as Zeke's. Carl the Hammer's namesake weapon was still firmly in his grasp.

The carpenter's tool was all he had to protect himself. It was a good one, a Belknap Bluegrass hammer, made in Louisville, Kentucky—good for anything: tacking down roofs, house-building, or cracking a man's head wide open.

Hand-to-hand fighting only dictated you could win, and a tool like the hammer was especially welcome.

It took Lucas a moment to accept the fact that everything else that had been left for him was lost.

The bay gelding with the rifle in the scabbard and perhaps any remaining instructions from the person, or persons, who had seen fit to orchestrate his escape, was gone, lost just like the Negro. Zeke had seemed to know little of the plot, including the origin and the purveyor of the escape. It would be nice to know who was behind the ordeal, but like everything else, that was behind Lucas, a mystery now.

Even though there didn't seem to be anyone around, Lucas remained cautious. He lay on the ground, pushed up against the old tree trunk, trying his best to blend in, regaining his breath and strength slowly but surely. He was fairly certain that he wasn't mortally injured, that the buckshot wound wasn't going to hamper his escape. Once he was sure that he was able and safe, he'd find out how steady his legs were.

Insects buzzed inside of his ears, and Lucas started to fight them off the best he could without regard to showing his position. A bug or two lodged in an ear could drive a man to sheer madness.

Finally, he'd had enough. Lucas jumped with an attempt to outrun the army of biting bastard insects. He damn near swallowed a battalion of the mosquitoes as he propelled himself forward, taking a deep breath to give himself the energy to make a dash for dry ground. If he could find it.

But it was more than that that took his breath away. In the blink of an eye, he came face-to-face with a black man. A black man he immediately recognized as Zeke Henry. It was the second time that had happened—only this time it was a relief, not a concern.

"Well, there you is, Mistuh Fume. I was about to give you up for dead."

Lucas swatted at the air, trying to keep the insects away from his mouth and nose. "I thought the same thing about you."

"Well, here I is." Zeke smiled. His perfect white teeth gleamed in the sunlight like a lamp had just been lit on an ivory keyboard. "You's bleedin'."

"Just buckshot. You took it worse than me."

"I packed that bullet hole with the mud. It be a bit sore, and hurts some, but I'll be just fine till I can get it tended to. We can't dillydally; that wound ain't gonna stop me none, and it done slowed me as much as it will. Them mens can't be far, and they ain't gonna be none too friendly since we slipped away from them. Bounty or not, they gonna see us dead. At least me. You might bring a gold dollar or two if they takes you alive, but they are gonna beat you within an inch of your life beforehand. You don't look like you can put up much of a fight. Not this second."

Lucas looked around. There was no sign of Nashville. He didn't know if they were south of it, clear of the city entirely. All he could see was a rising crest of trees, leafed out tenderly, shielding his view. "I don't know where we're at, and even if I did, I wouldn't know what to do but run, hide in the first barn I come to, and filch a pie off a window to satisfy this deep hunger I got brewing in my empty stomach."

Zeke fidgeted and looked to the east, to the deepest part of the surrounding forest. "I can get us to a safe place, not too far from here, but hidden away enough to keep us safe for a bit. Them mens, or other guards and law, might come there, but they ain't gonna be welcome much. We can stay long enough to catch a rest and a bite to eats if we're lucky. You can come with me, or stays here if you like. You be okay with me, but a white man's presence always be cause for leeriness and troubles, so don't expect much of a welcome other than bein' safe. Long as you're with me you be okay, but you stray, then you be on your own and face what you may."

Lucas angled his gaze upward at Zeke curiously. The

Negro was a good head taller than him, and nearly twice as broad. He'd noticed this before, but hadn't truly taken in the man's size until right then.

There wasn't an ounce of fat to be seen on Zeke's body, just mud-covered muscles that looked like they'd been carved out of mountainside rock. There was no question that at one time Zeke had fetched a pretty penny at the slave market—if he had been bought and sold, and not born into an owner's stable. Lucas didn't know much of the man's story, and at the moment, it wasn't necessary to know more than he needed to. "Where else would I go?"

"Don't know. The horses be gone. We ain't got no weapons or papers to tell us what's next, or what to do, unless you gots a clue?"

Lucas shook his head no. "There are places I can check into once I'm able to travel about. People I could see, even though they might not be too happy to see me. And there may be some lines to follow, some caches to tap, if they're still hidden, not dug up, once I'm free of here, out from the shadows of the prison.

"Somebody wanted me out from behind bars pretty bad, though I have no idea who that might be, or why. There's no value to my freedom that I know of. Just the opposite. I've had to fight for my life more than once since the day I set foot in prison. Somebody has wanted me dead . . . not free. But I have a past that's filled with deception and unclear reasoning, so there's no surprise to either cause. It'll just take some time for me to put the pieces together."

"Then you're comin' with me?"

"You sure you don't know anything else other than what you've told me?"

"No, suh, Mistuh Fume. I ain't no fool's idiot, but I ain't that smart, neither. There was supposed to be instructions in them saddlebags, along with everything else we was to need to get you to safety. Somebody somewhere is gonna be expectin' you. The less I knew, the less that Carl and his hammer could beat out me. I told you everything. I swear on the Lord's Good Book that I don't know nothin' more than that. But there ain't no book to be had. You just has to take my word. That, and my deeds, is all I have to offer you as the truth. I ain't got no currency either way to kill you or see you free. Not now. But it be the right thing to do, keepin' you safe, that's all."

Lucas drew in a deep breath. What Zeke said made sense, and sounded true. This was a well-organized plan, one that looked like many Lucas had been involved in himself during the war and just after.

Most likely, if there had been instructions in the saddle-bags, they would have been encrypted on a sheet of paper that looked blank, the code written in milk and visible only when heated up with a distant flame.

He would've had to draw on some old skills if that had been the case, figuring out a code with no key. But he was assuming his benefactor was someone from the war, an old associate come to his rescue—finally. But that's all it was, an assumption. Truth was he had no clue who would want to see him free. No one came to mind. No one at all, not at the moment. It could be anyone he had known before, during, or after the war. Lucas knew he'd left a path littered with discarded friends and enemies since taking up spying as a career.

"I suppose I am coming with you," Lucas said, surprised by his own conclusion to continue to put his fate in the hands of an unknown Negro man. But it was the only choice he had. That or stand there and wait for the posse to show up. "I suppose I am." He stepped back and motioned for Zeke to take the lead and show him the way.

TWENTY-TWO

THE EDGE OF THE FOREST WAS FULL OF blooming dogwood trees, four-petal flowers, mostly white, but some pink, that would fade away and fall to the ground in a matter of days. They seemed to glow in the diffused late afternoon light, celebrating their brief life. Spring never lasted long enough.

Farther inside the forest, there were healthy stands of maple, beech, and yellow birch, all coming to life, too, welcoming longer days and increased warmth with a wardrobe of new leaves—green and unscathed, like all youthful things.

Lucas wished for some of the vigor he'd taken for granted earlier in his life. But there was no magic potion to be had that would restore him to his former self as quick as he needed it. He followed after Zeke the best he could as the Negro dodged in and out of trees on a game trail that would have been difficult to see under perfect circumstances.

It seemed the Negro had special sight, or an internal compass, guiding him through the dense clump of trees.

Lucas was envious of his confidence and sudden show of strength. It was like the gunshot to the shoulder had had little effect on Zeke. He had been restored by his time in the river, while Lucas felt beaten and drained.

Nettle had already grown up past the itchy stage, a good ways past the desirable state for the makings of a soup. It raked along Lucas's arms and hands, making the barb-tipped weeds hard to escape. The only way was to put his hands on his head, and that was no way to run. Surrender of any type was out of the question.

The thought of food nearly stopped Lucas in his tracks, but he kept going at that, too.

His pace slowed a bit, and Zeke noticed, looking over his shoulder. He said, "This ain't no place to stop, Mistuh Fume. That man be lookin' for us high and low. He be achin' for that hammer you took from him. It was his namesake, like a son, or kin. Chasin' after a man for money is one thing, but a grudge over a theft is another."

Lucas caught his breath. He was more out of shape than he had thought. "I was just thinking of food. Been a while since I took a meal. Those nettles reminded me of soup, all mixed in with chicken broth and spring ramps that my mammy used to make." He ignored Zeke's fear about Carl the Hammer. *Let him come*, Lucas thought, but didn't say. *Let him come.*

Zeke stiffened. "Mammies is good at things like that, but you ain't gonna be eatin' no meals 'less there's a feast waitin' in heaven for you, you keep standin' here dreamin' of somethin' you can't have at the moment. Ain't got time to hunt down a rabbit or pilfer a squirrel's nest for its helpless young. We the easy pickin's standin' here jawin' likes we got all the time in the world. But we be safe soon, I promises you that, Mistuh Fume, if we get to movin'. I promises that there's a fine meal waitin' on a fire at the end of this run. If we makes it there alive."

Silence settled between the two men, and the noise in the

forest rose up around them quickly. Birds and insects offered restrained shouts of their location or all-clear signals; it was hard to tell. Lucas had lost his touch with the ways of the forest.

"We needs to run now, Mistuh Fume," Zeke said. "Can you do that much? Run? Run like your whole life is passin' before your eyes?"

Lucas nodded, and without another word, Zeke turned and jumped into a run, almost at full speed from the very start.

It was clear that freedom had its price in comparison to the rote consistency of prison life. Inside, Lucas could always count on a cup of broth—sometimes with a roach, or indistinguishable sliver of meat floating on top—and a bit of bread, fried sometimes, at the same given time of the day, morning and night. His body had adjusted to the routine, to the expectation, just as much as his mind had. Now feeding himself was his own responsibility. Life outside the walls would be like learning to walk all over again.

He broke into a full run, but by the time he was up to full speed, Zeke was already a good twenty yards ahead of him. It was easier to see the path, but Lucas felt alone, more exposed than anything. He would have felt more secure if he'd had a gun, something more than the hammer, or been on a horse, like one of the two that had been left for them.

The forest grew darker and gloomier, only because the trees had become thicker, their leaves fully formed overhead. The ground was soft, not muddy, and it all melded into one blurry vision. Lucas focused on the back of Zeke's head, with constant glances at the path in front of him. The last thing he needed to do was put his foot into a groundhog hole and come up lame. If they were caught, he wanted to be able to put up a decent last fight.

After nearly half an hour at a steady pace, Zeke finally slowed, then stopped to face Lucas. He was barely panting, and there was hardly any sweat showing on his face or body. Zeke was a natural born runner.

"We close now, Mistuh Fume, but you must do as I ask of you. I knows that sounds strange, a request as such, but it be for your best interest if you heed my call. Can you do that?"

"Depends on what it is that you ask of me." Lucas struggled with his breath and immediately bent over and steadied his hands on his knees, looking up at Zeke.

"You just needs to do whatever it is I tells you. Don't speak unless you's spoke to, don't look no man in his eye, and don't ogle the womenfolk."

"Where exactly are you taking me?"

"To a Negro village. A place slaves and Negroes like me made a place for themselves once they was free. They don't like white folk much. Especially white folk like you who used to own 'em. Be that as it is, you be all right as long as you with me, but Carl the Hammer and any other of them mens, they will think twice about comin' there, I promises you that."

Wood smoke curled out of a rickety chimney made from empty tin cans. The cans had most likely packaged beans at one time and were probably foraged from the outskirts of an old battlefield. There were a few nearby. The house itself looked pieced together, too, from old wood from wagons, barn siding, or whatever else was available to put a roof over someone's head. It leaned to the right and was weathered gray. Whitewash looked to be a luxury for the structure. To say it was on the verge of collapse was an understatement. But yet, there were two chairs on the front porch, a brass spittoon that gleamed clean in the late afternoon sun, a clothesline strung from the roof support, and a spring garden just outside the kitchen door, freshly tilled and tended to with care. Not far off, a barn stood, or leaned just like the house, offering cover for whatever farming utensils had once been employed on the fallow land.

The house sat at the edge of the forest, facing an open field that was full of knee-high bottlebrush grass yet to set its seeds to bloom. Beyond the field, about the size of the open center of the prison, were more trees and a rising ridge in the distance that fell short of a mountain but was a considerable hill.

It looked like the house had been set there on its own and its inhabitants left to fend for themselves.

"You remember what it was that I asked of you?" Zeke said to Lucas.

Lucas stood shoulder to shoulder with Zeke, a bit in his shadow, and nodded. "Don't see as I have much of a choice unless I want to walk off on my own." They were standing just inside the trees, out of sight of anyone in the little cabin.

"You's free to go on your own now anytime you wants. I ain't your keeper."

"I know that."

Zeke walked forward without saying another word, his shoulders squared, his eyes focused on the porch. As soon as they both stepped out into the open, a dog started barking from inside the house. It was an alarm bark, but a weak one. There wasn't much question that the dog was as old and tired as the farm.

In the blink of an eye, a Negro stepped outside the front door, with an old cavalry unit twelve-gauge shotgun anchored firmly under his arm and pointed directly at Zeke and Lucas. An old dog followed, a skinny yellow hound, one eye clouded white with blindness.

The Negro looked as old and neglected as the cabin and the dog. His unshorn wiry hair was gray, salt-and-pepper, and he was thin as a fence rail, his arms no thicker than broomsticks. There was no arguing with the shotgun, though; it was cocked and ready to fire.

"What business you got here, boy?" the Negro on the porch said to Zeke.

"Ain't got no business at all. Just passin' through is all, hopin' for a swig of water if it can be spared, then we be on our way. We mean you no trouble, suh."

"No trouble, you say? Well, I might believe you if your friend there was a little darker skinned."

"Ain't my friend," Zeke said quickly. "Just a business associate."

The Negro with the shotgun laughed, and the barrel pumped up and down as he did. "And exactly what is this business you be in with a white man who look like he ain't got a pot to piss in?"

"We just gettin' up and runnin' at the moment."

"Well, there's the truth of it, at least. Ain't no question that you be runnin' from something. What's your name, boy?"

"Zeke. Zeke Henry, suh."

"Ain't got no cause to suh me, you can stop with that nonsense."

"Habit, that's all."

The Negro nodded. "And your friend, uh, business associate. What be his name?"

Zeke turned to Lucas and nodded, giving him the okay to speak. "Lucas Fume. My name is Lucas Fume."

"Fume, you say?"

"Yes, sir, Fume, from up Seven Oaks way."

"Never set foot on that land, and don't know no one that has. You ever whip a man, Lucas Fume? You ever beat a man like he was a mule just 'cause he looked at you, or your womenfolk in the wrong way? You ever a whip a man like me, Lucas Fume?"

"Not a Negro man, no sir, can't say that I ever have."

"Not a Negro man, you say?"

"That's what I said."

Zeke stood silently next to Lucas, eyeing him cautiously. He looked away, then up to the man on the porch. "We mean no one any harm. What's your name, suh?"

"Farricus Jackson. Most folk just call me Far Jackson. But you can call me Mr. Jackson, if you please. You ain't got no right to call me Far, and from what I can see, you won't be stayin' around long enough to earn that right."

"No, suh, Mr. Jackson, that be right. We ain't lookin' to stay."

Farricus Jackson stared at Zeke, and lowered the shotgun to his side. "You be that Zeke Henry from Franklin, ain't you? The one they made all that noise about some years ago."

"Yes, suh, Mr. Jackson, I was borned there, and lived there most all my life in that place."

"Well, at least you gots the courage to use your real name with me. That says somethin'. They say you raped that white woman, then left her for dead."

Zeke shook his head no. "Ain't how it happened, and you knows that. I loved that woman, and her father caught us together in a private place. He nearly beat her to death. She loved me, too." Zeke's voice trailed off, and he looked to the ground.

"I hear that girl can't remember one minute to the next," Farricus Jackson said. "Doesn't even know her name. Has a nurse at her side day and night. Sad, sad life for that girl now. Sure is. Lovin' you was worse than any sickness set on her from the Lord above."

"I heard that, too," Zeke said, still looking at the ground. "Death would have been better for her, but then they'd've strung me up right then and there. Lucky for me her daddy was a powerful man who cared what peoples outside his house thought. There was limit to his rage, and other peoples came runnin' once they heard the screams."

"Man's a senator now," Jackson said.

Zeke nodded, then looked over to Lucas, who was just staring at him. "We all have reasons for runnin', for wantin' to be free. Peoples got reasons to see me dead, too."

"Well," Farricus Jackson said, "there's a water pump beyond the barn. But then you best be off. Sheriff was here right before you wandered out of the woods. Said there was a ruckus up at the prison in Nashville, and some mens escaped. Negro and a white man. You don't know anything about that do you, Zeke Henry?"

"No, suh, Mr. Jackson. I sure don't. I sure don't. We're just on our way to Atlanta to tend to some business." Zeke smiled, then turned, nudged Lucas to follow him, and made his way toward the water pump behind the barn.

TWENTY-THREE

CHARLOTTE BROGAN SAT STARING OUT THE
window of the train. Relief washed over her as she recognized the first hint in the land that they were nearing St.
Louis. More shacks sat congregated together just off the
tracks, on the west side of the river; some most likely had
been washed away in a wet spring, but these were still standing on dry dirt, solid for the moment, even though the gray
sky promised to let loose with a load of rain sometime soon.

Life pulsed around the shacks, not quite towns, more like
the outer boroughs of New York, the settlements that had
sprung up as the Irish and their like moved away from the
East, stopping at the first sign of prosperity, desperate for
roots, for a sense of home. It was not an aspiration that
Charlotte shared, though she was quick to recognize it.

Chickens pecked about the ground for ticks and gravel,
and clothes hung drying on lines strung about crossways
and every other way, from one structure, or pole, to the other.
They looked like banners strung over Main Street for a

coming parade or celebration, but there was no holiday, at least that Charlotte knew of. This was just a glimpse of everyday life. There *was* some celebration to be found in that, she supposed.

A knock came at the door, drawing Charlotte's attention away from the window, reminding her that she may have left John Barlow's company, but she was not free of his control—or eyes. Her every move was watched, and kept track of, by the Celestials sent along in her service. The two door guards, Yen and Cheng, and her dresser and housemaid, Little Ling, were her constant companions.

Joe Straut and his foul-smelling sidekick, Finney Deets, were lurking close, too. Their loyalty to John Barlow, or Lanford Grips as they believed him to be, was unquestioned, just like the Celestials'. There was, however, no Bojack Wu to be wary of. He would not leave the side of the man he served. Charlotte knew little of the deal between the two men, how it came about. There were blank lines in her relationship with John. Months had passed, almost a year, after that horrible nightmare that she had stumbled into, when she had found the severed hands carefully arranged on the desk in a pool of blood, before she even knew that John Barlow was still alive. Bojack Wu was there then, and had been ever since. Neither man spoke of his bond to the other; it just existed, unquestioned. They were like a prince and his manservant going about their daily business.

Charlotte had no one to confide in, and no one to trust, at least not at the moment. But she was accustomed to finding herself in such circumstances. Her time in the war, under the tutelage of Rose O'Neal Greenhow in the school of spying, may God rest her gentle but greedy soul, had taught her the skills to survive on her own—and whom to trust and when. Now was not the time to allow anyone to know her intentions other than offering herself up as bait for Lucas Fume.

She was still surprised that John had acquiesced so easily to her request. He had said yes, with a nod and no words, almost too quickly. His eagerness to be free of her presence concerned her, had almost made her reconsider her plan, but then she thought she was being overdramatic, thinking too much about John's own motives and desires. She knew what was at stake for him, what his desires were . . . At least, she thought she did. He was all business. Wealth could replace his losses. But her desires, her plans, were tightly held.

Charlotte was certain she hadn't telegraphed her intentions. Hiding her true desires had always been one of her greatest gifts—that and learning from other people's errors. Like the dear, departed Mrs. Greenhow, whose death was caused by her desire for wealth, too, and the refusal to let her gold sink to the bottom of the ocean during a storm. Charlotte would have never made that mistake. She would have let go of the gold and kept her life. Once you know how to accumulate something, it becomes much, much easier as time goes on. The trick is to value time more than gold or any other currency.

The tap at the door came again, only this time it was a little more emphatic, anxious.

"Yes, yes, I am coming," Charlotte said aloud, as he pulled herself from the window, pulling her red silk wrapper across her chest, looping it tightly at the neck so she would not expose her best features to any man passing by, or to the Celestials for that matter. Regardless of their quietness, and averted eyes, they were still men—and men, in her experience, no matter the color of their skin, or origin of their birth, were always happy to sneak a glance at the forbidden. Or pursue a touch of the flesh if they thought the glimpse was intentional, an invitation, which at the moment, it most certainly would not be. Pleasure was the last thing on her mind.

Charlotte walked to the door, answered the knock with two raps, even in tone and pressure, then stood back and waited.

After a long second, the door opened and Little Ling stood centered just outside the frame, her head down, her clothes the same as they were every day: black tunic across a flat chest, restrained if there was any health there at all, a matter which was only speculation on Charlotte's part. Celestial women were shyer, more mysterious, about their bodies than any white woman Charlotte had ever met.

Little Ling's pants matched the tunic in color and lack of form, and she wore traditional wood sandals on her tiny feet. There was no jewelry on her hands or chest, no adornments or frills of any kind. Her ankles were exposed, but Celestials were invisible, not to be seen, or ogled, by proper gentlemen, so there was little or no offense taken at the sight of her skin.

"Missy Charlotte is in need of me?" Little Ling asked, her eyes still to the ground. Her shiny coal-black hair was pulled tight and woven intricately into a pigtail that fell to her waist.

"Yes, Little Ling, I must be prepared to depart the train, and I mustn't look hurried."

"Yes, yes, of course, Missy." Little Ling looked to Yen and Cheng, who stood in their positions on either side of the door. They nodded an acceptance in unison, never saying a word, allowing her to enter the berth.

Charlotte stepped back and allowed the girl inside.

Little Ling couldn't have been more than fifteen years old, if that, and was lucky to be in the employ of Lanford Grips, instead of a fouler man who would see Little Ling's innocence and obvious purity as an opportunity to make money. Being a maid, of sorts, was a much better life than lying on her back as a whore.

Charlotte closed the door, glad again to be free of Yen's and Cheng's eyes and ears. "Are you well today, Little Ling?"

"Oh, yes, Missy." Little Ling bowed, smiled briefly on the way up, then scurried to the wardrobe against the far wall and opened the door cautiously as the train rocked back and forth.

"And you have been fed this morning?" Charlotte asked. "Eaten a fine breakfast?"

Little Ling hesitated. "Yes." It was a whisper, into the wardrobe.

"Little Ling, we have talked of this before. You mustn't fib to me."

"I do not fib, Missy."

"You just do not tell me the whole truth."

"Worrying about Little Ling is for Little Ling, not for Missy. I have everything I need and would not dream of complaining."

Charlotte walked to the table next to the bed and picked up an apple that sat in a bowl that had been brought with her breakfast. "You are not my slave, Little Ling. You are not anyone's slave. Those days are past for everyone in this country. You know that, yes?"

"Yes, Missy, Little Ling knows she is free to go whenever she want to and wherever she want to. But she doesn't want to. She likey Missy."

"But you have nowhere to go, right? That is the truth of it? So here is better than out there?" Charlotte pointed out the window, at the passing shantytowns.

Little Ling still stood facing the interior of the wardrobe, staring at the huge variety of dresses, skirts, and jackets that hung there, not looking about her or commenting further. There was silence in the room, but the noise of the train was constant and always impeded any solitude or quiet mood, if there was one.

The locomotive whistled and began to slow. The car jerked backward then forward, causing Charlotte to steady herself against the table. Once she was sure of herself, she walked over to the girl and handed her the apple. "Here, you must eat this, Little Ling. The day will be long. There is much to do once we arrive at the hotel."

The girl did not take the fruit. She looked up into Charlotte's eyes with tears welling in her own. "We will be late, Missy."

Charlotte pushed the apple toward her. "This is not our

stop. Now, eat the apple and tell me again of your home country. I can tell that you are longing for it on this gloomy day."

Little Ling forced a smile, nodded, then took a tepid bite of the apple and swallowed it gently. "I was born in the Valley of the Sleeping Dragon. The mountains behind the orphanage I was born in are the humps on the dragon's back. His head slopes down into a hill, covered with a thick forest of trees to hide his sleeping eyes from the sun and the moon. A constant mist hangs over the valley, no matter the time of year. It is steam from the dragon's fiery heart escaping through the caves at the end of his long, narrow nose." Little Ling smiled then, her shoulders squarer. Her eyes were bright, but distant, and she took a more substantial bite of the apple as the memories pulled her into the past, across faraway shores.

"Go on," Charlotte said, sitting on the edge of the bed, staring intently at Little Ling, with care and concern in her eyes and voice. "Tell me more."

"I knew no other home than the orphanage and the nuns who ran it. Mother Superior was stern but had a very kind heart. But Sister Mary Catherine was most like a mother to me. She taught me to speak best English I can. Life was happy, but the fear of the dragon was strong, even though the nuns did their best to teach us otherwise, that our salvation waited for us in the strength of our belief, not in the dark regions of old tales that did not belong in the modern world. Sister Mary Catherine said we should respect our past, but she did so away from the ears of the others and their perfect black-and-white habits. She longed for her home, too, just like I longed to know where I came from." Little Ling looked wistfully to the ceiling, and then back to the apple. "You remind me of her at times, Missy, and that makes me happy. She never far away."

"You miss her?"

Little Ling nodded yes. "When she grew ill, she wished to come home, back to America, to see her family one last time. She brought me with her to this place called Tennessee. And it looked very much like my home, our home. Tall mountains and deep valleys. I thought that there must be dragons all over the world, sleeping about, waiting to be awakened. But then Sister died, and I was afraid of being alone, or worse. But Sister Mary Catherine had made arrangements for me to be of service to her faraway brother. I did not see him there by the grave, but a long way away, across the big river, living with a name I never hear before, not from Sister Mary Catherine, or you."

"And that is how you came to be here, with me. I knew who you were," Charlotte said, standing up. "Finish the apple, Little Ling. We have lots to do. I have to make my arrival known, and we must present ourselves to the proper ladies in St. Louis straight off the train so we can secure an invitation to the Fettermans' Spring Ball. I must attend it to get my name in the newspaper's social column."

"Yes, Missy, you will be the most beautiful woman in the room. Everyone will stare at your ripe red hair more than ever. I will see to it." Little Ling nodded again and bit into the apple ravenously.

"One other thing, Ling." Charlotte's tone grew serious and cold. "You must never tell that story to anyone again. Not even me. Do you understand why?"

Little Ling nodded yes and swallowed the last bite of apple deeply. "I do. The dragon still sleeps, but he will awake someday, and if I utter his true name aloud, even by accident, he will come for me, and tear me apart limb by limb until I die a miserable death. Then I will be thrown to the fires, and I will be no more. Dust on a land that is not my own. I fear my soul will wander lost forever trying to return to the Valley of the Sleeping Dragon."

"That is right, Little Ling. You mustn't ever forget that, for it is the truth, no matter how sad or scary that may be."

TWENTY-FOUR

ZEKE PUMPED WATER INTO THE TIN CUP TIED just below the faucet and handed it to Lucas. He took the cup reluctantly, sipped the water, and never took his eyes off Zeke. Fresh blood leached out from the wound in the Negro's shoulder, but the hulking man didn't seem to notice, or to be troubled by it, as he cupped his hand under the pump, filled it the best he could, and drank the water readily.

"You're lucky to be alive," Lucas finally said. "Much less not stuffed inside a prison for the rape of a white woman."

"Ain't no luck in never bein' able to see your one true love ever again. Not that she'd know me none. Not now. But I'd care for her anyways, I sure would."

"I doubt she wants for a thing."

"She was put in a prison, too."

A chicken coop sat off to the rear of the barn, the door open, and the chickens, a variety of bantams, clucked about.

A rooster eyed both men warily from the sagging roof of the coop, picking up one foot, then the other, like a solider preparing to march to war.

Lucas was in no mood to be spurred by an overprotective cock, and he doubted if Farricus Jackson would take too kindly to finding the rooster dead with a broken neck if that were to happen.

Beyond the coop, a narrow path disappeared into the deep forest. There was nothing much to see except the dark green overgrowth that had sprung up along the edge of the trees. It almost looked like someone had planted honey-suckle bushes, full of buzzing bees and other nectar-seeking insects, with the intention to use them as a wall, to hide something deep in the holler.

The water sated Lucas's thirst, and he let Zeke's words wonder off into the wind, refusing to be too sad about the events that had put the Negro behind bars. If his story was to be believed. Lucas let the cup drop away without saying another word about the senator's daughter, or the crime that had been committed. It was too early to take up a cause, or a partnership for that matter. The empty cup swung just above the wet ground like a pendulum.

"More, Mistuh Fume?"

Lucas shook his head no. "So, this is your big plan? Bring us here and get us a drink?"

Zeke drew back, a flash of indignation crossing his face. He let the remaining water in his hand drain through his fingers and waste into the ground. "We just stoppin' to breathe, suh. We safe here. Far Jackson ain't gonna sic no dogs on us or let no man, white or black, do a thing like that here. He seen enough meanness in his long life, just like the rest of us, to know we just be passin' through. He know what it's like to be hunted down—and caught."

"You know him, then? You had to tell him your name."

"I had to tell him a lot of things since I brung a white

man to his doorstep. You think he gonna show a sign of recognition if I show him you a bad man? Negro had a right to be wary. Besides, I know lotsa folks, at one time."

"Safe you say?"

"Yes, suh, as safe as we gonna be in this state, and those close by."

"And this wasn't part of a plan, the escape plan?"

Zeke frowned. "I wished it was. But any letters that said what to do and where to go is lost now that that fine geldin' took to the hoof and runned off. I hopes no one of authority finds it."

"Instructions were likely written in code."

"Well," Zeke said, picking up the tin cup and filling it again, "more than one set of eyes knows how to read code writin' I imagine, don't you?"

"You know how to read it?"

"No, suh, but I can read words and books, I sure can. I don't make it known much, though. Some folks still see that as a crime, a Negro knowin' how to read. Even black folk can call uppity on the man readin' aloud. Unless it be the Good Book, of course. That is what we all learned to read from."

"A crime? Like miscegenation?"

Zeke shrugged and offered the cup back to Lucas.

He took it, then eyed the rooster, who had started to pace nervously back and forth across the roof. A few speckled hens pecked closer to Lucas's feet, and he was sure that the rooster was planning on a jump from the roof, sooner rather than later, to attack him and defend his hens.

"It's still a crime for a Negro to marry a white," Lucas said, then gulped down the water.

"A man can't pick the one he loves no more than a woman can. Sometimes, laws try to strangle the heart. But it don't work. At least in the light of day." Zeke followed Lucas's worried gaze toward the rooster. "Come on, now, we best get a move on before we get chased out of here. There's a place I'd like to be before the darkness catches up to us."

The thick woods rose up around them, making it more difficult to navigate than Lucas thought it would be. Tall nettles, mixed with fibrous jewelweed, yet to bloom its orange horn of plenty–like blooms, lined the path, reaching for whatever sunlight could penetrate the growing overhead. It wasn't a well-worn path, traveled daily by human feet, but it was barren of plants, tamped down into solid dirt. Most likely it was used by game more than men.

The path eased down the side of a ravine, and far off in the distance, Lucas could hear water washing over rocks, falling loud enough to make a consistent, but noisy, splash that echoed through the trees. There was no sign of any animals—no squirrels, deer, or rabbits—and the birdsong was occasional and muted, high above them or beyond. Only the call of a single wood thrush captured Lucas's attention, and that was only because the full-throated warbling song existed in his memory.

Thrushes had lived in the forest behind his childhood home. He used to sit on the porch and imitate their song with a whistle, trying to lure them out of the dense brush so he could see them up close and get a good look at them. It amazed him that something so small could be so loud. He had no inclination to do such a thing at the moment. He didn't want to draw any undue attention to their trek. They were far enough away from the Jackson farm to be out from under the man's protection, and it was hard telling who walked these woods. Zeke's story of his imprisonment was enlightening, if it was true, as to how intense the search for them both would be. There would be a lot of men who would want to see them both back in prison—or dead, dangling from one of the many tall trees that surrounded them.

Zeke led steadily, but he had begun to hold his hand over

the wound, applying as much pressure as he could muster. Earlier, after he had found Lucas hiding next to the tree on the bank, it had appeared that the wound had been cleansed and was not going to be a bother to the Negro. That didn't look to be the case now. Since Lucas had no clue where they were, or where they were headed, his concern for his own well-being grew by any declining sign Zeke offered up. Lucas was starting to worry that without the Negro's help he would die, and it was an odd set of circumstances that he found himself in.

"You sure you know where we are?" Lucas finally asked.

Zeke stopped and turned to face him. "Yes, suh, Mistuh Fume, I do. We on a path to safety. At least, as safe as we can be with no weapons."

"I've got a hammer."

"Won't do no good against the man's rifle or pistol, and the backup that rides with him."

"How come you didn't barter or borrow a gun from Farricus Jackson?"

Zeke forced a smile. "'Cause you the only thing I had to trade, and Far Jackson made it clear that he had no use for no white man under his feet."

"You think that's funny?"

"Well, suh, sayin' such a thing at one time would've got me whupped, or worst, but not now. You a fair man, with a decent sense about you. I figure I can josh you now and then when things get tense."

"I wouldn't push it."

"Yes, suh, I'll keep that in mind." And with that, Zeke turned and forced his way forward, his step certain, and maybe just a little bit lighter. He whistled into the sky, and somewhere close, the wood thrush whistled back.

TWENTY-FIVE

JOE STRAUT HAD NEVER BEEN FOND OF ST. Louis, but he was glad to be out from under the scrutiny of Lanford Grips and his unsettling shadow, Bojack Wu. There were still Chinese to deal with, the two that always stood guard outside Grips's door had been sent along on this trip, though Straut had no clue what their orders were. He didn't speak their language. For that matter, he didn't even know their names. Didn't care to. They weren't his to command, or look out for. Their agenda was as unknown to him as his was to them. At least, that's the way he thought it was, hoped it was. For all he knew, they were Lanford Grips's ears and eyes on this trip, with orders kill as soon as something went wrong.

"It all starts here, don't it, Sarge?" Finney Deets said. He stood shoulder to shoulder with Straut, staring at Union Depot, a small Gothic train station in the center of St. Louis that was rumored to be slated for replacement by a bigger station to accommodate the traffic and the train lines heading west. The depot had been built in haste, and it had been wholly underestimated in its size and service. That was one of the reasons Straut didn't like St. Louis. It changed before your very eyes, buildings being built and torn down so fast you didn't know where you were from one day to the next. He could never get his bearings, and that unsettled him.

"You need a bath," Straut said, not taking his eyes off the entrance to the depot. The structure and its future were less his concern than was his own personal comfort at the present. High finance and growth were best left to men like Lanford Grips who knew how to make one dollar turn into ten.

"Beg your pardon?" Deets said.

"I said you need a bath. You stink. You need it spelled out any clearer than that?"

"Well, I'll be. What's got you in a mood, Sarge? You ain't never said such a surly thing to me before."

"You smell like a cowboy fresh off the trail. Look at all these fine folks. You're an embarrassment. If I'd've knowed you stunk like the south end of a northbound horse, I would've paid myself for you to dip into those fine Turkish baths back at the Coates House Hotel in Kansas City." Straut paved the way with his hand, not pointing at anyone directly, but sweeping a big half circle in front of both of them.

There was a crowd of finely clothed men and women getting off the train, and more waiting to get on. The chatter was noisy, like the sound of a flock of birds set to the sky for the pure pleasure of flying, not in alarm. The women were all gussied up in their fancy spoon bonnets and silk bustled dresses made of colors that would make a peacock blush—and the men were dressed in fine frock coats and bowlers, tailored and cut to fit them perfectly. Sunday best for most folk, but something told Straut most of this crowd had a week's worth of suits and dresses in their wardrobes, while he was lucky to have an extra pair of drawers. That was the other thing he didn't like about cities. It was easy to see what other folks had and you didn't. He always felt unworthy, less than, not better than dirt, and he didn't like that feeling at all.

"I see them," Deets said. "Don't mean I got to put on airs like 'em. Besides, I ain't got no fresh collars. I'm a simple man, just like you, Sarge. Fashion ain't required to do the deeds I'm hired to do. I carry all I own in a small satchel just like you. Since when did we have to concern ourselves about what other folks think about us?"

"And what deeds are those?"

"Whatever you say they are."

"Cities make me nervous. I see things that I don't understand is all, Deets. Just makes me nervous, that's all. You just get the brunt of my displeasure. I'll try to watch myself."

"Takes a big man to see that, Sarge."

Straut ignored the comment, or at least acted like he did. He didn't want to alienate Deets. It wasn't his way of leading; he'd just let his mind take control of his mouth when he shouldn't have.

Deets filled in the silence without missing another beat, clearing the air the best he could. "We ain't gonna be here long, and that's a good thing. Maybe your mood'll change once we get where we're goin' and get back on a horse. I'm always better on a horse, ain't you, Sarge?"

Straut exhaled loudly, but said nothing. Deets was right. He was in a mood. The trip from Kansas City to St. Louis had been sweaty for everyone in the common seats. Unlike his other charge at the moment, Charlotte Brogan, who'd had the luxury of her own berth and an attendant to see to her every need and want.

Straut didn't like the Brogan woman much. She was like one of those kaleidoscope pictures, distant and apt to change depending on the light, depending on how you looked at her. One second she was soft and kind, the next she was cunning and cold as ice. Not that he'd had a whole lot of dealings with her. Charlotte Brogan was a mysterious woman, red hair and all, and Straut would be glad to leave her behind in St. Louis.

"Why don't you run and get us a newspaper while we wait, Deets," Straut said, digging into his pocket for a coin.

"I thought you wanted me to get a bath?"

"No time for that. But first thing once we set foot in Tennessee, while I'm takin' care of livery business, you're off to the suds, you understand?"

"Yes, Sarge, sure thing." Deets held out his hand, and Straut dropped a nickel into it.

"Get yourself some of that rock candy you're so fond of. Shouldn't be too hard to find. It's going to be a long ride to those spots on the map the Boss gave me."

Deets smiled, exposing two missing bottom teeth and a mouthful of others that were beginning to rot. He clasped his hand around the coin much like a little boy would and ran off into the crowd without saying another word.

Straut was glad to be free of the smell Deets emitted, though it took several minutes for it to fully dissipate. Deets was as ripe as a stinkbug burst open in the still desert air. Now that he was gone, Straut could breathe normal air mixed with the normal train smells—steam and wood smoke, along with grease on the wheels—and the toilet waters the womenfolk bathed in that floated into the city air, making any man accustomed to the wide open range forget that the natural world even existed.

"Why, Mr. Straut, I was hoping to see you before we were off," Charlotte Brogan said, startling Straut out of his thoughts.

Straut jumped, then quickly doffed his hat. The Colt Open Top he wore on his side jingled, drawing the Brogan woman's attention for a brief second. But she said nothing, just looked back up to Straut expectantly. "Ma'am," he said. "Looks like you'll be needin' that parasol for more than keeping the sun out of your eyes."

"And off my skin. Dear, me, I burn so easily, and that would be just a horrible occurrence, don't you think?"

"If you say so, ma'am."

Charlotte Brogan smiled, and then glanced to Little Ling, who was holding the parasol, a burgundy silk to match the fancy dress Charlotte was wearing, to keep the sun off her Missy's alabaster white skin as much as possible. "I am so lucky to have Little Ling in my company. I understand that you'll be traveling on, Mr. Straut."

"Yes, ma'am, to Nashville and beyond. I was waiting to see you off."

"Well, thank you, that wasn't necessary. Kind, but not necessary. Nashville's a ways away isn't it? Have you been back east since the war?"

Straut shook his head no. The question made him uncomfortable.

Charlotte Brogan sighed aloud, more dramatically than Straut had expected. "Alas, neither have I. I miss the familiar ways and voices of my old home, but business demands that I stay here. Do you like the city, Mr. Straut? You seem nervous."

"I'm always happier on the trail, ma'am. I had my fill of cities, and the throngs that pulse inside them, a long time ago."

"Pity. Cities are where the action is."

"I will leave that to those who know how to navigate it better than I do," Straut said—he was stiff, speaking as respectfully as he could find it in himself to do.

Straut was a tall man, so he had the advantage of long sight that most didn't have. He could see Deets heading back toward him, weaving through the crowd, parting it with his foul odor, chomping on a fresh chunk of rock candy. Only there was no joy on Finney Deets's face like Straut had expected. He was void of any emotion, and his face was paler than it had been before he'd gone on his errand to fetch the newspaper.

"Well, Mr. Straut, I must be moving on," Charlotte Brogan said, as she eyed the Chinese guards coming toward her, pulling a dolly loaded with suitcases and hatboxes. "Yen and Cheng have arrived with my things. We must be on our way to the White House Hotel. Have you ever stayed there, Mr. Straut? If you haven't, you really must. It is divine. Just divine. It really is a grand old hotel, one of the finest. The oysters are carted up directly from New Orleans. Oh my, I've just made my mouth water. Come, Little Ling, we must be on our way. Have a good trip, Mr. Straut. I hope you are successful with your dealings in Tennessee." And without saying another word, Charlotte Brogan paraded off with Little Ling scurrying after her, trying to keep the parasol over the Brogan woman's head.

Gray clouds overhead threatened rain but hadn't produced any precipitation yet. It wouldn't be long though. Thunder rumbled in the distance.

Yen and Cheng pushed by Straut without offering any recognition, either. At least he knew their names now. Not that it mattered. He really hoped to never see them again. They made him more nervous than Charlotte Brogan ever could.

"You best look at this, Sarge." Deets handed a copy of the *Daily Journal* to Straut. The newspaper had just recently begun to run hand-drawn illustrations.

Straut took the paper, unfolded it, and glanced over the top of it quickly to make sure that Charlotte Brogan and her troop of attendants were out of earshot. Satisfied, he looked at the paper, ignoring the odoriferous reintroduction of Deets's presence the best he could.

"It's them people, Sarge," Deets said, dropping his voice as low as he could, into an audible whisper.

"What people, Deets? I don't know what you're talking about, and you best just forget what you're even thinkin', you understand me?" A tremor of recognition ran through Straut's entire body as he digested the news the paper delivered not just to him, but to the rest of the world.

Deets had good reason to be afraid. It was the three people that they'd hidden under the bridge, instead of cutting up and burning like they had been instructed to do. One man was a banker, the other was his brother, a land agent, and the third was the land agent's wife. All set out on a business trip to Kansas City that had gone horribly wrong. At least that's what the paper said. That and that the U.S. Marshals were looking into the murders. The victims' names were all the same, Wilmington, which didn't mean anything to Straut.

"But what if the Boss finds out we didn't do what we was supposed to? What are we supposed to do if the marshals catch up to us?"

"The Boss will see to it that we're fine. Besides, we're on our way to Tennessee. We'll be a long way from that bridge and this city by the time they start to look for us, if they figure it out." Straut took a deep breath. "The only way out of this is to do what we're supposed to now. If we bring Lucas Fume back to the Boss like he wants, then we can save our own necks. If we don't, well, I don't know about you, but I'm walkin' straight into the nearest U.S. Marshals office and turnin' myself in. They'll go a lot easier on us than the Boss will, if it comes to that."

"So, we act like nothin' is the matter?"

Straut nodded yes and tapped the map in his breast pocket. "We're going after Lucas Fume, plain and simple. And we'll find him. I swear that to you. We ain't got no choice now. Not that we did before . . ."

TWENTY-SIX

LUCAS AND ZEKE ROUNDED A CURVE IN THE
trail at a steady pace, with Zeke still in the lead. It was easy
for anyone who had spent any time walking in a thick woods
to tell that a clearing lay straight ahead.

The ravine was about to come to a stop at the bottom of
a gorge, and Lucas had no idea where he was. All he knew
was that he had put his trust in Zeke Henry, a Negro of tall,
threatening proportions who had seen him to freedom, taken
a shot for him, and now led him deep into the forest with a
promise of safety.

Even if Lucas was a generous man and a kindhearted
soul, he would have had reservations about putting his fate
in this man's hands. But at the moment, he didn't seem to
have any choice—and that situation was very much like the
situation he had just escaped from. It had been a long time
since he had been a master of his own destiny.

Their trek came to a quick stop, one that it appeared neither man had been planning on. One second the way forward

was easy to see, and then in the blink of an eye, it was blocked. Blocked by another Negro holding an eight-gauge shotgun, leveled at them both. The unknown Negro had appeared from behind the base of a wide oak tree, like a wraith conjured from a children's tale, fierce-looking, but with the hint of a bumbler about his actions. Still, he was ably armed, holding a big, long gun, with his finger pressed purposefully on the trigger. If the man had burped, the gun would have gone off whether he wanted it to or not.

"You two best just stop right there," the Negro said. He was about a head shorter than Zeke but had about fifty pounds on him. The path-blocker was chunky, like he'd been eating bread pudding morning, noon, and night for all of his years. There were no men of heft in prison, at least ones that had been there awhile, so seeing someone so luxuriously healthy took Lucas aback.

It would have been easy to underestimate the man, consider him jolly and unprepared for a fight, except that Lucas was weak and not up for another fight. Zeke, too, for that matter. Truth be told, they could both hardly stand up and face the man. They were at his behest and command for as long as the shotgun remained in his flabby, skillet-sized hands.

Lucas had learned a long time ago to never underestimate any man who had the gift of stealth and was pointing a gun at your head, no matter the look on the man's face or his assumed nature. Instinctively, and without being told to, both Lucas and Zeke put their hands into the air and surrendered.

"That would be more like it," the Negro said. "Now, who was the one that whistled himself in here?"

"I did," Zeke said. "Been here before. Stopped up at Far Jackson's place so's y'all knowed we was comin'."

"We heard. Why you think I'm standin' here? Don't you figure I got better things to do as the day moves toward night than to come out here and see you in—or away? I had plans for the evening . . ."

Like eating dinner, Lucas thought but didn't say. The slight wind that had worked its way to the bottom of the ravine had shifted, and he smelled the first hint of wood smoke, the first promise of comfort and safety—of home, which he had tried not to think of since his free feet hit the ground running. He didn't know if he could ever go there, back to the place of his boyhood, back to his father's land and the place of his mother's burial, even once he was better, standing on his own two feet. If he lived that long.

"Don't mean to be a bother," Zeke said.

"Well, you *are* a bother. You'll bring trouble to us. We don't need no more trouble than we already got, and we shore don't need no more mouths to feed. There's hardly enough food to feed us all the way it is."

Zeke stepped forward, not stopping until his chest was pressed hard against the barrel of the man's shotgun. "I come a long way to be here, suh, and my friend and I are in need of some care and some rest. My daddy—"

"Don't you think I knows who your daddy was, Zeke Henry?" the Negro demanded, cutting Zeke off before he had the opportunity to finish his sentence. "And don't you think Far Jackson already done told us what he knows about the events of this day, and the identity and plight of your white friend there? Just 'cause your daddy helped lay the foundation to the church here don't means we owe you a doggone thing. Especially when you come a-cartin' trouble, like you're rabbits lookin' for a hole to hide in. There's hounds sniffin' after your feet. Both of ya's, and we have peace, at least more than we ever had, and your currency is lost at the till, dead and buried, and paid up in full the way I see it. You got powerful enemies, Zeke Henry. Him, too, far as that goes. But your enemies got hate in their hearts and fear in their minds. Most dangerous kinds, you ask me."

Lucas stepped forward and stopped next to Zeke. "Take him, then, to wherever it is you speak of. He's been shot and needs tending to. If I can just get a bit of bread and some fresh water, I'll be on my way. I won't trouble you none, or bring you anything you're not prepared for. It's been a long day, and Zeke here risked his life to save my own. Take him. I'll go on, and that will be that. You'll not be troubled by my pursuers if I'm not here."

Zeke glanced over to Lucas, but said nothing. Neither did the Negro with the eight-gauge. The smell of the wood smoke became stronger, only it was different, mixed with the powerful smell of simmering beans and bacon frying in a hot skillet over an open fire. Lucas's hunger screamed to be sated, but he ignored it. He stood rigid, waiting to see what the Negro would do with his offer.

"Compassion or contrition?" the Negro said, as he lowered the shotgun, allowing his finger to fall off the trigger for the first time since he'd appeared. "It matters none. Of course we'll tend to Zeke Henry's wound, but it is you, Mistuh Lucas Fume, that worries us. There is little known of you other than your family name, though none of our folk share it here like they do Jackson, Johnson, or even Henry, the surnames of the mens who bought us, sold us, then raged against us once't we was freed. There are no Fumes here, Mistuh Lucas. But you is welcome to come in for a spell. Rest up, then be on your way to wherever you may be headin'. We can't risk you stayin' here long, and no offense, you're a hard shade to hide."

Lucas drew in a deep breath that he didn't realize was relief until he exhaled freely. "What is your name, sir? And where are we?"

"Sulley Johnson is what they call me. Sulley Joe Johnson. And you is in the heart of the forest, at the bottom of Benjamin Hide's Gorge. There's a settlement of us here, freedmen mostly that have been that way since long before the great day of Emancipation came upon us. We been callin' it Libertyville since the day Zeke Henry's daddy run off from Mastuh Henry's place over Franklin way and founded it with the others he was runnin' with, or met up with on the way. My grandpappy was one of 'em, so we got some history, me an Zeke Henry. We sure do."

"I never heard of Libertyville," Lucas said.

"Ain't on no map," Zeke said, before Sulley Johnson could say anything, cutting him off in kind. "And it moves some, when the need arises, even now, even in these days of freedom. But trust me, Mistuh Fume, you be safe here. At least for the time bein'."

"Come on now," Sulley said, "Let's get you both looked at, and some dinner in your bellies. I've been standin' here jawin' too long the way it is." He turned then and trotted down the trail toward the smell of the wood smoke, fearful he'd miss dinner, the eight-gauge thrown over his shoulder, relaxed and jiggling, the way paved clear for Lucas and Zeke to follow him and make their way into Libertyville.

The only real building in the town was the church sitting at the end of the road that led into Libertyville. A jagged limestone wall, grayed with weather and time, sat opposite the church and a collection of tents that surrounded it. The wall reached nearly a hundred feet in the air, with half a roof hanging over the deep cut in the earth, like half a cantilevered bridge that was never finished or had broken away in another age. The natural-made roof offered shade, protection from the weather, and obscured the view of anyone looking straight down. Most of the tents were under the roof. The location of the secret settlement had been carefully chosen by its founders.

The church itself was in good repair, whitewashed recently, with two shiny windows on each side of the double doors that led inside. The doors were arched and one was hand-carved with a scene of the ark and its occupants braving a storm, rising on a tide, toward a dove carved on the other door, with an olive branch firmly ensconced in its beak. The story was apt, offering anyone who entered the building a new beginning. There was no steeple, just a simple cross on a cupola at the peak of the roof. The cross's shadow fell forward, reaching out on the road until it disappeared into the shade from the forest.

The tents that made up the rest of Libertyville were mostly white canvas, very much like the ones used in the war, and were of various sizes. One large tent stood next to the church. The flap was shredded; the tent was obviously past its prime. Green mold had begun to grow at the base, along with black mildew that streaked down the roof to the side. A sign that read LIBERTYVILLE MERCANTILE was anchored over the door with two wood pegs tied through holes in the canvas. A few churns sat outside the door, and from a distance, Lucas could see reams of fabric, shelves full of tin cups, and all the normal hardware, dinnerware, and tools a man would expect to find in a normal mercantile in a normal town.

Other signs lightened Lucas's steps, announcing a livery in the largest tent, next to a dry goods store, a barber, and a bathhouse.

Libertyville looked self-sufficient, but the supplies had to come from somewhere. There were ways about the tent village that made no sense to Lucas, but civilization had never looked so good, even if there wasn't another white person to be seen. He was uncomfortable, but he was not afraid. Zeke and Sulley had given him the confidence to follow them into the small town with a welcome step. Truth be told, he probably couldn't have gone much farther in the shape he was in. He was on the verge of collapse.

A few Negroes milled about outside of the tents, eyeing Lucas curiously, but saying nothing to any of the three men. They'd stare, then go about their business, walking away, sweeping the slate rock clean of dirt at the entrance to their tent, like everything was normal, even though they knew it wasn't.

Lucas was sure every man, woman, and child in Libertyville had known they were coming even before they'd arrived at Far Jackson's place. There was no question that there were eyes and ears in the forest, hidden from sight, much as in the old days, a perimeter set far and wide to protect the camp.

The smells of wood smoke and frying bacon were stronger than ever now, and there was a great amount of hope in Lucas's mind, and stomach, that the worst of their journey was over.

"You fellers are to stay in Miss Lainie's tent till Far Jackson can see fit to come down an' decide what to do with both of ya's," Sulley said, stopping in front of a tent that had a sign out front that said ROOMS and nothing else. The flap was closed, and there was no sound coming from the inside.

Now that Lucas stopped to notice, there were hardly any sounds around him at all. No horses neighing, no birds singing or men walking through the mud. It was like the whole world had come to a stop and decided to gaze on the back of his neck. Lucas stood up straighter at the thought. He knew no one had cause to trust him, and most of them probably had more than one reason to hate him. But he meant no one any harm. Only he couldn't express that, couldn't say that. He knew his place, and what was expected of him. Manners had not left him, nor had the sense of irony, of knowing the world had turned upside down. Lucas was like a baby learning how to walk and talk in a foreign country. A foreign country that he had been at war with since the day of his birth, even though he wasn't aware of it then—but he sure was now.

Sulley continued on, "Sorry there, Mistuh Fume, you have to stay out back in a room to yourself. I hope that doesn't offend you none, but you must surely understand why. Miss Lainie has a forgivin' heart, but you're likely to make more than a few folks nervous, if you ain't already figured that much out."

Lucas nodded yes. "That'll be fine. I'm accustomed to being alone."

"Miss Lainie, or one of her girls, will bring you a meal, and set you to a bath. You might want to consider a trip to the barber, Mistuh Fume, too. They be lookin' for a man with a head of long hair over his shoulders and a full beard, won't they now?"

"I suppose so," Lucas said. "But I have no money to pay for a thing, or a service. We have the clothes on our backs, and that's all."

"Well," Sulley Johnson said, "then I expect you'll just have to owe us a debt, now won't you, Lucas Fume?"

TWENTY-SEVEN

AN EMPTY WOOD TUB SAT IN THE MIDDLE OF the tent. The inside of it was still moist from recent use, but that was the only sign of any occupancy—which suited Lucas just fine. He was glad to be inside, alone, free of Sulley and Zeke, out of the weather, and away from staring eyes.

Prison had forced him into solitude, and now he longed for the comfort of it. He took a deep, weak breath and truly relaxed for the first time since he'd left his cell, the first time since the efforts of his escape could be deemed successful. He still could not believe his good fortune, even though he still had no answers as to who was behind his escape and why it had been orchestrated.

A cot sat along the outside wall, with a pile of blankets made up neatly on it to offer some softness and a clean uncovered feather pillow centered at the head. A simple wood table sat at the foot of the cot, with only a closed tin mess kit and a tin cup sitting on top of it. Each utensil showed some age in its dents and scuffs, but looked fully functional otherwise. The kit was another item that had most likely seen service by a Confederate soldier years before; it had probably been discarded, stolen, or sold for pennies at the local mercantile.

Everything Lucas needed was inside the tidy, well-organized tent, save a meal and hot water, but he assumed—and hoped—they would be coming soon. His manners had precluded him asking before he left Sulley's company.

He didn't have to wait long. He didn't even have time to sit at the table, in the single chair that was offered as hard comfort. His whole body ached, but it was his feet and legs that hurt the worst. They weren't used to so much exercise in one day.

The flap pushed open, and a middle-aged Negro woman made her way confidently inside the tent. Lucas assumed that this was Miss Lainie, the woman that Sulley had spoken of, the proprietor of the establishment he found himself in . . . though up until that moment he had not taken into full consideration what kind of establishment it really was. He had thought it was exactly what the sign said: ROOMS. Now he wasn't so sure. For all he knew, he now found himself in Libertyville's one and only whorehouse. Every town, big or small, had one.

"Well, looka here what Zeke Henry done brunged us," the woman said. She was about the same height as Lucas, so they looked each other in the eye and sized each other up quickly, without any obvious discernment on either's part. "You a little rickety, ain't you? Thin around the gills and in serious need of a bath if I do say so myself." She continued circling around Lucas. She came to a stop once she'd made a full revolution, and smiled. Her teeth were perfectly aligned and white as a freshly boiled sheet.

"Well, I apologize, ma'am, but it's been a difficult day," Lucas offered, never breaking eye contact with her. "I'm assuming you're Miss Lainie?"

"That would be me." She was a slender woman, dressed comfortably in the kind of yellow cotton wrapper that most women wore around the house, but which was formal enough to receive guests in. Everything about the woman suggested that she was clean and particular about herself. Her hair was cut evenly and pulled back behind her head in a long braid that disappeared under her collar, without a stray bit of wiry black hair to be seen, or any of the spiral of gray that worked its way back from her right temple, either. Her skin was the color of a bushel of fresh picked chestnuts, without a wrinkle or blemish on it. Miss Lainie was shapely, too, and not too proper to show it. The wrapper was cut open at the top, allowing her neck to be fully seen, though the well-fitted garb, cut at the waist, did cover her ankles and feet.

There was a beauty and confidence in the Negro woman that Lucas found unsettling. Freedom seemed to suit her just fine. Or maybe she was just comfortable among her own, safe in Libertyville, allowed to be whatever it was that she wanted to be, or needed to be.

Miss Lainie smelled of fresh soap, a hint of spring-flavored femininity that Lucas recognized immediately. Sweet fragrance was one of the many things that he had enjoyed in the past, in his previous life, without realizing it until it had been taken away from him.

"I'm pleased to meet you, Miss Lainie," Lucas said. "I hope to not bring you any trouble, and I'll be on my way as soon as I am able."

"Oh, you'll bring us trouble, Lucas Fume. You already done that. As far as the length of your stay, well, I don't imagine that's up to either one of us, now, is it? Far Jackson has say about such things, and so do you. I don't expect you'll leave until you're up to it, or run out in the middle of the night. There's nothing holding you here but your own will. Can't say which instance will come first. I'd offer you a piece of solid advice, though."

"And what would that be?"

"Sleep with one eye open. Some folks'd just as soon see you dead as see you walk out of here standing up straight as a cock robin in spring."

"No one knows me here."

Miss Lainie nodded. "That's true, or so you says. But you knows we're here. You think you got trust on your side? Not here. Just keep that in mind. Just 'cause you be free don't mean you be safe. We all in that boat together now, no matter what we called, or where we come from."

"I've had plenty of practice sleeping light in the places I've been."

"Well, that hammer ought to be enough of a protector if the need arises. I don't see no reason to relieve you of it."

Lucas glanced down at the hammer tucked in his belt. There was no way he was parting with it. Not to Miss Lainie, not to anybody without a fight. "There'll be a man coming looking for it."

"Well, from the looks of you, you'll knows just what to do with it when he show up. You ain't got no firearms?"

"No, ma'am, those were lost, as well as our horses."

"You in some shape then, ain't you?"

"Seems that way."

"Good thing Zeke Henry was with you and knew where to come."

"Yes, ma'am, I suppose that is a good thing."

Miss Lainie cocked her head to the side curiously. "You don't seem to believe that."

"I got questions, that's all. I'm not a big believer in luck or fate," Lucas answered dryly.

A knock came on the door flap of the tent, interrupting the conversation. It sounded more like a light slap on the canvas, but it got it Miss Lainie's attention right away. "That you, Avadine?"

"Yes'm," a female voice came from outside. It was a tiny voice, with the ring of a familiar brogue and twang that touched Lucas's ears with surprise. Something vibrated deep in him. Recognition, longing, a memory. He wasn't sure which.

Miss Lainie walked to the flap, leaving Lucas to stand where he was, curious.

"Well, come on in here," Miss Lainie said. "I expect this man is famished beyond belief. You ain't doin' him, or me, no good by bein' bashful."

"Just waiting, ma'am." The flap pulled back, and a girl walked into the tent carrying a tray of food. A piece of beef that was still sizzling, a small crock of steaming beans, a side of collards steeped in bacon grease, and a healthy end cut of cornbread sat squarely on a white porcelain plate.

It wasn't the food that most stirred Lucas's attention, though. It was the girl. To his surprise, she was white, half a head shorter than Miss Lainie, just as clean and cared for, dressed in a simple white housedress, covering her slender body to the knees. She was barefoot, and looked young, somewhere between a girl and a woman. Her green eyes betrayed her age, but offered both hesitancy and wisdom, allowing Lucas to assume that she had lived a little bit more than her initial appearance might have suggested.

Avadine's brown hair was nearly the same shade as the Negro woman's skin, chestnut-brown, pulled back and braided, too, only her braid showed outside the dress and hung midway to her waist.

Lucas looked away once he realized he was staring at the girl. When he looked back at her, he met her eyes again, and saw now that they were in fact as green as the highland hills, and it was that, and her voice, that gave her origins away. She had home country in her blood; there was no mistaking Scotland to a Scot.

Lucas was nearly speechless. It had been a long time since he had been in the company of women, especially beautiful women.

TWENTY-EIGHT

THE WHITE HOUSE HOTEL WAS NOT WHITE AT all, nor did it look like the seat of government in Washington. The simple square building was built with red brick, stood three stories tall, and offered a widow's walk all the way around the roof. The only thing white on the hotel was the cupola, and the sign itself, the color of it so bright and clean it could be seen from blocks away, even on a gray, dreary day, such as the one when Charlotte Brogan rode toward the hotel as a destination, dry as a bone, peeking from behind a thick curtain in a spectacular four-horse carriage most often used for dignitaries, special guests, or funerals.

Disappointment had overcome Charlotte. She had planned on a making a grand entrance, notable to anyone who paid attention to such things. An invitation to the Fettermans' Spring Ball was not securely hers, and she could not assume that one would come—especially if no one knew she was in town.

Little Ling sat inside the carriage, opposite Charlotte, staring at the floor. The curtains on the windows were drawn to keep the weather out now that Charlotte was satisfied they were on their way. Yen and Cheng, the remainder of her entourage, rode outside, wearing slickers, armed with their hands, feet, and firearms hidden somewhere on their person; their duty and loyalty to her was unquestioned—not worried about. A pair of Negro teamsters, dressed in formal black suits, top hats, and covered, too, in slickers, drove the carriage with great care, navigating the ruts and the mud slowly and skillfully, doing their best to make the ride to the hotel as comfortable and short as possible.

"You are quiet, Little Ling. Is there something the matter?" Charlotte asked. The carriage was big and comfortable. The seats were thick and as luxurious as could be expected, covered in red velvet, contrasting against the shiny black interior and flooring. The lighting was poor, muted, but it was easy for Charlotte to see the sadness on the Chinese girl's face.

"No, Missy." Little Ling looked up. Her eyes were wet with tears that had yet to break free and stream down her cheek. "I am just thinking of the last time I was in St. Louis. I was with Sister Mary Catherine on her final journey home. I was afraid, that is all."

"And you're afraid now? Oh dear, whatever of?"

Little Ling nodded her head yes. "Dreams and nightmares. Nothing real, I know, Missy, but dreams and nightmares nonetheless."

Charlotte smiled, reached across the space between them, and took Little Ling's small hand into hers. Her flesh was cold. "I have dreams and nightmares, too. All too often, of late, but you are correct. They are not real. Just our fears and memories playing tricks on us. We are on a happy journey now, and at its end is a fine ball, a grand time, a celebration. I promise you, Little Ling, this will be an experience you will never forget."

The girl forced a smile. She seemed to relax as her hand grew warm in Charlotte's grasp. "You are right. It's just that . . ." Little Ling stopped speaking, like she was about to spill a secret, or say something that should be reserved for her own kind, in the right place.

"Just what?"

Little Ling took a deep breath and pulled her hand away. "It's just that I keep dreaming of crows."

Charlotte shrugged. She was confused. The ways of the Celestials were lost on Charlotte, but she liked Little Ling, cared for her, as much as that was possible, and tried to understand her the best she could.

"Lots of crows," Little Ling continued, "flocks and flocks of crows circling over the ball, the celebration you are so happy about. So many crows that the sky is black and alive, and noisy with all their squawks and calls. The sky throbs with black wings, and open beaks, hungry for food, for blood, even though they do not sip it for sustenance, Missy, and the dream frightens me. Leaves me cold."

"It is just a bad dream, Little Ling. It means nothing, I promise."

"No, Missy, you no understand. In my country, crows are messengers, birds of omen. They carry souls to heaven or to hell. Death rides on their wings, either way. That is why they are black."

The inside of the hotel room was just a lavish as Charlotte remembered it to be. The rooms in the White House Hotel rivaled any fancy room this side of New York. Those hotels and that city were in a league of their own, and the gauge of all others. She longed to return to New York, and to Washington for that matter, but that would not be on her agenda anytime soon. At least, not until she accomplished what she had set out to do.

Little Ling hurried about once they had arrived, unpacking

Charlotte's suitcases, making the bedroom and the suite's adjoining sitting room as comfortable as possible. The girl knew the routine, knew where everything went and must be found by her lady. Charlotte had trained her well and much to her own pleasure, with an even hand, unlike some of the women of her caliber. They were downright mean to their girls.

Charlotte barely noticed the girl's chores; they would have a discussion after everything was in its place. And a treat of some kind if all was well. She couldn't get the thought of oysters out of her mind.

She walked over to the window and looked out toward the city from the third-floor room. Swirling storm clouds marched toward her from the west. Rain blew sideways, like buckets thrown toward a fire, hoping to put it out. Thunder boomed, and an occasional streak of lightning reached from the sky and exploded on the earth, shaking it, rattling the fragile glass in the window. She shivered and clutched her arms together, the images of Little Ling's nightmare still fresh in her mind. She soon exhaled, an attempt to calm herself down. She understood Little Ling's fears.

Charlotte had her own dreams and nightmares to contend with, though they had been fewer since she left Kansas City, since she had felt a slight bit of freedom, and the satisfaction of maneuvering her way out of John Barlow's presence. Or was it Lanford Grips? One was the other, and the other was the one, but the persona of Grips seemed more distant, colder, more unpredictable. They all had been actors in the war; the stages varied, but they shared the great hope that their performances had gone unnoticed. Spies, even women spies, were thrown in prison or, worse, like Mary Surratt, hanged in the end. It was no surprise that John had become someone else, something else, since losing his hands. He sought to build his wealth in their place. His ambition was obvious, pure, and without conscience. That's what frightened Charlotte. Once John Barlow had learned to kill as well as he could lie, everything had changed.

She shivered again, knowing full well that as long as Yen and Cheng stood outside of her door she was still under his control. His prisoner. His employee. His. Just his. To do anything with that he wanted, anything he could think of, and she had no choice, no escape. They were bound by their deeds, by their past, by their present, by their own desires. She was no killer. At least, with a direct hand. That test had not come to her yet, and she hoped it never would.

Another clap of thunder exploded, causing Charlotte to jump. But it pulled her out of her thoughts, and she turned to Little Ling, pale with the sudden fright she had inflicted on herself, and by the storm that had arrived much sooner than she had anticipated it would.

"There will be strawberries this time of year, Little Ling. Do you like strawberries?" Charlotte asked, steadying the tremble in her voice.

Little Ling closed the door on the large wardrobe that stood in the corner of the room. It latched heavily, echoing off the white plaster walls and high ceiling. "Yes, Missy, of course, berries of any kind are most welcome. We rarely get them on our table."

"Then we shall have a bowlful sent up, and we shall have the pleasure of tasting the season of freshness on our tongues, along with some fresh oysters, straight from New Orleans. Won't that be nice?"

"That would be very special," Little Ling said. Sweat clustered at her temple, dampening stray black hair against her soft yellow skin.

Charlotte had no time to do or say anything else. A knock on the door exploded through the room as if thunder itself had arrived on her doorstep. Two long, one short. A request to enter. She was expecting no visitors, and since the storm had ruined her entrance, she was convinced that no one of importance, or otherwise, was aware of her arrival. Her assumption was wrong. At first she was thrilled at the prospect of a visitor. Until she realized that she still wore her traveling clothes, that she was not decent to receive anyone. Why, there must have still been dirt on her face from the ride to the hotel from the train station.

The knock came again. More emphatic this time. Charlotte stood stricken, until Little Ling intervened. She must have seen the panic on her lady's face. "I get it, Missy. You wash up quick, and I keep them at the door as long as I can."

"Good," Charlotte whispered, and hurried over to the bowl and pitcher that stood waiting on the washstand. The bowl had been filled with fresh water. Freshly picked violets soaked on top of the water, and the sight of them relieved Charlotte, gave her momentary pleasure. At least the aroma of her clothes, soiled as they were with travel, would be less offensive.

Charlotte heard Little Ling open the door. She had her back to it, preparing herself as best, and as quickly, as she could. But she stopped moving as soon as she heard footsteps push inside the room, stopped breathing when she realized to whom they belonged.

"This is a fine room, Charlotte," Lanford Grips said. "I hope the journey here was comfortable for you."

TWENTY-NINE

LUCAS GRIPPED THE KNIFE AND FORK tightly, his manners less a concern than the urgency he felt to taste the decent food before him. The aroma of the perfectly cooked piece of beef was overwhelming, triggering memories of long lost meals at the family table, and a desire that bordered on madness, tinged with a euphoria that had been missing from Lucas's life for a very long time. He tore into the steak like he hadn't eaten a decent meal in years—which was the truth—and he could hardly cut it with the dull knife that had been provided for him. He managed to tear a piece off, and he stuffed it into his mouth ravenously. He had almost forgotten how to chew real meat. Flavor exploded inside his mouth, and he gobbled up another piece of the steak before the first one had successfully slid down his throat.

"You best slow down there, Mr. Fume," Avadine said. Miss Lainie had departed without saying a word, leaving Avadine to tend to Lucas's needs, which at first seemed inappropriate.

The act remained unprotested by both of them. Avadine didn't seem bothered by the fact that she'd been left alone with a strange man. It seemed very normal to her. "There's plenty more where that comes from."

Lucas cast the girl a hard look. His reaction was that of a little boy unaccustomed to being corrected. He cut off another piece of meat defiantly and pushed it into his already full mouth, never breaking her gaze.

Avadine shook her head with disgust and frustration. "Have it your way then. Choke to death before you can go any farther. Miss Lainie is coolin' a fine apple pie. She saved them apples deep in the root cellar for somethin' special. They are the last of the batch. Won't be no more till fall. Be a shame for ya to miss out on such a fine pie, now, wouldn't it? Especially considerin' they was saved just for you—even though we didn't know that at the time." There was a huskiness in her voice that Lucas hadn't noticed until then, a harder edge to her Scottish brogue that suggested she had come over from the home country and not just been raised among those who spoke in the old tongue, as he had been.

Lucas swallowed deeply and pushed the food down with a healthy gulp of cold springwater from the tin cup. He set the cup down more heavily than he'd intended to.

Water dripped unattended out of the corner of his mouth. The first bite of food hit his stomach, and all he wanted was more. That and to be left alone. But his manners were not all lost to the moment, even though he truly desired Avadine to leave. He wanted to eat in solitude. Just as he had not had a decent meal in a long time, he had not had the pleasure of eating it alone. He was more accustomed to hunching over food like a hawk, cowling it protectively, certain that someone would steal it. The mess hall in the prison was a cathedral of madness, thievery, and fear. He didn't miss it, and he wanted to enjoy his good fortune by himself—though he was conflicted to a degree. He enjoyed being in the presence of a woman, too.

Lucas still recognized that he was a guest in the village, and whether Miss Lainie was present or her girl in her stead, they were still women; women who had taken him in at their own peril. Maybe by their own choice, maybe not, but peril still lurked outside the tent, regardless of who owned the result of the decision to take him in. "I apologize," he finally said. "I have forgotten my manners."

"There is no need. I, too, have been weak, worried, and hungry from being on the run. You will do yourself a favor to heed my warning, though, Mr. Fume. Slow down, or you'll make yourself sick. You are safe here. The clock does not tick, unless you want it to."

"Why should I believe you?"

"Why shouldn't you?" Avadine stood firm, off to his right, her back to the closed tent flap, facing him directly. It was easy to see that she was still unsure of him, that she had her own escape plan measured out if the need arose to use it. "No one here has given you cause to distrust, or suspect any harmful intent."

The girl's response surprised Lucas. He had found himself in situations like this before where he knew no one, trusted no one, didn't know the lay of the land—all by design—and been comfortable in any environment that he'd put himself into. He'd found his way then, his confidence bolstered by his past experience, his mastery of disguise, and his ability to more than once jump from a country preacher's full book of knowledge and voice to imitating a senator or highborn businessman. But those skills were lost, locked up, the key tossed away. He could barely remember how to hold a knife, much less how to fake confidence.

"I will take you at face value then, and trust that the pie that awaits will be half as good as this meat is," Lucas answered, allowing a smile to cross his face.

Avadine's shoulders drooped as she relaxed. She grabbed a pitcher of water and refilled the cup. "You should take your time, enjoy what is here for you. I can see that your journey has been long and difficult."

Lucas nodded, but didn't feel compelled to tell the girl his story of the day. He was certain she knew most of it, all that mattered anyway. "How did you come to be here?"

"Here?"

"In Libertyville. Yes. I can hear my father's home country in your voice."

Avadine drew back, and Lucas immediately missed the freshness of her presence. He wanted to reach out and touch her skin, her hand. It looked like satin, her fingers clean, perfect. But he restrained himself.

"That is a longer story than we have time for," Avadine said.

"But you do not belong here."

"Why? Because I'm not a Negro? A freed slave, still at risk of hanging just because of who I am, where I come from? Because of things over which I had no control? Is that why I shouldn't be here? Because my skin is white and not black?"

Lucas looked away, back to his plate of food. Her indignation surprised him, made him immediately ashamed of the question. "I'm sorry. I didn't mean to offend you. I am a guest in this place and have been shown nothing but kindness."

"You didn't offend me, Mr. Fume—"

"Lucas. Please call me Lucas."

Avadine studied his face for a long moment. It seemed it was her turn to decide whether or not she could trust what she was seeing and hearing. "Mr. Lucas, then."

"If it must be that."

"It must."

Lucas nodded, then took up the spoon and dipped it into a healthy pile of collards. The greens were perfectly cooked, with just enough bacon grease melted in them to take away their natural bitterness.

Avadine set the water pitcher down. "You must know that all those that are bound to masters and landowners are not of African origin. They have white skin as well as black. Passage is bought and paid for, along with domestic expectations for month or years. Costs accumulate and are added to the time required to be served upon arrival—with the possibility of permanent enslavement. Tricks to the unsuspecting, who come from one bad situation with the hope of a better life, only to find themselves in something far worse than they could have ever imagined. That practice grew worse once the war was over, once there was emancipation for the African-blooded slaves. Freedom did not come for all, Mr. Lucas.

"I was left with no choice but to run and break free of the situation I'd been put in. There are men looking for me, too. The longer I stay here, the easier it is for them to find me. There are still laws that allow for indentured servitude, for innocence and dreams to be bought and sold, a human being bound to another forever, and I have no desire to face the consequences of my one true act of sanity."

"Sanity?"

"Yes, sanity. It was only for a moment, a chance to break free. I took it, and was helped here by a network of folk, Negro and white, who are still fighting the good fight for equality and freedom for all."

"You had reason to escape, to know the fear of looking over your shoulder instead of what you were left to face?"

"Yes, there was more fear in the staying. All of us here in Libertyville are free to come and go as we please, just as you are, but there are those of us who will never know true freedom. Not like some do. You and I share that place, I think—the long desire to breathe fresh air, looking to the sun and knowing there is no one underneath it being given coin to capture and drag you back into the darkness. We are not free, but we are better off than we were." Avadine's voice was soft, wistful, but there was not a sad look on her face. Her cheeks were set in place, hard with anger and determination.

"Go on now, Mr. Lucas," she said, "eat your meal. I will leave you to your peace and quiet. If you need to relieve yourself, there is a privy just beyond the door. You'll see it, even in the darkness."

"I'd rather you stay."

"Don't worry, I won't be far." And with that, she disappeared out the flap of the tent, barely leaving a trace of her presence. Only her sweet fragrance lingered.

Lucas settled into the tub and allowed himself to slide as far down as he could, under the water, hot and steaming, so that all of the world disappeared.

Avadine had come and gone, filling the tub, cleaning away his dirty dishes, bringing him fresh, clean clothes, but never lingering. It was as if she had said all she needed to and understood Lucas's unexpressed needs as much, or more, than he did himself.

There was no sound under the water. No hum of life outside, no hard-beating heart, just the nothingness of water-clogged ears. Lingering in a bath was a delight, a luxury, like the delicious food he had been provided, and the accumulating feeling of comfort and safety. But Lucas was wise enough to know that everything could change in a moment. He was not going to totally let his guard down. The hammer lay in the bottom of the tub, always within reach of his fingers, if the need to use it arose.

His mind wandered, and he returned to the surface, taking in a deep breath, but not moving to leave the water. There were still aches and pains to address. His body and mind were still weak, beaten down by his time in prison, and the effort to escape it.

He wiped the water from his eyes and found the tent empty, the only addition a perfectly cut piece of apple pie sitting in the middle of the table, with a steaming cup of chicory coffee sitting next to it. There was no sign of Avadine, or anyone

else for that matter. Time had marched on, and the sun had
settled over the horizon, offering the first hint of night. A
candle burned on the table. A small flame that barely illu-
minated the inside of the tent.

He smiled and slid back down into the water, his head
just above the surface. He was satisfied for the moment that
everything was what it was supposed to be, what he thought
it was, where it was supposed to be.

Lucas knew that before he could move on, he had to heal,
had to restore his strength and mind. There were places to
go, people to see, questions to answer . . . but first there was
a bath, a piece of pie, and the sight of a woman's shadow,
lingering just outside the tent, her ear turned to the flap, to
serve a need, or cry out in alarm—he hoped—if there was
reason to call for help.

The pie was every bit as tasty as Lucas had hoped it would
be. Beyond that, he fell onto the cot, and slept, slept peace-
fully, unmoving, with both eyes and ears closed off to the
world. He was convinced that he was safe enough to trust
what he saw before him. There were no demons in his sleep,
no nightmares to fight off. Just a restful emptiness that left
him famished when he awoke the next day.

There was a plate of fried eggs, bacon, and johnnycakes
sitting on the table, along with more chicory coffee. The tub
was full of fresh, hot water, and everything about the tent had
been tidied up. He quickly dressed, found his way outside,
and was immediately surprised by the brightness of the sun.
The position of it was higher than he'd expected. It was almost
midday. Luckily, he saw no one; he did his business and made
his way back inside where he was comfortable, safe.

He ate the breakfast alone, a little slower but still unable
to restrain himself from eating like there would be no more.
Then he disrobed and made his way back to the tub to soak

away the soreness that overnight had risen to the surface of the skin and to the edge of every joint in his body.

For two days, Lucas did nothing but eat, sleep, and soak in the hot tub, only leaving the tent when he needed to, and then returning as quickly as he could. The barber, a little Negro man, John Drakeman, who talked with a lisp because a piece of his tongue had been cut away, came to him, shaved his beard away, and cut his hair short, to the latest fashion.

After that he felt lighter, like someone else. He settled into the safety of the tent, making it a cell of recovery, knowing that he could leave at any time he wanted to—and was able. He did not see Zeke, or Miss Lainie, or Far Jackson. The only contact with the outside world he had was Avadine, who eased in and out of the tent respectfully, carrying with her his material needs and nothing more. She spoke when she was spoken to, but didn't offer to linger and engage herself in small talk. It was obvious that she had instructions to serve and nothing more.

But Lucas could not help himself from noticing her and quickly found himself longing for her presence. The tent was very much like a prison, albeit a comfortable one, when she was gone.

Finally, on the third day, well into the morning, the flap of the tent opened and Far Jackson walked in.

Lucas had expected, had hoped, it would be Avadine, so he was caught a little off guard when the skinny old man entered the tent. He stood up immediately.

"Sit down, sit down there, Fume. I ain't no general," Far Jackson said. He was alone. The flap slapped shut behind him. "You looks almost human now that John Drakeman done his shearin' on you."

"I'm feeling much better, thank you."

"Good. I sees that Miss Lainie and her girl has done good for you."

"They have been more than generous. I don't know how

I'll ever be able to repay them—you, I guess—for the kindness I've been shown."

"I ain't here to settle no accounts. Not yet. I 'spect that day will come soon. But not today."

Lucas cocked his head to the right. Something in Far Jackson's tone troubled him. "What's the matter?"

"That Carl the Hammer is a good tracker. Zeke done throwed him off your trail twice, but I think they's goin' to figure out the two of yous has split up and start lookin' closer to the prison sooner rather than later."

"I thought Zeke was still here," Lucas said. "Resting up, like me. He was shot, needed tended to."

"You ever see a bull shot and stumble. Hell, no. That bull still charge at you if you're on his land. Zeke was looked at, and then chose to run on and do what he could to give you time to heal yourself up."

Lucas exhaled, then looked to the ground. "Why are you doing this?"

"Because it's the right thing to do. Beyond that," Far Jackson shrugged his shoulders, "Seven Oaks way, your home place, still have shadows that fall deep into this here woods. If you was thinkin' of makin' your way home, I'd advise against it. There's people waitin' for you there."

THIRTY

THE TRAIN DEPARTED ST. LOUIS TOWARD
Nashville late in the day. A decent rainstorm had followed
them out of town—thunder, lightning, rain blowing
sideways—but it was dry as a bone inside the passenger car.
The windows were squared to the tops of their frames,
closed tight, with most of the blinds drawn. Lighting was
dim, gray and shadowy, pierced frequently by surprising
flashes of lightning. The storm was less a worry to the few
passengers who had already nodded off to sleep than it was
to Joe Straut. He hated storms and thunder. They reminded
him of the war. Sometimes he saw ghosts in the shadows
left behind by the lightning bolts—ghosts of men he had
killed, come back to haunt him, to collect what he owed
them. A life—he thought he owed those men a life, even
though it had been wartime. Some men took to drink to
stave off the madness, the visions, the fear, but not him.
Straut sucked it up, found work, tried to do the right thing
when he could.

The seats in the passenger car were hard and uncomfortable. There would be no fancy berths for Joe Straut and Finney Deets. Straut had not expected such a thing. As it was, he was just glad to get out of St. Louis alive. He wondered if the news of the discovery of the three bodies had made its way to Kansas City, to the Boss's eyes and ears. A strong clap of thunder burst unexpectedly over the train, causing Straut to shiver. He closed his eyes, trying to fight away his fear, his failure, but there was no answer in the dark recesses of his mind, so he opened his eyes to face the reality he'd put himself in: looking over his shoulder, waiting for the other shoe to drop.

He sat directly across from a tired-looking woman in her late twenties who was trying to calm down two irascible young girls. The girls looked like identical twins, blond hair knotted at the tops of their heads and flowing down perfectly over their shoulders, with a series of ribbons tied randomly about; one had white ribbons, the other yellow. They both wore light wool knee-length skirts the color of summer wheat about to be thrashed and white high-neck blouses, and their shoes looked new. There was hardly a scuff on the girls anywhere, which could not be said for their mother, or at least Straut assumed the woman was their mother. She had the same shape face as the girls, and she shared the same deep blue eyes, the color that Straut imagined the ocean to be, but he knew he was probably wrong. It looked like all of the woman's assets had been used to adorn the children in her charge, with little left for herself. Either way, she looked tired, and hardly up to a long trip of any kind. Straut didn't know what her story was, where she was going and why, and he didn't want to know, either.

The girl with yellow ribbons was picking on the other one, pulling the white ribbons from her perfect curls. Straut was not amused, nor was he looking forward to spending hundreds of miles in the company of two spoiled brats. At the moment, he would've preferred to be stowed away in one of the freight cars up near the locomotive. He could be left alone there, to smoke if he so desired, or think, or be free of wandering eyes. Over and above the privacy of freight cars, Straut preferred the solitude of horses, even though the travel was slower.

They were far enough away from the station for the train to settle into a steady speed, and the rock and pull of the car had become normal. Balance was easily accounted for, at least for those accustomed to riding on trains. Straut stood up without warning, and Deets, who was sitting next to him, was surprised by the move.

"Where you goin', Sarge?"

"I need to get some fresh air."

"Air smells fine to me," Finney Deets said, with a smile that made the twin girls stop what they were doing and cringe in unison. They turned up their noses at the sight of Deets's jagged and yellow teeth. Deets closed his mouth as soon as he noticed their reaction, and stood up shoulder to shoulder with Straut. "I think I'll come with you."

"Suit yourself." Straut walked away, toward the back exit of the car. The woman said something apologetically, but her words were muffled by the train's forward motion and the continuing storm. The apology didn't slow Straut. Nor did it provoke a response. He ignored the woman and her two brats, and every other passenger in the car who stared at him, or cast a judgmental look, as he made his way to the door and the fresh air that awaited.

A small covered vestibule allowed Straut to step outside and close the door, once Deets had exited the car behind him.

Rain immediately pelted both men, but neither of them acted to shield themselves. "Feels good, don't it?" Deets said.

"I think you should get off at the next stop, Deets."

"What for, Sarge?"

"I got a little money on me. You need to go. Just go. Clean yourself up, cut your hair, buy a new suit and horse, and find a new life. Start over. Ain't you got dreams?"

"I don't want a new life, Sarge. I like the one I got."

"If you stick with me, it might end sooner than you'd like, I can tell you that. Land's openin' up, and there's opportunity out there for the takin'. A man like you could do well for himself on twenty acres."

"I ain't no farmer, Sarge. I had enough of that life when I was a boy. I ain't lazy or nothin'. Hard work don't scare me none. It's just that I can't grow a pea in perfect dirt. I don't have that kind of luck. Come to think of it, I don't have much luck at all when I'm out on my own."

"Bad luck paired you with me."

"Says you," Deets said.

"I just think you ought to give it some thought, Deets, that's all. Get out of here, before things turn bad—"

"You mean before the Boss catches up to us? I thought you meant to take him Lucas Fume's head and settle the mistake with those folks straight out?"

"I still intend to do that, if I can find Fume, if this map is any help, but I'd just as soon face that day on my own. You was just followin' orders, doin' what I told you to do. There's no crime in that."

"It woulda been an awful thing burnin' them folks up arm by arm, leg by leg."

"Well, that's what the Boss wanted . . ."

The train slowed more than usual as they rounded a curve in the tracks. It was too dark to see why, and the track was lined thick with trees. Even with fresh spring leaves, they provided a heavy curtain to the world beyond.

For a second the action of the engineer puzzled Straut, until the curve allowed him to see forward as the locomotive powered down and slowed to an eventual stop. It was then that he saw the pile of rubble that had been placed across the tracks and set on fire. He took a deep breath and reached for the Colt Open Top on his hip just as the first shot was fired into the air.

"Get inside, Deets, and make sure nothin' happens to

them little girls," Straut said, swinging down off the vestibule and onto the ground.

"You think it's a robbery, Sarge?"

"I hope so."

"What? You think it's men workin' for the Boss comin' after us?" Deets's face was pale with fear.

"Go on, now, do what I told you. I'll see what this is, don't you worry."

Another shot rang out up near the locomotive, and Straut could see the shadows of horsemen playing out on the side of the train. The fire raged upward, casting light almost to his feet. When he turned back to make sure Deets had done what he'd been told, he found himself staring at an empty vestibule.

Finney Deets had disappeared inside without saying another word.

THIRTY-ONE

LUCAS SAT ON THE COT LOOKING AT THE
floor. The ground was worn thin, giving him cause to consider how long the tent had actually been there. Libertyville might have given the impression that it was a mobile, temporary kind of town, but the brown grass under his feet betrayed that notion. It had been tramped down and was now part of the hard, dry soil; nothing more than a floor to walk on.

The Negroes were putting down roots whether they knew, or wanted to admit, it. Just like he had in prison. Truth be told, Lucas had thought he would die inside his cell, his death no cause for mourning, his suffering ended, and the truth and justice of his sentence, or the lack thereof, lost in the darkness, buried in an unmarked grave just inside the gate.

He was surprised by his good fortune to be free of those dank, putrid walls, and he grew more curious by the hour about the mind behind his escape. No matter how many ways he considered it, things just didn't add up, but his freedom, or a type of it, was hard to deny.

Outside, the night was mostly silent. A few insects buzzed beyond the tent flap, and a happy male redbird whistled from a nearby tree, boasting that his accomplishments for the day were nearly done, unlike the mournful whip-poor-will who had yet to hum a note in the settling darkness. But the whip-poor-will would cry out soon if the last few nights were any indication of the night bird's habits. The previous nights had been filled with the low, lonesome call. There had only been one, and no reply, over and over again until the wee hours in the morning gave the bird cause to retreat, or give up. Lucas knew the call, had heard the whip-poor-will all his life, but had never realized how lonely its song was until now.

There was no foot or horse traffic coming and going down the main street of Libertyville. The day's commerce was done, put to bed. On previous nights in the village there had followed music and laughter, the clinking of ale glasses, the smell of a slow-roasting pig. Laughter and a comfortable easiness had hung over the village like a thick fog that refused to dissipate—all of the noises were foreign to Lucas's ears.

Life pulsated around him as if he had never been locked away, but he had forgotten what being free did to the senses, how aware it made you feel, how it stirred memories, revived pain and loss, and the desire to set things right. Anger brewed deep inside him, rising slowly to the surface, ready to burst out at any given moment. His temper had always been his Achilles' heel, and even now he knew no way to control it. Even though his body was free, his mind was still in prison.

The silence outside felt more like relief than a demanded reaction or a retreat. There was a natural rhythm in Libertyville, an obvious cadence to the days and seasons, and the longer Lucas was there, even though he had, by his own choice, spent most of his time in the tent, the more he began to get a sense of the place. But he knew that to do that fully he would have to walk the streets in daylight just like the rest of the freedmen in the secret village. Maybe to-morrow, now that he was feeling more like himself.

Recuperation had come to him quickly under the care of Miss Lainie and Avadine. Food, a hot consistent bath, a daily shave, a fresh haircut, and more sleep than any man had a right to had been a great recipe for restoration.

There had never been a moment when Lucas didn't realize how lucky he was to have found himself in the place where he had landed. But that good fortune was also tinged with the sad realization that he could not go home even if he wanted to. But what Far Jackson did not know, could not know, was that that curse had been cast a long time ago. Lucas had been disowned by his family, shunned for the murder of John Barlow. He was dead to his father, and that had been the worst thing to accept overall. There was no way to know now if his father was alive or dead. Word had stopped once the irons were clamped around Lucas's ankles and wrists. Being thrown in prison was like being tossed out to sea, lost on a raft, never knowing the fate of the others who were on the ship of life with you.

A tap came at the flap, taking Lucas's attention away from the hard dirt floor, and from his worries. Without waiting for a word of acknowledgment from Lucas, it opened, causing the lone oil lamp in the tent to flicker slightly.

He had drawn in a breath, but no words had come out of his mouth. He really did not want any company, was in no mood for conversation, but he was glad when the interloper who appeared inside the tent, almost magically, turned out to be Avadine.

"I wasn't expecting to see you until the morning," Lucas said, standing up.

Avadine never disturbed him after his dinner. She collected his plates from the previous meal when she brought his breakfast the next day. It was always her who showed up, never Miss Lainie. There was no question that he was Avadine's charge—and he was glad of it.

There was nothing in her hands now, no plate of food or pitcher of water. The motive behind her unscheduled, and unusual, appearance was unclear.

Avadine turned to make sure the tent flap was secure, then faced Lucas. "I was concerned about you," she said. Her voice was just above a whisper, the huskiness down a note, offering an unexpected softness that was usually not there.

Lucas made no effort to move. He drank in the sight of her with surprise and restrained delight. She was like the discovery of a fine jewel that had suddenly appeared unexpectedly in a boring, nonproductive gold mine.

Avadine was dressed simply, in a white linen sack dress that could have easily been mistaken for a shift, a simple woman's undergarment. The dress fell to just below her knees, the sleeves short, the neck not cut too low to show any of her bodily features, and her feet were bare. Her dark brown hair glimmered from fresh washing and brushing, even in the dim light, and flowed comfortably over her shoulders.

A hint of toilet water accompanied Avadine into the tent, a pleasing fragrance that had made its way almost instantly to Lucas's nose, reminding him again how much he'd missed the simple pleasure of being in the company of a woman.

"I'm fine," Lucas said. "Better than I have been in a long time. There's no need to worry about me. You and Miss Lainie have shown me a great kindness. My feet feel solid on the ground for the first time in a long time."

Avadine, too, stood still in her place. A full body length separated the two of them, but neither of them moved to fill the space. Her shoulders were relaxed, and she stared at him, not breaking eye contact.

The tips of Lucas's fingers tingled slightly with nervousness. Avadine had come and gone from his tent on many occasions over the last few days, but she had been all business—tending to his food and comfort but rarely lingering—never giving him the impression that she was interested in anything other than what her job demanded of her. She was as concise and regulated as a young private wishing to prove himself to some unknown sergeant.

Every time Avadine appeared, Lucas secretly wanted the outside world to disappear so they could spend more time alone together. Time with no duties, or worry, or pain to consider. He wished for a normal moment even though he couldn't bring himself to say so out loud. There was nothing normal about healing in a tent in a hidden village, on the run from prison for a crime he didn't commit.

"I'm fine," Lucas repeated, cutting the silence between them.

Avadine blinked when Lucas responded, but she did not look away; her deep green eyes were vulnerable but direct. There was something on her mind. Surprisingly, at least to himself, Lucas didn't look away, either. He had never been a shy man or a bumbler around women, but he was out of practice. His days of swagger, intrigue, and courting women were long behind him.

"You look much better than you did when you first came into town, but the scowl on your face has yet to leave," Avadine said. "No man will recognize you now, that should be a comfort, but I had hoped your eyes would soften over time so I could see the real man inside. Anger distorts even the purest heart."

"You're a poet."

"I can read books and faces, if that's what you're suggestin'."

"Anger's a habit I picked up in prison. My scowl helped keep the rats away."

"There are no rats here."

"That's true. I have yet to see one."

"But you're always on the lookout for one?"

"I am a man of many habits. I know my own, mostly, so yes, I am always on the lookout for a rat. They are loathsome creatures. Smart and curious. Patient, too. They will bite you in your sleep, take a nibble at a time until they are sated and you are full of madness."

"I know a rat's habits, too. But does knowing your own ways make it easier to see another man's ways?"

"Something like that. I'm sure it does."

"Or a woman's?"

"I have watched you closely," Lucas said. The volume in his voice trailed off. He had let his restraint fall away, and he was afraid that he had said more than he should, that he had said something that Avadine might take offense to.

To his relief, Avadine smiled. Her lips were moist, her teeth almost as perfect as Zeke's, but not quite as white. Still, she had a beautiful smile, and Lucas was filled with pleasure by the sight.

"Why do you think I am here?" Avadine whispered. She took one step toward Lucas, stopped, and cocked her ear to the tent flap, as if to listen for some warning, a secret command, or a sign that there was someone standing close by, spying on them.

Before Lucas could respond to her question, Avadine leaned forward, pulled the simple sack dress over her head, and tossed it easily to the floor.

If there had been any air stored up in Lucas's lungs, it escaped with the surprise of her action.

Avadine stood naked before him, staring directly into his eyes, the expression on her face void of any of emotion. It was like she was a blank canvas, waiting for his reaction to her, waiting to see if he approved or felt the same way she did. There was no question what her intention was.

Lucas did not move; he was frozen in place. He regulated his breath the best he could, all the while allowing the tingling in the tips of his fingers to find its way through his entire body. He couldn't have ignored the stimulating surge throughout his body if he had tried.

Avadine stepped forward, but Lucas shook his head no

and put his hand out gently. "Wait, let me look at you," he said in a whisper.

A half smile crossed Avadine's face. "I hope you like what you see."

"It's been a very long time since I have seen a woman without clothes and with a welcoming urge in her eyes. I don't want to miss a thing." His breathing had quickened slightly, and his heart raced. A plate of decent food had sent him into a ravenous frenzy, and he had not considered what his reaction would be if he was faced with a beautiful woman offering herself to him, too. If he did not restrain his desire, he would devour her in a rush, and that would be shame, a waste.

"I know. 'Tis obvious." Avadine glanced down at the growing bulge in his pants. "I will respect your wish." She smiled, the gleam in her eyes suddenly mischievous. "Take your time. We have all night."

The flame in the lamp regulated itself, settling the light to a constant glow. It was low, allowing for clear sight, but Lucas wanted to see Avadine clearer. He did not dare turn up the flame and cast her silhouette against the wall of the tent, allowing it to be viewed from the street. He wanted her all to himself.

It had been his concern upon first seeing her that she was young, too young, more a girl than a woman. But with her clothes off, it was clear to see that that thought had been misguided, perhaps on purpose, so he would not allow himself any more desire than he already had.

Avadine was more woman than girl, much closer to twenty, or older, than he had first imagined. She was proportioned perfectly, with commanding breasts and hard nipples and a perfect tuft of glimmering brown hair between her legs. There was no doubt that she was young, had not borne a child, but she was far from innocent, far from being a little girl. It was too late to ask her her age, or worry about the appropriateness of the moment—her actions told Lucas that he was not her first lover, nor would he be her last. But none of that mattered to him. Not now. He didn't want her to leave. He wanted to touch her, smell her, taste her, feel her underneath him.

Without saying another word, Lucas slipped off his shirt, undid his pants, and let them fall to the ground. He had been prepared to sleep, but that was now the furthest thing from his mind. Avadine had awoken his desires, his needs, and he meant to fulfill them as much as she did.

He stepped forward, and in a breath, Avadine was in his arms, skin pressed hard against skin, their mouths locked together, tongues searching and darting with joy, their hunger and touch unrestrained. It was a quick start to a hopeful journey, and Lucas was already sure that one night was not going to be long enough to go to the places he wanted to go with Avadine.

THIRTY-TWO

JOE STRAUT EDGED ALONG THE LAST PASSEN-
ger car with a load in the chamber of his Colt Open Top and
six more in the cylinder. It was an advantage he'd learned
when he'd worn a uniform and fought for the cause. From
the looks of things, he was going to need every cartridge he
had on him, and then some.

It was hard to say where they were, somewhere in Missouri, in the land of bushwhackers and Jesse James, or on-
ward, into Tennessee, a place Straut cared little for, had
fought in more than once and lost handily, but was glad to
be heading to, all things considered. He wanted to be as far
away from St. Louis as possible.

Darkness had fallen, and the entire sky was black and
empty—the rain had moved on. If there were stars above,
Straut couldn't see them. Nor did he care if they existed. The
fire in front of the locomotive had his full attention. The pulsing orange flames gave Straut a gauge of distance, and a distant view of what was happening. It was a pocket of unnatural

light in the middle of darkness, but not enough to let him know entirely what the motive for the trouble really was.

It looked to be a typical robbery. But the who's, what's, and why's were unknown. Truth was, all he cared about was making sure that the stop wasn't about him and Deets, that Lanford Grips hadn't sent a posse of hired men after him. His failure to chop up those rich people and dispose of them properly hung over him heavily since he'd seen the notice of their deaths in the newspaper. Robbers could take every goddamned penny and dollar on the train for all he cared if that's all this was.

Shadows suddenly danced on the side of the locomotive, black against black, but the movement and silhouette of man on a horse was hard to mistake. The rider's identity was still lost in the darkness, but his intent was clear.

Before Straut could wonder about anything else, a muzzle flash exploded from the end of a gun, then the report of a rifle reached his ears, followed by another and another and another.

The rider had shot directly into the open window of the locomotive. If there was any man left standing inside at the engineer's station, it would be a minor miracle. Either way, Straut let out a long sigh of relief and stopped his crawl along the train. This wasn't about him. He wanted nothing to do with whatever was going on in the locomotive. Besides, the train probably deserved to be robbed. It wasn't like he had never thought about doing such a thing himself. He just hadn't ever been that desperate. Not yet, anyway.

The lone rider whooped and hollered, and two more black silhouettes appeared from out of the dark woods that butted up along the railroad tracks, riders on horses, and like the first, they were too far away for Straut to make out any definite features.

The three riders huddled together, and Straut knew that they were preparing to execute the second part of their plan. There was most likely a payroll or treasure box somewhere on the train, and they surely meant to find it. The best thing Straut thought he could do was go back to where he came from, blend in with Finney Deets, and let the robbers do what needed doing. Then he could get on with his own plans. Find Lucas Fume and return him to the Boss—dead or alive—preferably dead, head in hand. It was the only way he knew how to stay alive himself. Running was foolish. A man like Lanford Grips had more resources than Straut could imagine. Looking over your shoulder was no way to live. No way to live at all.

Straut kept the Colt Open Top in hand and made his way back to the passenger car, doing his best to stay in the shadows. The last thing he wanted to do was draw any undue attention to himself.

As he turned to board the car, shots rang out behind him, this time at the opposite end of the train from the locomotive. Two more riders appeared at the back of the train, carrying torches. These riders were taking it slow, peering in windows, like they were looking for something . . . or someone. They were firing shots in the air to get attention, and to be taken seriously. That didn't sit well with Straut. He hurried back inside the car, garnering everyone's attention as he entered.

A little towheaded boy, most likely about ten, grabbed ahold of Straut's sleeve as he headed for his seat. "What is it, mister? A train robbery?" There was no excitement or enthusiasm in the boy's voice. He was afraid and had edged as close to his mother as he could get without climbing into her lap.

Straut stopped, even though he didn't want to. He eyed Deets, who'd made it back to his seat just like he'd been told. They made eye contact, and Straut nodded subtly. He was glad to see Deets, glad he hadn't just taken off as Straut had earlier suggested. Backup might be needed in a situation like this, but the time would come when he'd insist Deets go out on his own. There was no question about that.

Straut turned his attention back to the boy. "It's nothing to worry about, son. Just a tree down on the tracks. Must have been struck by lightning. I'm sure we'll be gettin' along soon."

"I heard gunshots," the boy said. "And it ain't rainin' outside no more. How was there lightning when there wasn't no thunder?"

Straut tugged forward, stepping out of the boy's grip. "I told you, there ain't nothin' to worry about."

"My pa's got a gun. I'm not worried."

Straut looked over his shoulder to the boy's father and stopped. The father looked like a boy himself, barely old enough to shave, with a brand-new bowler on his head, and rimless spectacles on his eyes to see where he was going. Looked like a lawyer or a teacher of some kind. It was obvious to Straut that the father wasn't the kind of man who handled a gun on an everyday basis.

"Well, if it comes that, son, I hope your pa here has enough sense not to use that gun foolishly, or if he don't have to," Straut said, glaring at the man. "A bad man ain't afraid of no nervous nelly, and it just might make things more difficult for all of us, if it comes to that."

The man stiffened and held Straut's gaze. "I'll do whatever I have to to protect my family." He grabbed his wife's hand. She was a prim and proper young thing, wearing a new blue gingham dress. Her glasses looked just like her husband's. They were a matching pair of wide-eyed fear and anticipation.

Straut retreated between the seats and leaned down to the man, aware that everyone in the train was watching, and listening, to him. "You pull out that gun, mister, and you're a dead man. Your family, too, if I'm a betting man. I don't think this is a show. Those fellas out there look serious. Real serious. Now, you just keep your courage to yourself and your mouth shut, and everything'll be all right."

"You lied," the boy said. "You said there was a tree down in front of the tracks."

"Ain't a lie," Straut answered. "I just didn't say what else was out there." He looked back to the boy's father. "I'm tellin' you the truth. Things turn ugly, I'm only gonna worry about savin' my own skin. You understand? You do somethin' stupid, then you and yours are on your own. Ain't no sense in dyin' in the middle of God knows where for no cause."

"Don't you worry about us. I've got us this far. Our journey to the West didn't work out. I'll get us back east if it's the last thing I do. Back where people got manners, and respectable men can be counted on to honor their promises."

Straut exhaled with frustration and pulled away. He didn't bother to look back to the man's wife. He knew the fear that was painted on her face, had seen it in a woman's eyes more times than he cared to admit. She had no choice but to keep her mouth shut and her feet planted in place. Her husband had been filled with hope at the opportunity moving out west had once offered them, but now he was defeated, returning home bitter and afraid, still looking for a way to prove his worth to her—and himself. Straut wanted nothing more to do with that than he did the robbery that he'd found himself in the middle of.

The inside of the passenger car suddenly felt hot and humid. Straut lumbered down the aisle and sat down heavily next to Deets.

The twin girls that were there before had not moved. They sat next to their mother, quiet, eyes to the floor, like they had been admonished, gotten into some kind of trouble. Straut was glad to see them behaving. The last thing he was in the mood for was dealing with another smart-mouthed brat.

"Bad men are coming," the girl with the yellow ribbons said, eyeing Straut as if he knew everything there was to know.

"You just sit and mind your manners, little miss. Everything'll be all right. We'll be on our way again before you know it," Straut replied. He nudged Deets in the side with his elbow.

"What?" Deets said. "I didn't say nothin'."

"No use," Straut said.

Riders passed by the window, off in a hurry like wolves in the night chasing innocent prey. But before Straut could let out a sigh of relief, the men turned back and came to a stop just outside the car.

"You think they're lookin' for us, don't you, Sarge?" Deets asked in a whisper—but the girl with the white ribbons heard him.

Straut glared hard at the girl with an intended, but silent, threat for her to keep her mouth shut. She recoiled, and stuck her tongue out at him.

"I'll think that until we do what needs doing to clear up our set of problems with the Boss, most likely we're going to keep being in the wrong place at the wrong time."

"I hope they shoot you both," the girl with the white ribbons in her hair said.

"Matilda!" the mother said. "That is not nice. You be a proper little girl, and sit there with your mouth shut."

"But they're bad men, Momma," Matilda said.

"We don't know that." The mother looked at both Straut and Deets a little closer. "The bad men are outside. These are not bad men."

"They smell," Matilda said.

Before anyone could say anything else, the door to the passenger car burst open, and the two tall riders pushed inside. They both wore black dusters, black hats, and black boots so they would be difficult to see in the moonless night. Both men held revolvers in the air in each hand. Straut calculated the odds and the bullets, and wasn't encouraged by either.

"This here is a robbery," the first man said. He pulled the trigger of the gun in his right hand to solidify his point—even though it was unnecessary. Every man, woman, and child inside the passenger car had known what was going on the moment the train came to a stop. All Straut had done when he came back inside the car was validate everyone's fears—including his own.

The gunshot easily pierced the roof of the railcar and echoed loudly inside the confined space. Women screamed. Babies cried. And Joe Straut sat stiffly on the bench seat next to Deets, annoyed by the robber's unnecessary action.

The smell of exploded gunpowder filled every nostril in the hot car. To make things worse, the man fired the gun in his opposite hand, as well, then laughed out loud in its wake. It was a wicked laugh. More than Straut could take. He didn't give the robbers a chance to demand all of the money and jewelry, or the nervous nelly a chance to prove his worth to anyone.

In a swift move, spinning off the seat into a kneel, all the while pulling his gun from its holster, Joe Straut fired at the obnoxious laughing robber, hitting him square in the forehead with the first shot. The second shot thudded into his accomplice's forehead before he had a chance to react or fire in retribution.

Straut unloaded the remaining cartridges in his Colt Open Top on the two men as they collapsed to the floor in a pile of bloody useless flesh. By the time silence had returned to the car—most all of the passengers were stunned by Straut's act—he was standing up pulling at Deets's collar. "Come on, let's go."

"Where?"

"Those fellas have two horses. We need to get as far away from here as fast as we can," Straut said, heading for the door, his grip tight on Deets, ignoring all of the passengers, especially the nervous nelly and his family, the best he could.

THIRTY-THREE

CHARLOTTE BROGAN FELT THE WIND GO OUT of her lungs at the sight of Lanford Grips. A shiver ran up her spine so forcefully that it nearly knocked her off her feet.

"Dear, dear, Charlotte, why, you look like you just saw a ghost," Grips said. There was a high tone of aristocracy in Lanford Grips's voice. A note of Tennessee royalty that could not be hidden no matter how hard he tried. Not that he had ever attempted such a thing when he spoke to her. He didn't have to hide the fact that he'd grown up in privilege, his father a man of high power. She knew every nuance in his voice. No matter what he said, she heard John Barlow. No matter how he changed his appearance, either with clothes, lifts in his shoes, a haircut, or an added mustache, she saw John Barlow. For her own good, she tried to play along, to see and hear Lanford Grips. But there was no deceiving herself. She had known the man since he was a boy, had been close friends with his two sisters. There was also no escaping the flaws in his character—even though she had thought that was what she had just done. St. Louis had offered her the hope of freedom, and now it had been taken from her.

"I thought you were staying in Kansas City to attend to business," Charlotte said, picking up a fan from the nearest table and fanning her face casually. She knew better than to show fear to an angry dog. The look on Lanford Grips's face could not be misinterpreted. He was annoyed, agitated at something, and she did not want to be the object of his rage.

Bojack Wu stood stiffly off to Grips's side. The door behind him was closed, the message clear that the exit from the room was blocked. The only way out was to jump from the window. The thought of falling to her death or, worse, surviving with a great injury was too much to consider. Charlotte had no choice but to face whatever it was that Lanford Grips or John Barlow had in mind for her. She was at his mercy. *God, how I hate his split personalities, but once a spy, always a spy*, she thought, though she could never say it out loud.

Little Ling had frozen in place, too, once Grips and Bojack Wu entered the room. Charlotte could not ignore the discomfort on the girl's face. "Go on, Little Ling, do what needs doing. Mr. Grips is welcome here."

"Yes, yes," Grips said, "carry on. I am only here for a moment. Just long enough to ask Miss Brogan for the pleasure of her company at the upcoming Fettermans' Ball. The society tongue-waggers are all abuzz about your arrival in St. Louis, Charlotte. I can't imagine that you intended to go to the ball without an escort? That would be such a tragedy."

Charlotte's mouth went dry. "You know what my intentions are, Lanford. They have not changed since I arrived in the city, and an invitation has not yet been offered."

"It will be, don't worry."

"I always worry about such things, you know that, Lanford." Charlotte placed as much emphasis on "Lanford" as she could, halting just at the point of overdoing it.

"Do I really know your intentions, dear Charlotte?"

"Of course you do. I had hoped to attract a certain suitor to the ball. Was that not the reason for my journey?"

"Yes, yes, of course. But I would like to offer my services in reserve. Just in case there is something along the way that prevents your expected suitor from arriving on time. How would that look, Charlotte, for you to walk into the ball unattended? Your youthful allure would be lost. Your time past. No one likes a has-been, dear."

Charlotte feigned a blush. "Why, of course, I would be honored to attend the Fettermans' Ball with you, Lanford. I am aware of your long-standing business relationship with the family. It would be an honor to be on your arm." She looked down to the floor then, noticing as she lowered her gaze that Lanford Grips wore his best gloves, offering the illusion that he was of a full body and mind. His hands looked normal, unless one questioned his need for such stiff gloves at this time of year. She ignored his slight about her age and stature, as well. A spider's web was being spun, and she was not going to get caught up in it. A fool she was not.

"Good. I assumed you would accept," Grips said, with a wry smile. "The ball could be interesting if your plan comes to fruition. But you should be aware there may be a distraction before you set foot onto the floor."

The air was stale in the room. It smelled of mold and must, as if it had not been occupied for a long time. There was no breeze, no whirling fan to distribute the humidity.

Charlotte had not noticed the discomfort until that very moment. "And what exactly is this distraction you speak of? Is it something I should be concerned about?" she asked.

"No, of course not. Just a simple misunderstanding that will be worked out once the perpetrators of the alleged misdeed are apprehended and returned to St. Louis," Grips said, as a sneer crossed his face. "It seems that I have employed some less than desirable characters, and I must save face by turning them in to the authorities for their heinous crimes.

Your association with me may be reflected in the eyes of those you covet. Just a fair warning is all."

"You are being cryptic, Lanford."

"I don't want you to worry, dear Charlotte. I know how much you enjoy the pomp of a good ball."

"It has been a while."

"Yes. Just realize there is more to be concerned about than your probable suitor, who may, or may not, show up here in St. Louis in time to provide a proper escort."

"I'm glad you have brought this to my attention, Lanford, so I will know how to proceed with my wardrobe."

"Just be cautious. My enemies are your enemies."

"It has always been that way," Charlotte said.

"Which is why you have my trust and protection, dear. Ours is a long and winding path, and I do not wish this situation to keep us from obtaining our goals."

"We will achieve what we set out to do, Lanford. You have my word on that," Charlotte said.

"I know." Lanford Grips nodded, and Bojack Wu stepped forward and offered Charlotte a copy of the current day's newspaper. As usual, the bodyguard bore no emotion on his face. He offered no good grace or happiness to see Charlotte.

She took the paper and opened it, seeing right away that there were three depictions, two men and a woman of high stature who had been found murdered and left behind under a railroad bridge to rot. Charlotte recognized the trio that had been tempted by innumerable riches in the distant West. She tried not to show any surprise, any emotion at all. It was not the first time business associates of Lanford's had come to a bad end, though she did not know the circumstances of the deaths involved. But she was sure of one thing: Lanford Grips wasn't telling her the truth. Or the entire truth. He never had.

"Bojack Wu will accompany you on any journey you may take while you're here in the city," Grips said. "Your safety is of utmost importance to me."

"I understand," Charlotte said. "What of Yen and Cheng?"

"It is their charge to bring the employees who have put our reputation in such peril to justice. It is the least I can do to aid the efforts of the local authorities. It is such a tragedy to see three enterprising citizens killed in their prime, for nothing more than the trinkets of gold they carried on their persons."

"They were killed for their jewelry and personal possessions?" Charlotte said, as her hand came up to her necklace. She stroked the pearls gently. "Who would do such a thing?"

"Straut and Deets," Grips said.

"Are you certain? They seem like such good men and have been in your employ for a very long time."

"Oh, yes, dear, I am absolutely certain that they are the perpetrators of this crime. I have offered myself to the authorities as a witness. I saw them carrying the bodies away in the night. Joe Straut and Finney Deets will hang for their crime, and we will be there to watch them fall into the depths of hell, where they most surely belong."

Charlotte studied Grips's face and said nothing more. If she had doubted him before, then she positively disbelieved him now. His face was white and pale, and he was sweating more than normal.

"Everything you need to know is on the front page of the newspaper, Charlotte. Now, I must be off. I have other fires to put out. I'm certain we will have a lot to discuss at dinner."

"Yes, of course," Charlotte said.

With that, Lanford Grips turned and stood before the door. In a flash, Bojack Wu slid past him and opened the door easily, allowing him to exit the room without uttering another word.

Charlotte did not breathe a sigh of relief until the door closed, and she heard the lock slide into place.

THIRTY-FOUR

THE DARKNESS OF NIGHT EASED INTO THE
light of day, and Lucas woke up to find his bed empty of
anyone but himself. Avadine had left at some point during
the night, leaving him in a comfortable sleep, feeling much
more satisfied and content than he could have ever imagined
a few short days before. Just to make sure he had not
dreamed the encounter with the beautiful brown-haired girl
who spoke in the tongue of the old country, he grabbed up
the bedding closest to his face and inhaled deeply. The scent
of a woman was unmistakable. The sweetness of toilet water
and pleasure lingered in Lucas's nose, promising to arouse
him again if he did not stop breathing it in.

He let go of the bedding and stood up. He was hungry,
famished from the night of lovemaking. But he didn't feel
weak. Just the opposite. There was an old, familiar strength
flowing through his veins. He felt hail and fit, as if his former
self had returned from a long, dark journey. It was good to

be alive, and that was as much a change in his mind and body as anything else.

The soft morning sun glowed warmly outside the tent, beckoning him. As did the smell of firewood being stoked, and bacon frying in a skillet. He could hear the sizzle of the meat, almost taste the succulent strips of pork side on the tip of his tongue. His stomach growled, demanding attention. He chuckled at his own situation. He let the hard-won smile linger longer than he might have in the past.

Lucas threw on his clothes and, for the first time ever, stepped outside of his tent like he truly belonged in Libertyville. But he didn't go far. The path to the outhouse was the only certain path that he'd traveled since he had arrived in the village. He stood outside the tent, close enough to dash inside at the first hint of trouble, much like a prison mouse, with which he was all too familiar.

Sulley Johnson was standing just beyond the tent, hunched over a fire, tending to the bacon that had helped draw Lucas out of his tent. The bacon lay flat on a skillet hanging on a tripod. Pulsing orange coals breathed in and out underneath the skillet, their life long and purposeful. The air smelled full of abundance.

"Well, looka here, it's Mistuh Lucas Fume all fit and clean. I hardly recognized you with your hair shorn and your face free of that thick bramble of whiskas you was wearing when I first sawed you on the path in. You done walked out of the dark and into the sun. That pale skin will be tender now, you be aware of that."

Lucas stopped and smiled at the man the best he could. He had to relieve himself in a bad way. "Good mornin', Mr. Johnson. Thank you for the advice, I'll heed your fair warning."

"Most folks just call me Sulley. Momma calls me Sultan Joseph Johnson when she mad at me, but I tries to stay away from her bad side. Got aim with a switch like a frog's tongue after a dragonfly. It be deadly if it hits ya square in the back of the head. Momma thinks she can still whup me, and I just lets her keep thinkin' that. She old and needs to think she can still do somethin' worthy. What about you, Mistuh Lucas? You up for a fine day of worthiness?"

Lucas fidgeted, nodded, mumbled an agreement, then hurried off to the outhouse and did his business. When he returned, Far Jackson was standing next to Sulley, along with another Negro man that Lucas did not know and had never seen before.

The unknown Negro was a bit taller than Far Jackson, and a few years younger, but not much. A thin patch of wiry white hair sprouted from under his lip. He looked like a skinny elder, too, a man weathered by time and worry. He had the look of an ex-slave. Every man and woman in the village did. It didn't take much for Lucas to feel out of place.

Something in the air had changed. The bacon was out of the skillet and on a plate in Sulley's big hand. There was a look of concern on all three men's faces.

"Mornin' there, Fume," Far Jackson said. The other man stood next to him and said nothing, just looked at the ground. "Set the plate down, Sulley, this ain't no time to be thinkin' about food."

Lucas came to a stop before the men and stood stiffly. "Is there a problem?"

Jackson nodded yes. "This here's J'rome Smitson. He come from a little place just outside the gorge. Got 'im a nice little stretch a land like I does. Has some chickens, goats. Pays no mind to anyone else, like most all of us. We don't want no troubles. The land gives us enough of that tryin' to feed those that need fed. We just wants a quiet life, and to be left alone. But the night riders come last night to Smitson's place and changed all that."

Sulley shivered and dropped the plate. Bacon spilled

across the ground, but the big man did nothing to retrieve it. He just stared at it.

"Good to meet you Mr. Smitson," Lucas said, offering his hand and all the while eyeing Sulley curiously.

Jerome Smitson glared at Lucas and ignored the handshake. His eyes were red, like there was blood let loose somewhere inside of them, and his cheeks drooped with sadness and defeat. Smitson's face looked accustomed to those feelings, but the lines looked like they might have dug deeper under his eyes recently. A scar cut across his forehead, and it resembled the same kind of scar that Lucas had seen on a lot of Negroes' backs.

"They was lookin' for you," Smitson said. "Ain't nothin' left of my life but ashes now."

"I had nothing to do with that," Lucas said.

"The hell you didn't," Smitson said.

Far Jackson eased between the two men. "Now, don't be goin' hog wild on this here man, J'rome. He be our guest. You got a complaint of that, you take it up wit' me."

"In due time, Jackson, in due time."

Lucas exhaled deeply and stepped back away, toward the entrance of the tent. He had no fight with the man before him. "What are these night riders you speak of?"

"Klan," Far Jackson said. "Ku Klux Klan. Men dressed in sheets settin' the countryside ablaze. War ain't over for them, but they hide their faces in the hood of a ghost. Lawd, just to speak of such a thing sets my teeth a-chatter. They be lookin' for you, Mistuh Lucas, but they really after Zeke, and those that offer him aid. Klan been makin' noise for a long time, but you escapin' with Zeke got them all riled up."

Smitson nodded. "They just usin' my place to prove they's serious. They find Zeke, he be a-danglin' from a tree before you can say Johnny come marchin' home. You, too, if you with him. No matter what your name be. There be big a reward on your head now, and even some mens of color might be desperate enough to claim it."

It was then that a certain movement in the distance caught Lucas's eye. The roof of a white tent wavered, then collapsed, disappearing from sight. "You're striking camp?"

"It's time to go," Far Jackson said. "We probably done stayed here longer than we should have the way it is."

Lucas could barely form the words that were swirling in his mind, but they finally came out. "Everybody's leaving?"

"Yes, everybody." It wasn't a man's voice. It was a woman's—Miss Lainie's stern voice—and she was standing directly behind Lucas.

Lucas turned and faced the woman. The blood drained from his head to his toes before he could offer anything else. It took all of the strength he had to stay standing.

"We all gonna have to go before night falls," Miss Lainie said, "even you."

Far Jackson nodded. "That's right. Take your post, Sulley. Keep a sharp eye out. There's men ridin' in the day, too, but they got the law on their side. You know what to do at the first sign of trouble."

"Yes, suh, I sure does. Whistle louder'n I ever whistled before." Sulley cast a woeful glance at the bacon on the ground, then tore off, disappearing into the nearby thicket without saying another word.

"You best go to your tent and wait, Mistuh Lucas," Far Jackson ordered. There was no mistaking his tone.

There had been a time in recent history when a Negro ordering a white man about was cause for punishment, or just plain unheard of. But Lucas offered no reprisal. It was Far Jackson's place to look out for. There was no questioning that.

Lucas nodded silently, his knees still weak. He looked to Jerome Smitson and thought to offer an apology, but he couldn't find the words.

The road suddenly grew busy with carts and nervous

horses darting about. Another tent fell from sight, and the perfect morning turned dark and uncertain. Panic tasted far worse than the bacon on the ground ever would have.

Lucas had very little to gather up. He had escaped prison with only the clothes on his back. All that he owned now was what had been given to him by the people of Libertyville, and the hammer that had seen him and Zeke free of the posse. There was no doubt in Lucas's mind that Carl the Hammer was still on his trail. And, obviously, drawing closer.

The inside of the tent seemed more like a prison cell than it ever had before. Lucas felt helpless, at risk, and he longed to see Avadine. His greatest fear at that moment was that he would never see her again.

A shadow moved toward the flap of the tent. There were muffled sounds outside. Nothing that indicated alarm, just the hurried deconstruction of Libertyville.

Lucas grabbed the hammer, arming himself for the worst, hoping for the best—which of course, would have been an appearance by Avadine.

He was disappointed, but only marginally so. Lucas was glad to see Zeke Henry enter the tent.

"You ain't gonna be needin' that hammer for me, Mistuh Lucas," Zeke said, offering a hearty smile. "But I be glad to see you standin' upright."

Lucas returned the smile. Zeke stood stiffly just inside the tent. His head nearly rubbed the roof. "I was concerned about you. But you look healthy, too, all things considered," Lucas said.

Zeke tapped his shoulder. "I was fine once they digged that lead out of my flesh. Ain't got time to let a little discomfort come between me and the grave. I always was a fast healer. Skin don't like to be open. It tries to close up soon as it's tore." He stared Lucas in the eye, then flicked his head toward the outside. "Come on, I got somethin' for ya to see," he said, then made his way back out of the tent.

Lucas followed Zeke outside and stopped shortly beyond the flap. Nearly every other tent in Libertyville had vanished. The view was clear all of the way to the church. Wagons and their teams moved about in all directions, ferrying the citizens of the town to points unknown. But that was not what Zeke had wanted Lucas to see.

The big Negro stood next to a horse, a very familiar bay gelding.

"You found him," Lucas said.

Zeke nodded his head up and down, the smile on his face solid, like it would never fall away. "The satchel inside the saddlebag be intact, too. Papers inside for you to see, but the funny thing is, they's blank."

"Doesn't surprise me," Lucas said, walking up to the horse. The gelding snorted and lowered its head slightly, then pulled it back up. Lucas patted the horse's neck and made his way to the first saddlebag. "I told you they probably would be, and I was right about that."

"They be on the other side of the horse," Zeke said, watching Lucas closely. "Why don't blank papers surprise ya none? I thought they'd be instructions for you to follow."

Lucas made his way to the other side of the bay gelding carefully, unsure of the horse's nature. He didn't want to spook it. "It was a common way in the war of sending messages. Most likely, the note was written in milk, in code of some sort that will appear when the paper is heated. Whoever put you up to this is somebody that knows me, knows my past, my skills. If it is blank, as you say, then this is a heartening turn of events. I know exactly what to do."

"You think you knows who it is that planned your escape?"

"Hard to say. I knew a lot of people in the war, doing what I did." Lucas steadied the horse, then opened the saddlebag and pulled out the satchel. "Good boy," he said softly as he walked away from the horse, back toward the tent.

Zeke followed after him silently. Neither man said another word until they were inside. As conflicted as Lucas was about the fate of Libertyville, he was hopeful that some of his questions would soon be answered.

"You were lucky to find the horse," Lucas said.

"Went lookin' for it. Was the only way there'd be any clue as to what was to come next for you. I'da failed myself if you was left to the winds."

"I'm hopeful, too."

Lucas opened the satchel and found one single piece of paper and nothing else. No cash, no weapons of any sort, nothing. He pulled out the paper and examined it, and as Zeke had said, at first glance it looked blank. He quickly found a match by the lamp and struck it to life, then waved it cautiously under the paper. For a long moment, it continued to look blank, and there was a kernel of fear in Lucas's mind that the paper had gotten too wet and the milk had washed away—but the saddlebag was dry. Finally, letters began to appear:

GLEK YXOILT FP XIFSB

Lucas recognized the code immediately, and set the paper down and started to decipher the hidden message.

"Well, I'll be . . ." Zeke said. "You do know that magic." It wasn't a question; it was a statement, tinged with surprise.

"It's not magic. Just a basic spy code. When simple messages like this were passed, they were usually passed within the same camp, but coded for security concerns. Anybody could be a spy; even the most basic orders were encrypted. This code seems to be based on the principal of moving letters forward or backward in their place. The most common would be to move three back for each letter. If someone else found that horse, they would have just seen a blank piece of paper . . . unless they had the same kind of experience that I do. And that seems unlikely these days."

"So's you can read it?"

"I can. I just need a minute to make sure I'm right in my thinking. I'm a little rusty at this. The war's been over for a long time," Lucas said.

His heart began to beat faster as he made progress with each letter, using his fingers as counters. The outside world disappeared. If there was any noise in the street beyond, he couldn't hear it. Especially once he figured out the message.

Lucas's entire body went numb, and his face felt like all of the blood drained out of it at once.

"Well," Zeke said, "what's it say?"

Lucas could barely get his mouth to work. Everything inside it was dry. "It says . . ." he stuttered. "It says John Barlow is alive."

PART III

Vengeance at Sundown

Back into the chamber turning, all my soul within me burning, Soon again I heard a tapping somewhat louder than before.

—EDGAR ALLAN POE, "THE RAVEN"

THIRTY-FIVE

SLEEP DID NOT COME EASILY TO CHARLOTTE Brogan. The bed was big enough to put two kings in, and it was comfortable enough, firm but soft enough to fit around her, hold her safely like a cocoon—she just couldn't find a spot to settle into.

The thick velvet draperies were pulled tight across the third-floor windows, though even that would not have mattered. The night had turned dark, the moon obscured by a thick blanket of clouds. She could barely see her hand in front of her face as she tossed and turned.

When sleep finally did come, her dreams took her to places that she did not want to go; the past held nothing but pain and discomfort for her.

The first thing she saw was old moss hanging from skeletal branches of monstrous old trees. Trees that she knew well. They lined the road that led to her home. Home to the plantation. A place she had not returned to in many years. At least physically. Nightmares pulled her back as often as they could.

She knew she was alone. On the road. Facing the house. An observer of the past. There was no discernible noise. It was as if her ears were stuffed with cotton. Silence abounded, though there seemed to be a distant rush of air vibrating just out of reach. The was no way to identify where it originated.

Charlotte tossed and turned in the physical world, tried to wake herself up, to no avail. She had no choice but to exist inside the dream, let it take her where it would. It was always the way of such things. Had been that way for many years.

She had seen many men returning home after the war a shell of their former selves. Some called it Soldier's Heart. They were affected by what they'd seen, by what they'd done, by the explosions and rifle fire. But no one spoke of such a thing for the women of the war. Message carriers. Delivery agents. Spies who gave all, including their bodies, in service of the cause—whether it was Confederate or Union. Women fought in the war, too, but most never fired a gun—at least on the battlefields. Still, how many deaths were laid at the hands of women who ferried information and revealed troop movements to the colonels and captains of the brigades?

Charlotte feared those ghosts who came after her in sleep, in her dreams and nightmares. There was no redemption, no offering to erase the deeds committed in the past. Her soul was damned, and she knew it. Knew that to be the certain truth from the dreams she was forced to endure, night after night, time after time—especially when she was afraid for her own safety in her waking life.

Now she stood before the house of her birth, the place where it all began, where her story and life intertwined with John Barlow's and Lucas Fume's and would be altered forever. All of their parents had traveled in the same circle, and the three of them, just out of childhood, had been thrown together. Lucas had been short and muscular as a boy, a face carved like a young god's. John had been sickly, thin as a rail, fussed over by all those who came into contact with him. He appeared weak, but even then he knew how to get what he wanted, when he wanted it. Manipulation came naturally to him. But it was Lucas who took her breath away—no matter how much John Barlow tried to win her heart, and try he did, nothing could compare to Lucas's effort, which had taken very little—to John's chagrin.

Fate had brought her home to taunt her, punish her for her misdeeds, by showing her what once was, and what could have been if she had made different choices in her youth. That was the way of her dreams. Hell was what she didn't do, what she didn't say when she should have . . .

The house was grand, two stories with three pillars carved of the oldest and tallest oaks to be found on the land. A balcony overlooked the grand porch, offering a wide view of the valley from her second-floor bedroom. Cotton fields. Acres upon acres of woodland timber. A bounty of natural resources to be cultivated and sold to the highest bidder—it was all never-ending, like it would never run out.

The house was surrounded by magnolia bushes, allowing for secret passageways to be made by children and slaves alike. The paint was fresh, and it seemed sometimes, especially in the light of a full moon, that the house glowed white, like a beacon set on the edge of the nearby swamp.

A shallow river cut through the land, leaving the swamp in its wake most years, years when there was plenty—or too much—rain. The swamp was a spooky place even in the daytime. It held its secrets out in the open, there to see for anyone who dared to venture into it and face the miserable swarms of insects and whatever lived just underneath the surface, ready to pull you under. Rows and rows of slave shacks sat just off the edge of the swamp.

Charlotte had feared water ever since she could remember, and was never more overjoyed than the first time she saw the dry, open plains of Kansas and beyond. If she never saw another body of water in her life, it would be too soon.

Most of the furniture in the grand house, called Harper's Belle, named after its famed architect, Wilfred Altune Harper, and because of its shape—the back curved narrowly into a kitchen, while the front was wide—had been shipped over from Europe, primarily Italy. Charlotte's mother held a strong fondness for Italy, even though she had never visited the country.

Charlotte always thought her mother wanted to be a model for a marble statue, to have her likeness carved in stone so that she would live on forever in some form, never age, never have to die. But that did not happen. By the time such a thing could be afforded, her mother was wracked with sickness; a cancer ate at her bones, making her brittle and weak. There were few that remembered her mother's beauty by then, but Charlotte did. She couldn't forget it. She always feared the same thing would happen to her.

The distant air turned into a sudden wind, wrapping around Charlotte, blowing her red hair all about her face and tugging at her long skirt and petticoats. Storm clouds hung over Harper's Belle, and Charlotte recognized the wind, knew it was from the north, offering the first chill of winter, but no snow.

Thunder exploded overhead, rattling her toes and driving a sharp pain straight up her back. It was the drums of war beating in her ears, the fight against slavery, the Northern Aggression, the battle for the very soul of the soil she stood on. In her waking moments, she knew the outcome of that struggle, but in her nightmare, she only knew that the battle lines were being drawn. She had feared being pulled into the war, just as she feared slipping into the swamp. She nearly drowned once, saved by a black hand, a Negro slave whose name she never knew. He ran off not long after, never to be seen again.

Charlotte knew where she stood: The dream taunted her with the aftermath of her mother's funeral. She was distraught, but relieved that the suffering was over. A thick pall had dropped over Harper's Belle, and its white glow had dimmed gray with her mother's sickness.

The Negro door butler, Simon Don, stood with his white-gloved hands clasped together, his head down, eyes cast to the ground. His black frock coat and pants stood in stark contrast to the red front door. Even in the graying storm, there was no missing him.

Charlotte's heart fluttered at the recognition. Simon Don had been with the family long before she was born. He gave her a wide path, and a kind of acceptance that she could never get from either of her parents, living or dead.

She walked up on the porch, suddenly aware of the weight of her funeral clothes. "Simon Don," she whispered. "It is so good to see you."

The Negro looked up, directly into her eyes. His own eyes were bloodshot, red with the aftermath of tears. "We wuz worried about ya, Miss Charlotte, a storm's a-comin'."

"I took the long way home."

"Alone."

"It is what I wanted, Simon Don."

"I suppose it was," the doorman said, offering a slight smile, his approval of her independent nature. "Mr. Lucas is waitin' in the parlor for you."

Charlotte nodded. "I expected he would be. And Father?"

"In his study."

"Nursing a bottle of whiskey, I imagine."

Simon Don looked away quickly, then back to Charlotte directly. "Mr. John came calling, too, but stalked off once he looked upon Mr. Lucas's horse." The butler ticked his head to the left so Charlotte would look upon the familiar solid black gelding tied to the post.

Charlotte sighed. "I suppose I should have expected that, too." She forced a smile, nodded, and Simon Don opened the door to let her inside.

The smell of food greeted her nose; a fresh-cooked roast with carrots and potatoes, offset by the comforting aroma of an apple pie baking in the pit of the fireplace in the far-off kitchen. Whispers and murmurs filled the grand entrance, and Charlotte paid no one any mind. All eyes were upon her, of course, mourners come from the graveyard to pay their respects and eat a fine meal at her father's expense. She was in no mood to be social. She made a beeline to the parlor, walked in, and closed the door heavily behind her.

Lucas Fume stood behind the piano, fiddling with the keys, not playing any known song, just pecking at the occasional note. Charlotte's sudden entrance stopped him, caused him to look up, surprised. "You are bound and determined to set tongues wagging today, aren't you?" he asked. "What will the world think with us alone, unchaperoned?"

Charlotte stopped in the middle of the room. A marble statue occupied each corner, all nude females, headless, armless, making her feel like she really wasn't the only woman in the room. "If there is one day when I couldn't care less what people have to say, then today is that day. They will consider me grief-stricken. Or not. I could not care one whit less what they have to say. I want to be in your company at the moment, not anyone else's."

"And they would be correct? You are grief-stricken, not in your right mind?"

"Yes, of course. Of course." Charlotte drew in a deep breath, sucking in the air of the past, the smell of her home, and the sight of Lucas Fume as she liked to remember him—when he was young, untouched by the war, still wide-eyed, hopeful, and woefully in love with her. She could do nothing wrong in his eyes. Not then. Betrayal would come later. All in the name of war and wealth.

They were the same age, sixteen, the prospect of adulthood within reach but still far enough away not to be a worry. But the adult urges were there. For them both, though they were hardly ever in private company long enough to explore them.

Lucas stood stiffly in place behind the piano, and Charlotte remained in the center of the room, staring at him.

He was dressed all in black, perfect in his mourning as in anything else. He had long black hair, wavy, with curls that fell over the back of his collar. There was a hint of beard on his face, young and tender, but not too threatening, not like his father's beard that seemed to fall halfway to his chest. Lucas's eyes were almost the color of his suit, of the mood of the day, black onyx—but on closer inspection, which Charlotte took every opportunity she could to make, they were really just a deep, deep blue. A canyon in the sea that she had to restrain herself from diving into.

"We shouldn't be alone," Lucas whispered. "Not today."

"You don't really mean that."

"No, I don't."

There were more murmurs outside the door, but it sounded like a distant storm to Charlotte—the thunder coming closer, like it was drawn to her. She stepped toward Lucas just as he stepped toward her. It was almost like she were floating, being guided by something other than her own will. She had little understanding of destiny, of fate, or of the power of desire, when she was a girl.

All she knew was that in the blink of an eye she was exactly where she wanted to be, wrapped in Lucas Fume's arms, her mouth searching out his, and his searching out hers. They kissed deeply, and she pressed into him in a way she never had before, signaling her need for him in a way she never had. God, she wanted him to take her away. Just take her. She understood that much.

And then the next moment . . . everything changed.

Charlotte awoke, and sat straight up in bed, only to find what she had found so long ago in the past: John Barlow standing in the doorway, finding her half-dressed, her skin exposed in a shameful way, and glaring at her with hate and jealousy in his eyes. His broken heart had never healed, only grown darker, angrier, and just as in the past, Charlotte was afraid of what John Barlow was capable of. Very afraid.

THIRTY-SIX

ZEKE HANDED LUCAS A COLT SINGLE-ACTION Army revolver. The weapon looked brand-new, like it had never been fired. The silver plating shone, even inside the dim light of the tent, causing Lucas to question the gun's origins, but as with the reappearance of the bay gelding, he was going to leave those questions for later, or unasked altogether. All that mattered now was that he had a horse, a gun, and the knowledge that John Barlow was still alive—if he were to believe the message that the code had revealed to him.

Everything that had led up to that moment—the well-planned and well-executed escape, along with the horses set for a getaway, even though that didn't quite work out as it was intended, and Zeke's efforts, along with his knowledge and thoughtfulness—had brought Lucas to Libertyville and led him to fully believe in the validity of the note.

It would have been helpful if there had been more information, but Lucas knew that what was written was all that he needed to know for the moment. He wasn't the only one with code-breaking skills in the world. The bay gelding could have easily fallen into the wrong hands. Whether the message would have made sense to anyone else was another question. But there were obviously still people left in the world to whom it mattered that John Barlow still breathed and walked on the surface of the earth. Deception has long roots and does not die easily.

John Barlow is alive, Lucas thought again. The words reverberated inside his mind more as an affirmation than a shock. He was savoring them one letter at a time.

His gut had told him all along that the ploy that had seen him to prison stunk like a week-old carp left out in the sun to rot. There had been no body, just a pair of severed hands, speculated to be Barlow's, based on the scars he'd accumulated in the war. The murder, if it could be called that, just hadn't felt right from the start. The more Lucas cried out about his innocence, the more he was punished. Now he was left to wonder what had become of the timber business he'd operated in partnership with Barlow—and where in the world Barlow was and, most importantly, what the hell he was up to.

No matter what, the world had to continue to believe that John Barlow was dead or there would be no cause to imprison Lucas, and his family would not have reason to disown him, turn their backs on his very being. But someone knew the truth. Someone wanted Lucas out of prison. And that someone wanted Lucas to find John Barlow. Lucas just had to figure out who that someone was, and why they wanted these things. More specifically, why now?

Lucas turned the Colt over in his hand and examined the gun a little closer. The black grips were comfortable, and the weight of the six-inch barrel balanced nicely in his hand. The playing field was slowly becoming more even. Having a gun would make leaving Libertyville a little easier. It would give him the confidence he would need to face whatever it was he was heading toward. He knew one thing for certain, as he lifted the empty revolver up and aimed it at the barren back wall of the tent: No matter what happened, when he faced John Barlow, one of them was going to die.

"Looks fancy," Lucas said, drawing the Colt back, opening the empty cylinder and spinning it, then eyeing the gun with admiration.

Zeke stood stiffly a few feet away. He had remained silent after Lucas read the code aloud, never taking his eyes off him. "Standard issue for the army now. There be another one on the horse, along with a repeater rifle in the scabbard. Cartridges are easy to load, and I can shows you how to use it, if you like."

"I think I can figure it out. A gun's a gun."

"Well, then, I've done all I needed to do." Zeke turned and headed toward the closed flap of the tent.

"Wait." Lucas put the Colt on the table next to the piece of paper. "Aren't you coming with me?"

Zeke stopped. "Where to?"

"I've got to find John Barlow."

"John Barlow ain't none of my bizness, Mistuh Lucas. Why I got to go after him? No offense or nuthin', but I figure I got troubles of my own—without the Barlows. Far Jackson done told you my story. I never laid a bad hand on that woman. I loved her. That was my only crime."

"Once word gets out beyond Tennessee that we escaped the prison, you'll be associated with me, and somehow they found a way to link us together. I don't think that's a mistake. You were chosen to break me out of prison for a reason. I just don't know what that reason is. Yet. Barlow's a cunning man. I've known him most all of my life, and I was in business with him. He'll go to any length to keep his betrayal a secret, far as I can tell. It isn't just going to be the law or the Klan looking for us that worries me. He'll have his men after us, too. We need to find him before he finds us. It's that simple."

"And how's you gonna do that? How you gonna find this man that don't want to be found?"

A frustrated look crossed Lucas's face, then disappeared just as quickly as it came. "In the old days, there were caches of money and instructions hidden in predetermined spots. The only clue that the code held was the fact that whoever wrote it knew I'd know what to do with it once I found it. There's a few spots between here and Atlanta that we used regularly for drops. First thing we would do would be to check them, see if there's anything there. If I'm a betting man, and I am, then I think we'll find everything we need in one of those old caches."

Zeke stared warily at Lucas. "Two peoples is easier to track than just one. No offense, it sound like a risky plan to me."

"I'm in your debt, Zeke, and I'd like to repay you. Barlow's coming after you, too, just because you helped me see the light of day. But you're right, two horses are easier to find than one, and all those folks will be looking for us. I've changed my appearance as best I can, but there's not much we can do about yours."

"White man and a Negro travelin' together will draw certain attention these days, Mistuh Lucas. I think it be best if we goes our separate ways, but if you thinks that you still needs my help, then I can come along wit you, at least into Atlanta. All I knows is that we need to flee here as soon as we can. That posse be close, and them night riders will most likely shows up here as soon as the darkness eat away the daylight. They gonna be surprised when there ain't no one heres for them to scare or torture. Far Jackson never would let no one build a cabin on his land, and this be why. Folks still need to scurry quick no matter what them fellas in Washington say. Free ain't so free right here."

"I've got a good-bye to say before we leave," Lucas said.

"Most everybody be gone, Mistuh Lucas. It be like a bad storm is a-comin', and I brought it here. People ain't gonna forget that I'm the one whose fault it is they had to move on. Even if you find her, she might be a sight mad at the prospect of the uprootin' that's goin' on."

"I hope you're wrong, Zeke. I sure hope you're wrong." Lucas tucked the Colt in his belt and walked out the flap of the tent, leaving Zeke standing there to consider what was to come next for them both.

THIRTY-SEVEN

MOST ALL OF THE PEOPLE OF LIBERTYVILLE were gone. The land was open all the way from Lucas's tent to the one lone building that had stood as the anchor to the village. The church that Zeke's father had helped to build stood alone in the gorge now, its back to the fortress-like wall of eons-old limestone. Late morning shadows danced off the church heavily, coloring it gray and dreary instead of the hopeful whitewash that had gleamed the first time Lucas saw it. The limestone wall looked black, the cleavage of the rocks even blacker with shadows, but the sky was blue, dotted with thin, intermittent clouds, offering a clear day beyond the hidden village, which was as much a good thing as it was a bad thing.

The bacon remained on the ground just where Sulley had dropped it. It was covered with a horde of ants, scurrying around happily, busily, enjoying the bounty that had fallen out of the sky. But most everything else that Lucas had grown accustomed to seeing was gone. There were no tents, no tripods to cook on, and the fire pits had been filled in, and the outhouses removed. To where, Lucas wasn't certain, nor did it matter much. Zeke was right. It was like Libertyville had almost never existed.

The main road was still evident, but it led straight up to the church, like the road ought to be there regardless. The ground around the church, though, was rubbed raw in places, the grass long dead. It looked like *something* had been there, but if a man, or a posse, rode by in a hurry, he or they would likely be surprised to know that a whole village had once sat there.

The bay gelding stood in place dutifully, tied to a hitching post along with another horse, a black gelding with a white diamond shape on its nose, packed and ready to go. A duplicate rifle stuck out of the black gelding's scabbard, and the saddlebags were stuffed full, just like the bay's. They would be slowed some by the weight, another concern to take into consideration when the time came. Lucas was just glad to see the horses packed and ready to go.

A few tents still stood behind Lucas, toward the path that had led into Libertyville, where Sulley stood watch in the forest, ready to alert those that remained. Ashes in a fire pit smoldered by the road. Steam rose up into the air instead of smoke, in front of one of the distant tents. Two wagons, fixed with a team of healthy Springfield mules, sat outside the tent, loaded with furniture and trunks in preparation for the journey to come. But there was no one to be seen milling about, and no noise coming from inside the tent.

Lucas stood facing the tent, trying to decide if he should make his way to it or load the Colt he had stuffed in his belt. The gun butted up against the hammer, a piece that was rarely out of Lucas's sight inside the tent and always on his person when he left it.

Before Lucas had a chance to move, Miss Lainie walked out, carrying a sheet bundled up with a load of clothes stuffed inside it. She stopped immediately and glared at Lucas.

"Varmints. You varmints just go on and get the hell out of here while you still can. If I had a shotgun, I'd pepper your asses good and proper so's you wouldn't think twice about stayin' round here. You ain't welcome no more, ya hear. You ain't welcome by none of us."

Lucas squared his shoulders, put off loading the Colt, and walked toward Miss Lainie. He stopped a few feet directly in front of her. "I need to say good-bye to Avadine."

"She gone."

"You're a bad liar," Lucas said.

Miss Lainie had no chance to offer a response. An explosion of pigeons pierced through the canopy of the nearby woods. The sudden appearance of the thick flock of birds was followed by a single gunshot from the same vicinity, only inside the trees, out of sight. The pigeons scattered in different directions, the prism of colors on their wings and bellies flashing in the direct sunlight like a mirror hung in the sky, a brief warning to take shelter.

A panicked look crossed Miss Lainie's face. She glanced back to the woods, toward Sulley's post, then to the church. Lucas followed her gaze, and understood her concern immediately.

Avadine stood in the arched doorway of the church, the expression on her face obscured by shadows. She looked like a statue, frozen in place and time, that Lucas hadn't noticed before. But he knew Avadine was more than a statue—she was alive, and full of fear.

"I have to see to Sulley, you take care of her," Miss Lainie whispered as she turned to make a dash back to the tent. But she wasn't quick enough.

Three riders rushed down the path at full speed, their horses lathered with sweat from a long, hard run. All three beasts looked enraged, nostrils flared and black eyes fixed on the distance, just like their masters'.

The trio broke out of the darkness of the trees with guns blazing. Their thunder was deafening, shattering the peace of the gorge. The air was quickly filled with the smell of gunpowder and hate. No one had to say anything. Lucas knew that his presence had brought the men to Libertyville.

The first shot hit the dirt at Miss Lainie's feet. The second one hit her square in the chest, just above the heart. The bullet's impact lifted her completely off her feet and knocked her a good five feet backward. She fell to the ground in an explosion of dust and blood.

The attack caught Lucas unaware, but not Zeke. The big Negro dove to the ground, then crawled directly toward the black horse. "Get down, Mistuh Lucas. Get down. This be war."

But Lucas stood in place like nothing was happening, still staring at Avadine standing in the doorway. Shots exploded at his feet and hit the wagon outside of Miss Lainie's tent. He motioned for Avadine to go, and didn't move until the door to the church closed, until Avadine disappeared from his sight.

Satisfied that Avadine was safe for the moment, Lucas jumped to the ground and rolled back and forth haphazardly, like he was trying to douse a fire on his pants. Puffs of dirt exploded around him as he tried to make a difficult target of himself.

Zeke made it to the bay gelding and the black diamond horse, grabbed his rifle, then untied the horses. They tore off in the opposite direction from the three men, fleeing the gunshots as quickly as they could.

The horses fleeing distracted the three men, and Lucas crawled over next to the outside wall of his tent. He edged up alongside it as close as he could, allowing full sight of the road when he peeked out to see what was happening.

The riders made their way down the main road, all three firing their weapons at the horses. One of them was holding a torch, a long stick with a healthy flame atop it. Lucas recognized the rider in the lead, the one holding the torch, right away. It was Carl the Hammer.

There was no helping Miss Lainie. She hadn't moved since she was first shot, and Lucas didn't know whether she was dead or alive. The Negro woman lay still as a corpse, completely out in the open.

Zeke fired back at the trio of riders. He'd taken up a standing position on the other side of Lucas's tent. It didn't offer any viable cover, but the three riders looked surprised to be shot at.

Zeke hit the first one, a small man, riding with the reins of his horse stuck between his teeth, firing his pistols haphazardly. The man teetered, but kept firing—until Zeke shot him again, catching him in the shoulder, knocking him off the horse. The man landed in the middle of the road with a thud. His weapons spiraled out of his grasp.

The other two men slowed their rides, as panic replaced the rage on their faces. Each man's eyes darted about for cover, but there was none. They were directly in the middle of the road between the church and the woods from which they'd come.

Zeke called out, not loud, but direct enough to get Lucas's attention. "Mistuh Lucas, take this."

Lucas looked around the corner of the tent and caught another Colt Army. The empty one on his belt offered no help at the moment; the horses had run off with the ammunition on their backs. This gun was fully loaded.

Carl the Hammer yelled to the other man to make a run for the church, then gouged his horse with his muddy spurs, demanding every ounce of energy that the overworked animal had. The horse lowered its head, almost like it was diving toward the church, kicking up a cloud of dust in its wake.

Lucas aimed the Colt at the speeding horse and pulled the trigger. He missed Carl the Hammer. The gun was new to him, the sights not any more sure than his rusty shooting skills. He was battle-soft. His heart was racing faster than his thoughts, making his aim jittery. He took a deep breath and pulled the trigger again. This time he caught Carl the Hammer in the arm—but he still held on to the torch. It was like the man was glued in the saddle, unwavering in his mission to bring about as much death and destruction as he could.

Zeke shot the other man, caught out in the open on a slower horse. The second rider slumped over the front of his horse. The constant firing had left Zeke's rifle empty, and he had to reload, so there was no certainty in the deed—he couldn't finish the man off as quickly as he wanted to.

Lucas fired again, but missed, giving Carl the Hammer just enough time to make a last, hard run at the church. The horse's eyes looked like they were about to explode. With a deep, primal scream, Carl lobbed the torch to the roof.

The flame tumbled through the air, staying lit, and landed next to the cupola, just at the base of the cross.

Carl the Hammer shifted in the saddle, unsteady, and cut the horse back toward Lucas, firing his pistol as he came, all the while reaching for another sidearm with his opposite hand.

Lucas walked away from the tent, firing the Colt. It thumped into the angry rider's shoulder. The next shot took Carl the Hammer to the ground. Leaving Lucas one more cartridge.

The horse bucked and whinnied, trotted as best it could away from Carl, and promptly collapsed at the edge of a thin copse of weak horse chestnut trees

For a moment, it wasn't clear if Carl the Hammer was still alive. The dust settled, and like the other rider's, Carl's guns had flown out of his hands on impact. Once clarity returned, Carl eyed Lucas hatefully, his mouth twisted in pain and dryness, as he reached for the gun closest to his hand.

Lucas drew in another breath, and at the peak of it, he pulled the trigger of the Colt. The shot reverberated in his hand and echoed loudly before him, deafening him for a brief second. His aim was off just a bit. He hit Carl in the forearm, and he had been aiming for his head. He had always been better at breaking code than he was shooting a gun.

The wound stopped Carl the Hammer, stopped him like he had reached a wall and could not go any farther. But it was not a life-threatening wound. The pursuer still breathed.

Lucas walked up to the man and tossed the Colt to the side. It was empty of cartridges, no good to him anymore.

"I will hunt you into the bounds of hell, Lucas Fume, I promise you that," Carl the Hammer said. Bloody spittle spewed out of his mouth at the end of every word.

He reminded Lucas of a rat in his cell, trapped and unwilling to die. It was then that all the pain that he had seen Carl the Hammer inflict within the walls of the prison came rushing back to Lucas. It was one long, painful memory. There was only one way to rid himself of it. He unleashed the hammer from his belt, reared back on his heels, and threw it as hard he could, striking the man right between the eyes.

Carl the Hammer's forehead shattered as the hammer bounced away. A slight whine escaped his mouth, but beyond that, death was instant. Blood and brain escaped to the ground, soaking in.

There was no sound like the sound of a hammer smashing into a man's head, and it was not one that Lucas had ever heard, and not one he ever wanted to hear again. "I'll see you in hell, Carl," he said.

Lucas turned away just in time to see the flame take hold of the cupola and run straight up the cross, and all the while another arm of the flame tore across the old roof, jumping as joyously as it could at the opportunity to eat bare wood, just like the ants had jumped when they'd discovered the bacon on the ground.

Lucas ran to the door of the church and kicked it open with all of the strength he had left. Smoke was already snaking around the rafters, but there was no sign of the flames inside. It wouldn't be long, though. The acrid smell of fire was thick, and his eyes were tinged with tears that were not brought on by sadness but by the smoke.

Avadine stood in the center of the aisle that led up to the pulpit. She ran to Lucas and threw herself into his waiting arms. "I knew you'd come for me," she said.

"I have to go," Lucas said, nuzzling her thick mane of brown hair, holding her tight.

"I'll go with you."

The back wall of the church started to smoke heavily. Fire was running down the wall on the outside, just like on the roof, looking for a way inside.

Lucas pulled back and shook his head no. "Running is no way for you to live. Libertyville was a make-believe life compared to what it would be with me. Miss Lainie is hurt. They shot her. If she's still alive, she'll need your help."

The blood drained out of Avadine's face, giving her a sudden, sickly look. "She has to be alive."

"I'm sure Zeke's seeing to her. Come on now, we've got to go. This place is about to erupt into flames."

Lucas stood aside to let Avadine pass, but she wrapped her arms around him instead and pulled herself as close to him as she could. "I'll never see you again, will I?"

Lucas felt her warmth, her need for him, and his for her, but he knew better than to speculate, or to lie to her. Instead, he leaned down and kissed her deeply, kissed her like they were old lovers about to embark on another unrestrained, naked adventure. "Thank you for saving me," he said, pulling away.

He wanted to stay there, to be with her forever, but he knew it was an impossible desire. He was a wanted man, and he had a score to settle. His freedom relied on him staying alive and finding John Barlow. There was no place in that picture for Avadine. Not now. And who knew what would happen if he was successful in his quest?

Fire broke ravenously through the roof and back wall at the same time. "We have to go," Lucas said more forcefully this time, giving her no choice but to obey him.

They ran out of the burning church together, their eyes stinging from the smoke, their vision blurry, their lungs heavy, but they did not stop until they were far enough away from the fire to not feel the heat of it.

Zeke was on the ground, leaning over Miss Lainie, his back to them. She was still, unmoving. "Go to her," Lucas said to Avadine. "She needs you now more than ever. She's done far more for you than I ever can."

"What about you?"

"I have to get the horses."

"But . . ."

"There'll be more men coming, Avadine. These were just the lead scouts. They found us, and when they don't return when they're supposed to, a bigger posse will follow. We have to go, or we'll all die."

Avadine started to say something, but no words came out. A tear ran down her face, cutting a curvy path through dirt and ashes, suggesting a scar on her skin that would never fade. She ran then, ran toward Miss Lainie and Zeke without looking back.

Lucas tore out, too, skirting the burning church, wishing like hell he could douse the fire. It was a signal, a direct landmark for the posse to ride toward. Carl the Hammer had let the world know where he was, and it was as much the fire as the three men's presence that convinced Lucas that there was another imminent threat.

Luckily, the horses weren't far. Lucas made his way to the bay gelding, who noticed him but did not spook. He dug into the saddlebag, found the cartridges for the Colt that was still stuffed in his belt, and loaded it as quickly as he could. Then he mounted the gelding, grabbed the reins of the black diamond horse, and made his way back to Zeke and Avadine.

Miss Lainie's eyes were open; she was alive. Zeke stood up as Lucas drew the horses to a stop next to them. Avadine stayed on her knees, applying pressure to Miss Lainie's gunshot wound.

Miss Lainie tried to say something, but her words were silent. Lucas wasn't sure what she meant to say, but he didn't feel inclined to get off the horse. He nodded to her. "Avadine will look after you, ma'am. Thank you for all you've done." He paused and looked away to the trees, distracted by something moving, then back. "Are you coming with me, Zeke?"

Zeke didn't answer. A gunshot did. Followed by another and another.

The posse that Lucas had feared would come exploded out of the forest, sooner rather than later. There were too many men to count.

Zeke jumped up on the black horse, pulled the rifle out of the scabbard, and shot three times at the roof of Miss Lainie's tent. It fell away, and another flock of pigeons exploded upward.

The eruption of birds surprised the posse, and they slowed and started shooting at the birds. But that was not the intent. Unlike the first release, which had been an alarm, this one was a request.

Stuffed in the crevices of the wall behind the burning church were all of the men of Libertyville, set and waiting with rifles. They started firing at the posse, causing them to stop in surprise and necessity, then retreat back into the woods.

"We got cover for a minute there, Mistuh Lucas. We got to go. Womenfolk'll be fine. Far Jackson ain't gonna let nothin' happen to them."

Lucas nodded, stared at Avadine, who stood up as he

pulled away, with more tears streaming down her face. "I'll wait for you," she called out, as the two horses sped away.

Lucas didn't hear her. All he heard was the crackling of fire, the *pop-pop* of gunshots, and the pounding of his horse's hooves fleeing an army of men who sought to kill him and Zeke.

THIRTY-EIGHT

CHARLOTTE BROGAN STOOD NEXT TO THE desk just as she had been instructed. She wasn't sure that she could keep her mouth shut during the coming meeting, even though she knew that's what Lanford Grips expected of her. It was only her presence that was needed, desired. Obedience was in her best interest. Her hands were clasped tightly together at her waist, and she could hardly breathe.

The top-floor suite where Charlotte stood was adjacent to her own hotel room, and it looked very similar; the same fine imported fabrics, the same swirling designs in the Turkish rugs, and the same European-influenced furniture—heavy, burled, dark wood that filled the room. All that was different was the ornate writing desk that sat just to the side of the barren fireplace—no logs, no grate, just an open hearth big enough to shove an ox into, with two stiff chairs sitting in front of it.

Lanford Grips sat behind the desk smugly, in an

appropriately high-backed chair most likely imported from France, since it was in the stately Louis XVI style, painted beige with open arms and a crown embroidered on the same color of silky fabric—that left Grips exposed for all the world to see. His hooks were covered in black leather gloves, tucked under the desk comfortably, resting on his knees. Only a man with curious eyes would spy the false append-ages and comment on them, and that would be an unfortu-nate flaw in said man's character. It would be unlikely that he would live to see the sun rise on another day if he pursued any undue questioning.

Grips was finely appointed in a black suit, tailored espe-cially for the impending meeting. His collar was the latest gates-ajar fashion, high and turned up like a bird's wing. He wore a daytime double-breasted waistcoat and a vest that was cut from a deep burgundy brocade cloth. The gold chains that held his watch in place stood out in the shadows cast by the early afternoon sun that was beaming into the room through the open draperies. Fresh pomade slicked Grips's perfectly cut hair back into a thin line that disap-peared under his collar. Lanford Grips glowed like he was the happiest man on earth. Which was hardly the case.

Nobody did stiff and formal as well as Lanford Grips as far as Charlotte was concerned. Nor was his expectation of her presentation any less than of his own. Little Ling had helped her into her newest outfit, consisting of two gray skirts that left a short train of a lighter shade of burgundy, with the larger back skirt fitted over her bustle. It was no mistake that the colors of her dress coordinated with Lan-ford Grips's outfit. While they weren't known as a romantic couple, there could be no mistaking that they were engaged in a deep business partnership.

Charlotte's undergarments held her tight, upright, and her posture was as proper as would be deemed acceptably fit for any occasion. Still, she was extremely uncomfortable. The skirts and jackets were heavy, and she was warmer than usual. It was all she could do to keep from sweating outright.

A tall wall clock ticked loudly, offering the only direct sound in the room. The clock accented the European furniture with its rosewood veneer, rippled molding, and octagon shape, offering eight days of time in one winding. The chimes were loud and distinct in announcements, and never seemed to stop. Charlotte had halted the pendulum of the clock in her room so she could sleep—or try to.

Sunlight from the open draperies struck renegade flecks of dust on occasion, making the direct light boring into the room look like a sky full of tiny stars that had dared to come out in the daylight.

Noise from the busy street below made its way upward, through the closed windows. The sound was muffled, but there was no mistaking the coming and going of carriages and wagons and stagecoaches—all bound for, or coming from, the West. The idea that Charlotte was on the cusp of, at the very beginning of, or at the very end of a million journeys was never far from her mind. St. Louis had a heartbeat like no other city she had ever been to. Dreams were born and fortunes were lost every day, at the gateway to the West. It was a matter of luck, timing, and smart business which way the fates would decide for a person.

Charlotte had her own plans to execute in St. Louis. But that's all they were at the moment—just plans. Unfortunately, her presence in the impending meeting had not been part of those plans.

She knew better than to try and strike up a conversation with Lanford. He was in no mood for small talk, and neither was she. A distinct tension had existed between the two of them since his surprise arrival St. Louis.

It was one thing to be under the continued watch of Yen and Cheng as she traveled from Kansas City, but it was entirely another to think of herself as not free to travel, to be prevented from coming and going as she pleased. But then, that had been the case for a long time, if Charlotte allowed herself to fully face the truth of her recent, and current, circumstances. Even her dreams seemed to tease her about her attachment to Lanford—to John Barlow—though they were foggy and nearly forgotten in the light of day. Nearly. Not entirely. The memories of their past together were never too far away, though she would be better served, especially at the moment, if she could forget everything that had happened between the two of them.

"I have something for you, Charlotte," Grips said, breaking the silence. He brought his right glove up and pushed a small box on the desk toward her. "A token of my appreciation."

Charlotte walked over the desk, curious, and opened the box, expecting a piece of jewelry, but she found a man's gold watch instead. She looked at Grips oddly, and he just returned a cold stare. "A watch?"

Grips shrugged. "An artifact that our friend, Joe Straut, missed in one of his duties. I thought it would be a good reminder for you."

"A reminder of what?"

"What can happen if you overlook something." Grips smiled then, sat back in the chair smugly, and tucked his gloved hooks back underneath the desk.

A cold chill traveled down Charlotte's spine, but she opened the watch anyway. It was a fine timepiece, clean and shiny, and opposite the face was a picture of a man and a woman that she recognized from the newspaper, from the train ride to Kansas City from St. Louis. There was an inscription on the back that read: *To my wonderful husband on the occasion of our marriage. 07/04/1871. JLW.*

"Should I know whose watch this is?" Charlotte asked, closing it and placing it back into the box.

"If you don't, you will soon enough. Soon enough."

A tap came at the door, interrupting the conversation, and Bojack Wu entered the room soft-footedly, his black

Chinese pantaloons and blouse as impeccable as usual, though he seemed a little more polished, too, for the occasion at hand.

"It is my pleasure to present to you the gentlemen you are expecting, sir," Bojack Wu said.

"Show them in," Lanford Grips said. He flicked his wrist in acceptance. Old habits were hard to break.

Bojack Wu bowed and walked out of the room backward, never breaking eye contact with Grips.

Charlotte stiffened, realigned her posture, and set her jaw in place. She didn't know how the businessmen would respond to her presence in the meeting. Expectations of women commonly called for them to be dismissed as unknowledgeable or to be treated casually—in this case, either action would be as much a mistake as a show of curiosity about Lanford Grips's hands, or lack thereof.

Bojack Wu ushered in the two gentlemen, one approaching old age with an air of erect dignity, while the other man was younger, frumpier, disheveled, like he had just walked out of the nearest saloon, even though it was morning. Not only did the younger man need a new tailor, he looked as if he needed a shave, a haircut, and was in serious need of a bath. Charlotte did her best not to turn up her nose at the smell he brought with him into the room. The odd thing about his appearance was that he carried a leather satchel that looked like it had just been tanned last week.

"I present Mr. Harrington Fetterman, executive vice president for the Union Pacific Railroad, and his associate, Hiram Pinter, esquire, attorney at law," Bojack Wu said. He bowed and swept his arm again, only this time toward Charlotte. "And may I present to you, gentlemen, Miss Charlotte Brogan, an associate of Mr. Grips."

Lanford Grips stood up but did not offer to shake hands with the men. Instead, Charlotte, well versed in the dance that was taking place, stepped forward and offered her hand to the older gentleman. "Please forgive Mr. Grips. An injury from the war prevents him from the simplest cordialities."

The older man nodded, stepped forward, then took Charlotte's hand and kissed it. "Harrington Fetterman at your service, ma'am. I am well aware of Mr. Grips's contribution to the cause. We have known one another for quite some time. But you, Miss Brogan, well, you are a breath of fresh air."

"Oh, please, call me Charlotte." She fluttered her eyelashes slightly. She loved to flirt with old men. Especially old men with money.

Hiram Pinter remained where he was and eyed Charlotte, Fetterman, and Lanford Grips suspiciously.

Fetterman stepped back, and Hiram Pinter stepped in but did not kiss Charlotte's hand. Instead, he took her hand in his and shook it gently, limply, then returned to his place next to his partner.

"Please, gentlemen, sit," Grips said, returning to his seat. "May I offer you some refreshments?"

Charlotte sat down in a chair next to the desk, and it was only after she was comfortably seated that Fetterman and Pinter took their places.

Harrington Fetterman immediately looked uncomfortable in the chair provided. He was a tall man, and the legs of the chair were low, forcing him to sit forward. His knees looked like they could touch his chin without much effort. "I hate to be a bearer of bad news, but we need to get down to business, Mr. Grips. The delays we have suffered can no longer be tolerated. Refreshments will be appreciated as a celebration once our deal is closed."

Grips smiled, nodded to Bojack Wu, sending him off, and leaned forward. "I assure you, Harrington, the need for the delay has been as difficult for me as it has been for you."

Hiram Pinter sat back, looked bored, and said nothing. His puffy face was void of any emotion, and Charlotte was sure he was going to tip over and pass out at any moment.

"Have you indeed acquired the deeds to the properties in question, Mr. Grips?" Fetterman demanded. "I have kept the wolves at bay as long as I can."

"I have the deed to the Wilmington forestlands in Minnesota," Grips said. He brought his gloves up and pushed a document to the edge of the desk, offering it to Fetterman.

Harrington Fetterman ignored the offer. Instead, Pinter leaned forward, took the paper, and started to examine it.

"As you know," Fetterman said, "the need for timber, especially the timber that you have offered to sell to us, is great as the railroad expands. There are a thousand miles to cover to complete the St. Louis–to–San Francisco line. The demand for delivery of that timber increases daily, and no matter our past relationship, I need to show immediate results, or this deal will be null and void."

"As you know, Harrington, I have been in this business for a very long time," Grips said. "And we have done business with the Union Pacific in almost every phase of construction of the railway. I assure you that I am aware of the demand."

"It is the supply that concerns us," Fetterman said. "Or the proper supply." He glanced over to Pinter.

The lawyer nodded. "The document looks to be in order, Mr. Fetterman," he said, then turned his attention to Grips. "But you realize that the two brothers that were equal shareholders in the Wilmington holdings were recently found murdered?"

"Yes, of course, a sad occurrence," Grips said.

"Murdered on a train in which you were traveling," Pinter said.

"I assure you, I have spoken to the authorities," Grips countered, "and I have given them all of the information they required, a full account of my whereabouts, with witnesses. The men responsible for this heinous crime will be brought to justice. I assure you I am doing everything I can to make sure that happens with great expediency."

"There will be an inquiry into the estate of the Wilmington

brothers," Pinter said, as he pulled papers out of the satchel and handed them to Grips. "A hold has been placed on all unfiled transactions conducted by the Wilmingtons before their unfortunate deaths. Your deed was signed on the train, and there is no sign of the money in their belongings."

Lanford Grips shook his head angrily. "They were robbed. It is very obvious what has happened here, and I have had nothing to do with any of this tragedy."

"I hate to question what is at hand, Mr. Grips, but is it really that obvious?" Harrington Fetterman said.

"Yes, it is," Charlotte said. All three men looked at her with great surprise, but that did not stop her. "May I remind you that Mr. Grips is a longtime associate of the current appropriation committee chairman in Washington, Senator Lancaster Barlow? Now, how would it appear for an associate of a man of such great stature and position to be involved in something as unsavory as you suggest? I met the Wilmingtons and was especially impressed with the wife of one of the brothers. Jennifer, I believe, was her name." She cast a quick glance to Grips, acknowledging that she had figured out who the watch belonged to. "I was saddened by their desire to sell all of their holdings in their trust. The opportunities the West presents put fool's gold in some eyes, and those three had the fever. They let their guard down, that is all, and their fancy wares attracted the attention of two unsavory men. It happens all of the time, gentlemen, as you well know. And, might I add, that I was in Mr. Grips's company from the moment the Wilmingtons boarded the train until they met with him. I assure you that he is innocent of anything other than being in the wrong place at the wrong time."

Harrington Fetterman stood up. "I am quite aware of Mr. Grips's long association with the Union Pacific Railroad, and with Senator Barlow, a man whom I call my friend, as well. But this additional delay, while the inquiry takes place, will most likely cost us our relationship, and the delivery of the timber will remain unfulfilled. Do you know how much money that will cost us, Mr. Grips?"

"Yes," Grips said, as he stood up, staring the older man directly in the eye. "I do. Exactly four hundred thousand dollars for every week that there is a delay in the movement west to San Francisco."

"Exactly."

"It is an amount that the railroad can ill afford to lose," Grips said.

"And you have a solution?"

Charlotte held her tongue, though she wanted to barge in.

"Yes," Lanford Grips said. "I will have the deed to the Fume holdings in Minnesota and Wisconsin in my possession in a matter of days. It is a transaction I have been working on for quite some time now."

"That holding has been unavailable to us since the unfortunate death of Senator Barlow's son, John. It was jointly owned by the man's killer. How is it possible now that it, all two million acres of timber, will be available to us?" Harrington Fetterman asked.

Charlotte stood then and smiled at the two men. "Upon the death of the killer, I will inherit the right to sell all of that timber, Mr. Fetterman. I am the sole beneficiary of Lucas Fume's estate. On the death of his father, it was all left to me."

Harrington Fetterman smiled with satisfaction. "Then all is well. I will expect to see you both at the annual ball this coming Saturday?"

"We wouldn't miss it for the world," Charlotte said with a smile, glad finally to have the invitation. "Not for the world."

THIRTY-NINE

DARKNESS SURROUNDED JOE STRAUT. THE
road was muddy from the recent rain, but the air smelled
clean as it pushed past his face. The horse underneath him
was a good one, a roan mare with a bitchy attitude that was
reasonably easy to contain. She'd bucked a bit when he'd
first urged her on, when he'd stolen her from the dead train
robbers, but she'd grown accustomed to his straightforward
handling pretty quickly. Straut had never been the kind of
man who took out his anger on a beast, big or small. This
one rode like it had been whipped regularly.

Straut was still under the assumption that the mare's previous owner was a robber and nothing more. Not a bounty
hunter. Not a killer on a mission. It was hard to tell if he was
right. Those eggs hadn't fully hatched yet. But one thing was
for certain, Joe Straut was keeping a keen eye on the trail
behind him.

Deets was about a half a length back there to his right,
pushing his horse, a thin gelding with tall legs and a gentler

demeanor than the horse Straut rode. The gelding was skittish, winced at thunder, either showing a lack of experience or, like the mare, that it had had a brutal, unspeakable past.

The two men had talked little. Fleeing was all that mattered. They didn't know where they were or where they were going—not directly. Once they got their bearings, Straut would consult the map and continue his search for Lucas Fume. But all that really mattered at the moment was that they get as far away from the train as they could as quickly as possible.

Caution hadn't been thrown to the wind in their escape. Just the opposite. Although Straut knew he'd just added enemies to a growing list, he could have joined in the mayhem, volunteered to help in the robbery—but revealing himself was not a risk he was willing to take then or anytime soon.

Straut turned his head to look behind him, took in a long gaze of darkness, wished he had vision that would cut through the night, but no such thing existed. He wasn't about to light a torch.

So far, no one was chasing them, or at least close enough to notice.

It was always a risky proposition running full out at night. There was little to see beyond the berm, just a continuous line of thick trees that blurred in the darkness. Occasionally, they would pass by a cabin beyond the road, a clearing cut out of the trees allowing entrance. Their unexpected presence always set off the worrisome bark of a lone dog. Other times, coyotes would yip in the distance, or something unidentifiable would cross ahead of them on the road, scurrying to get out of their way; maybe a coon or a fox caught unaware on a night's hunt. Owls hooted and screamed with regularity, and far away to the east, thunder rumbled. A streak of lightning would give brief vision to the cloudy night sky, then blackness would quickly return.

They rode hard until they could ride no more. Hour upon

hour. Long enough for the clouds to part and a thumbnail moon to poke out of nowhere, like an odd smile, dim and maniacal in its appearance, spurning Straut for his attempt to outrun Lanford Grips's grasp. But run he did, until his horse just plum fagged out, slowed, and whinnied to an angry, defiant stop. They had no choice but to make camp.

The sun nearly jumped up from the horizon, bringing with it a dense heat and humidity that Joe Straut had nearly forgotten existed.

Luckily, there had been a bedroll and a gum blanket among the supplies packed on the roan mare, suggesting a long ride instead of a local robbery to Straut—but that didn't surprise him. He was just glad that he didn't have to lie directly on the wet ground to catch a wink.

Deets still slept, curled up at the base of a young oak tree, the leaves and branches perfectly shaped like an open parasol. Straut envied the man's ability to stay in the land of slumber so easily. He had tried to sleep with one eye open, not wanting to journey into the next world unaware with a slit throat, or a bullet put to his head by an unidentified assassin. If he had his way, Straut would go out on a deathbed laid out long in the future. His current predicament didn't lend itself to that kind of future, one where the only way to escape was old age. But he could change that. Or at least try.

Straut woke up Deets. They cleaned their faces, took care of the necessary business demanded by morning itself, packed up, and continued to head south.

Both horses seemed more relaxed running in the daylight. They were rested, fed, and watered, and looked like loyal steeds, instead of two stolen horses. Straut shook his head at the idea. On top of everything else, he was a horse thief now. Just like there was an end to the road they were on, there was most certainly an end to a rope with his name on it, just waiting.

A cabin sat off in the distance, with smoke curling up lazily out of the chimney. Two healthy white milk cows chawed fresh grass in a lazy meadow that stretched down to a fast-running creek. A thin cloud of freshly hatched mayflies swayed over the creek on a slight, comfortable breeze. Hills abounded beyond the cabin, fresh and green, rolling out of sight, offering no clue as to where exactly they were. The air was full of the aroma of fresh-bloomed wild-flowers, causing Straut to consider the possibility of drunk-enness, and the hope that spring brought with it every year.

"I always wanted a place like this," Deets said. He'd sidled his gelding up next to Straut's mare. Neither horse seemed to mind. They appeared to like each other's company.

"Why didn't you find your way there?"

Deets shrugged. "I guess the war happened. Once't I went home, it wasn't there no more. I kind of had a sour stomach for a few years, if you know what I mean."

"I do," Straut said. "I surely do. But time's passed now. Maybe you ought to think about that kind of thing again."

"Settling down? What with all this trouble we got on our tails?"

"Seems like the best time to me."

"You still think we ought to go our separate ways, Sarge? That's it, ain't it?"

Straut nodded. "I do. Two men are easier to find than one."

"I ain't good at bein' on my own."

"I understand. It's just somethin' I want you to consider. Time just might come when it's best we split and go our own way. Will you at least think about that?"

"Well, I suppose so." Deets looked down at the horn of the saddle, then back to Straut. "What about you, Sarge? You ever want a place of your own, somethin' to tend to? A comfortable porch rail to kick up your feet on?"

Straut shook his head no, never taking his eyes off the cabin. "Ain't got no such hankerin' for home. I guess I lost the taste for it in the war, too."

"War changed everythin', you ask me."

"It did. We got a wide view now. The West is opened up, and there's plenty of ways for a man to renew himself beyond the big river. Maybe I'll just ride west once this is all over and see what all the fuss is. I'd like to see the mountains that pierce the clouds. The Yellowstone Valley sounds like a place of magic. I'd like to see that, too."

"Be a good way to live , I 'spect, out on your own," Deets said. "Especially if you ain't lookin' over your shoulder."

"My plan's still the same," Straut answered. He tapped his breast pocket, the map of drop spots that Lanford Grips had given him before sending them east. "Find Lucas Fume, and go from there. I figure the Boss'll want him more than us."

"I hope you're right," Deets said. "I sure hope you're right."

To Straut's surprise, the cabin was empty. The two men stood in the doorway, surveying the small, tidy room. A pan of beans sat on top of the Franklin stove in the center of it. The stove was warm to the touch, but not hot. Nothing, other than the pan, seemed to be out of place. The single bed in the far corner was made up with a quilt tucked in at the corners and a feather pillow atop it. Clean dishes were stacked on the cupboard, and the room smelled lived in, not old, musty, or abandoned.

"Go out to the barn and check on the horses," Straut said to Deets.

Deets looked at him oddly, let his hand slide down to his holster, then walked cautiously out the door.

The pan of beans bothered Straut. He couldn't keep from staring at it. Nothing in the cabin was out of place except the unfinished beans. They should have been stored or eaten. But it didn't look like there'd been a tussle of any kind. Most likely, whoever lived there had been called away unexpectedly. Still, he couldn't help but feel like he was missing something.

After several quiet minutes, Deets walked back inside with no noticeable expression on his face. "Ain't no horses out there. Fresh bag of feed had just been opened, and there was some day-old shit in the stall, but nothin' struck me as odd."

Straut nodded, then made his way to the cupboard and opened it. He leaned in and grabbed a couple of cans of the beans, then stood up, dug a nickel out of his pocket, and flipped it into the place where the beans had sat.

"What ya doin'?" Deets asked.

"I might be a lot of things, but I ain't no thief. Let's get out of here before whoever's place this is comes back to it."

"I sure wouldn't leave this place if I didn't have to."

"Me, neither," Joe Straut said solemnly. "Me, neither."

The day wore on, and they finally came to a small town that gave Straut his bearings. The town, Dyersburg, wasn't much to speak of, but it confirmed his sense that he was back inside the state of Tennessee. Nashville was two hundred miles east, and the way he figured it, they still had a good stretch of travel in front of them. He checked the map and found that he was closer to one of the drop spots than he was the city. It was still a day's ride away, at least. He'd have to give good care to the horses, and they'd have to sleep out on the side of the road, but that was all right with him. His gut told him that Lucas Fume was nowhere near Nashville by now, but it was only a feeling; he had no way to know for sure.

Straut and Deets kept their heads low and hats down, and made their way out of Dyersburg long before the sun began to drop below the horizon. As far as Straut could tell, no one gave them much notice. The town was bustling, with lots of people coming and going, and they hadn't done anything to draw any undue attention to themselves.

The road got quieter once they were away from the town, and they both hustled the horses up to speed, hoping to make up some miles before dark came on.

Nothing got in their way or gave them reason to worry. The farther they got away from the train, the more Joe Straut relaxed. But not so much that he didn't cast an occasional glance over his shoulder.

Night came and went, and the next morning found the pair packing up, preparing to leave their camp spot. The night before, they had happened upon a slight clearing that butted up against a deep, heavily wooded ravine. It was a perfect place to rest themselves and their horses. No one could see their camp from the road, and Straut had built a small, cautious fire as close to the edge of the ravine as he could get, not wanting to draw any attention. Before he went to sleep, he'd wondered about the occupant of the abandoned cabin. He hoped whoever it was had made it home safe.

Straut cinched his saddle one last time and froze just as he pulled back. He'd heard a twig snap behind him.

Deets was in his periphery, loading up his saddlebag, but didn't seem to hear anything. Straut eased his hand to his Colt Open Top. His finger found the grip just as he saw the shadow.

It was like a black cloud had passed in front of the morning sun, sucking all of the light out of the tranquil camp spot. But it was no cloud. It was a man. A Chinese man dressed in his traditional black garb, pigtail streaming behind him, his onyx eyes focused with deadly intent on Deets. It was either Yen or Cheng, Straut couldn't tell which, but the little man's moon face was familiar. And he was flying through the air. Or it looked like the Chinaman was flying, like he had acquired magic somehow—but in reality, he had jumped silently from the limb of a tall live oak that stretched out over the ravine. Somehow he'd been waiting for them to move about; he could have climbed up there during the night for all Straut knew.

There was no time to warn Deets. The attacker flew through the air with his right leg fully extended, his bare foot vertical, toes pointed to the sky while his other leg was tucked back. The heel of the Chinaman's foot caught Deets right behind the ear. Skin against skin exploded, sounded like thunder, followed by the unmistakable sound of cracking bone, a neck breaking.

The Chinaman did not recoil, but followed his position though, chopping his hands, slicing into Deets's body as it crumpled to the ground. There was a groan, a look of sudden surprise on Deets's face, and a recognition of fatal pain as Straut's sidekick tumbled forward to the ground. He had no idea what had hit him. His head bounced off a big rock, and blood exploded from his mouth, as he came to a final rest.

The Chinaman tucked into a roll and dove over the ravine, out of sight.

By the time this all had transpired, Straut had been able to fully grab his gun but not pull it free of the holster. His mind raced. He knew that if the man *was* Yen or Cheng, then the other one was not far away. Where there was one, there was one more, and Straut found himself in the open, his only cover the roan mare, who had sensed something was wrong as soon the Chinaman appeared above them.

Like Deets, Straut didn't see his attack coming. Before he could lift the gun, he was struck in the back, right between the shoulder blades. The force of the blow flung him forward into the empty saddle. His head nearly hit the horn. The horse screeched and bellowed, reacting to the surprise, then lurched forward into a reactionary run, legs kicking up in the air, screaming with alarm.

Consciousness had not left Straut, but he could barely breathe. Still, he had his senses about him. The horse had cushioned the blow, and he bounced backward. As he fell, he spun, raising the six-shooter, pulling the trigger at nothing but a blur as he stumbled to the side.

The shot was lucky. It caught the second Chinaman, who had most likely not been counting on Straut surviving the kick in the arm, just at the shoulder. The little man was close, and the shot knocked him off his feet, sending him flying flat on his back.

The wounded Chinaman looked like a turtle flipped over, struggling to right himself, trying to protect his openness, his weakness. Straut was too fast for Yen or Cheng to recover. He stopped his fall with his left hand, pulled the hammer back with his thumb, and fired again, shooting the Chinaman directly in the stomach.

Straut fired again and again, just to make sure the sneaky little bastard was dead.

There was no dust; the ground was still wet. But once the echo of the shots vanished, silence returned. Straut could hear his own heart beating and feel his fear growing inside. He expected to die at any second. When he tried to stand, pain shot through him like he'd been hit again—but he hadn't been. The attack had left him with some cracked ribs. He could barely stand, and he immediately fell to his knees on his first try. His eyes darted about looking for anything that moved. Nothing did. Deets was as still as the dead man that he was, and the Chinaman hadn't moved. Flies had already found him.

Another twig snapped—only this time it was over the ravine. Straut pulled himself up, crouched, and made his way to the edge of the ravine, right before it descended downward.

The other Chinaman was pulling himself up off the ground, out of a tangle of raspberry thickets that he had obviously dove into. His yellow-skinned face was covered in scratches that had just begun to bleed.

Straut didn't take time to consider his actions. He leveled the Colt downward and fanned it, firing off the remaining rounds in the cylinder.

The Chinaman tumbled backward, the shots riddling his body. He rolled to the bottom of the ravine, out of sight.

Straut collapsed forward, taking a deep breath, glad to

be alive, but sad that Deets hadn't taken his advice and left out on his own.

Nothing else mattered now but staying alive. Straut knew that Lanford Grips was going to keep coming after him until he was dead. That was all too clear.

There was only one thing left that Straut knew to do to make sure that didn't happen.

FORTY

LUCAS AND ZEKE RODE HARD, LEAVING LIB-
ertyville, or what was left of it, behind them. The horses
responded in kind, offering no hesitation or restraint. It was
as if the heavily loaded saddlebags didn't exist at all. They
were all running for their lives, with the smell of smoke,
gunpowder, and sadness blasted inside their nostrils and
minds.

The road ahead of them was clear and unhindered. Lucas
was acutely aware of everything that moved—flittering
birds, scurrying squirrels, or unknown creatures diving into
the underbrush that lined the road. His hand was never far
from the fully loaded Single-Action Colt at his side.

There was no time for regret, or to reconsider returning
for Avadine. She was in the best place she could be, pro-
tected by those that knew her best. Miss Lainie would need
caring for, if she lived through the day. Being hunted down
like an animal was no way for any woman to live. Still, it

pained Lucas to leave her behind. Regret was a familiar feeling, but one that he hadn't felt in a long time.

He urged the bay gelding on a little harder, wanting to be as far away from the battle at Libertyville as he could get. Zeke did the same, riding nose to nose with him, sometimes falling back, but never rushing out in the lead. Only Lucas knew where they were headed, and he was comfortable with the Negro watching his back. Zeke had proven himself over and over again.

They continued to run full out for as long as they could, pulling back only to consider the horses. By the time the afternoon sun started toward evening, Lucas had begun to look for a place to rest and water their mounts.

It didn't take long for the trees to open up to a meadow. A stand of cottonwoods stood in the distance, towering over the bend of a fast-running creek. Lucas slowed the gelding, looked over to Zeke, nodded to the trees, then exited the road on the first clear deer path he could find.

The bend offered the perfect place to rest. A head-high thicket of wild berries would hide them from the road and allow them to keep a lookout for anyone giving them chase. The horses welcomed the chance to stop, both flipping their tails and snorting happily as Lucas and Zeke dismounted.

"I'll water the horses, Mistuh Lucas," Zeke said, taking both sets of reins in his big hands.

Lucas nodded, making sure he had clear sight of the road from where he stood.

Birdsong returned around him. Waxwings darted about at the tops of trees, passing the time until the berries below ripened and offered them a fruitful bounty. It would be a while, long into summer, before that happened. Until then, the birds had to satisfy their appetites on the abundance of insects that survived off the creek. It felt good to stop, but this was by no means a way station or a spot to make camp.

Zeke tied off the horses and ambled back to Lucas. "You knows where we is?"

"About three stops out of Nashville."

"Close enough. Columbia ain't too far to the south, we keep headin' that ways."

Lucas shook his head no. "Nothing in Columbia for us."

"Goin' home would be a big mistake, Mistuh Lucas."

A tenseness rolled up Lucas's spine, and he stood stiffer. "There's nothing for me at Seven Oaks, or Harper's Belle for that matter. Once I was convicted of killing John Barlow, my father washed his hands of me. I had disparaged the family name with my heinous crime. I think that was the worst thing of all, losing my father and Charlotte. I don't know if either place still stands. I don't know anything."

"Do you wants to know?"

Lucas looked upon Zeke's face curiously. "My father was an aged man when I was dragged into prison. He may very well be dead by now. What do you know?"

"Nothin', no I don't knows nothin' about your folks. I surely don't. But I knows how these mens will hunt you, and that's where they'll be lookin' for you."

"And you?"

"Done found me in Libertyville. My father's blood ran through the foundation of that church. It be gone, and so is he. Home is where I stand, Mistuh Lucas. Just where I stand and breathe."

"Mine, too. Mine, too, Zeke."

They let a long silence fill the gap between them. It was a peaceful place that they had stumbled on. There were no buildings in sight, no cabins, barns, or fences to offer any evidence of humans in the world they stood in. The land rose up behind them, offering a dry spot in a wet season, and for a long second, Lucas thought it'd be a good place to build a home, settle into a life of solitude and hard work, bartering with the land in a harmonious way so that they both could prosper. But it was a fleeting thought. One he'd had more than once but let go. The settled life was not for him, though some days he sure wished it was.

"We need to head to Parker's Crossroads," Lucas said. "There was a battle there in the winter of '62. General Forrest was trapped after he destroyed a railroad line, slowing the Federals as they built up strength for Vicksburg. Forrest fought his way out of the battle by ordering his men to fight both ways, forward and back. There was a cache drop just beyond the lower river battery outside of Fort Donelson. It'll be the first place I check."

"And what if you is wrong? What if there ain't nothin' there?"

"Then it's on to Dyersburg, to an old hotel. There's a drop on the third floor just outside the attic door. Take up the plank, and there should be a treasure box there."

"You be bettin' that these places are still there," Zeke said.

"I am," Lucas answered. "I'm betting that the person who sent me the message, who arranged for us both to be free, knows how I think. It's all I know to do."

"Then it's what we do," Zeke said. "I'll go to this Parker's Crossroads with ya, but maybe not beyond."

Lucas nodded. "You're free to go on your own anytime you want, Zeke. I know staying with me is a risky proposition."

FORTY-ONE

LUCAS KNEW THAT THE BEST WAY TO GET TO Fort Donelson was to skirt the Cumberland River, but as with the escape, the spring rains would make that trek more difficult, not easier. A summer drought would have been a welcome gift, but there was no choice in the timing of this journey. He couldn't wait out the seasons.

There was no question that navigating the main roads, especially with Zeke at his side, would be difficult, and dangerous. A lot of eyes would be looking for them during the day, and during the night, as well. Lucas would rather face a law-abiding posse than the torch-bearing Klan riders any day. Neither would be his preference. He knew little of the Klan since they had grown in stature and fearsomeness during his time in prison. What little he did know about the organization had been learned at Libertyville. The Klan was a force to be feared. Marauders operating outside of the law always were.

It was nearly a hundred-mile ride west to Parker's

Crossroads and the fort, but as it was, they'd already made up some of the miles lost during their escape. If they carried any luck at all, it would be almost a two-day ride, pushing both horses as hard as they could go.

The farther away from Libertyville they got, the more Lucas was able to relax, to breathe a little easier. It felt good to have a horse underneath him. He hadn't lost his riding skills like he'd thought he might have. They came back pretty quickly.

Zeke had no trouble keeping up. Both horses seemed to be equitable modes of transportation. They rode until the sun dropped away from sight, leaving the world gray and full of shadows.

They found a spot to camp north of Columbia, off a dirt lane in a hidden meadow. Lucas was sore by the end of the day's ride, and his mood had turned sullen. The idea of never seeing Avadine again didn't sit well with him, and he worried about the outcome of the plight she was left behind in. Far Jackson was a smart man, but the whole village was up against odds that none of them knew the extent of. Still, there was no turning back. He ate some jerky, muttered to Zeke that he was tired, then collapsed onto his bedroll under a beech tree.

There were no nightmares or dreams to disturb Lucas's sleep. He felt safer out in the middle of nowhere, sleeping under the stars, than he ever had in prison.

Lucas awoke stiff, hungry, and unsure of where he was.

Zeke was up, packing his horse. The jerky and cold beans allowed for them to have a meal without lighting a fire. Once they were on their way, there'd be no sign that they'd ever stopped. It would be like they had never been there. More than once, Lucas was tempted to tell Zeke that he would have made a fine spy, but he withheld comment because of his understanding of the origin of the Negro's stealth skills.

"Good thing there was owls and insects about last night, Mistuh Lucas, otherwise you snorin' mighta brought a farmer out lookin' for a lost pig." Zeke smiled.

Lucas ran his hand through his hair and eyed the man narrowly. "You seem to know how to pick a bad time to pick at a man."

"I wakes up happy."

"Good for you." Lucas squinted into the distance, looked to the sky to check the weather. There was nothing to obscure his view, and there were no clouds in sight. Satisfied that there'd be nothing from above to hinder the day's ride, he made his way to the trees, relieved himself, then made his way back to the camp. "I figure we can make the fort by nightfall," he said.

Zeke nodded, then climbed onto the diamond-nosed gelding with ease. "If the good Lawd be willin'."

"All right, if you say so." Lucas rolled up his bed and followed suit onto the gelding.

Zeke stared at Lucas sadly but did not make any more comments.

They rode away as quickly as they had arrived, heading due west, their eyes peeled for any travelers coming from ahead or behind them. When they did stop, there was little conversation between the two men. Their mission was clear: Arrive at the old cache drop as soon as possible, in one piece, without drawing any attention to themselves, if that was possible.

Lucas knew that traveling to Fort Donelson might be a mistake. He could possibly be wrong, and there could be nothing waiting for them. If that were the case, then it would be on to the next one, and the next. It was all he knew to do.

Knowing what to do next would have been easier if the code had gone on to tell him where to go. But it hadn't. It had told him all that he really needed to know: John Barlow was alive.

If it was a trick, he'd jumped at it without taking a second look, taking the bait like a starving fish. If that was the case, it wouldn't have been the first time he'd been snookered. But he was willing to take the chance that he was right. With that consideration in mind, he pushed the bay gelding to run faster toward Fort Donelson, knowing full well that the horse wouldn't be worth much if they didn't make it there alive.

The lower battery still looked over the Cumberland River, though most of the cannons, originally seacoast artillery, had been carted off. The embrasures still stood—rock foundations with openings that had initially been constructed of sandbags and rawhide.

The cannons had been used to fight off Union ironclad and timberclad gunboats, protecting the supply routes to Clarksville and Nashville. That period of the war had been a busy time for Lucas, and as he made his way down the hill that overlooked the river and the long line of embrasures, he tried to fight off the memories. He was here for a reason, not to reminisce.

Dusk was quickly giving way to night, grayness easing into murky blackness. A quarter moon waxed upward, rising above a deep line of trees in the distance. Crickets chirped, and over the plain of grasses on the hill swallows swooped and dove for a quick evening meal of emerging insects. A soft breeze caressed the river, rising up the hill and offering a pleasant bit of relief from the warm day.

Other than the old cannon stands there was no sign that suggested there had once been a battle here. The earth had forgotten the heroics and the cowardice that had played itself out on that spot just a matter of years before. Lucas sighed. *If only the bloody madness was truly so easy to forget for humans as it was for the land.*

Zeke followed after Lucas slowly after tying off and hobbling the horses. "You sure you knows where you is, Mistuh Lucas?"

"I got us here, didn't I?"

"We was lucky to make it unbidden, without bein' approached none."

"That we were. Your skills and knowledge of the roads leading here saw to that."

"Those smarts was hard won."

"I'm sure they were," Lucas said, eyeing the embrasure closest to the river. It would have been the hardest one to reach during the time of war, making it the last place a Federal would think to look for a Confederate cache. He made his way there without looking back, confident that Zeke was following him.

Lucas touched the bottom of the foundation, limestone smoothed by time and weather, still warm from the day, then counted up three blocks. That one was loose, and it didn't take much effort to pull it away and open up a space that had already welcomed the darkness.

"You got any of those lucifers on you?" Lucas asked, staring into the hole, trying to see if anything was inside. There was no way he was sticking his hand into a dark hole if he didn't have to.

Zeke didn't answer directly. Instead, the evening turned light, briefly, in a small way, like a little star had fallen from the heavens, making its way down to the ground and stopping at eye level. Lucas and Zeke were head to head, both staring at the hole, lit by the wood match.

"Damn, it," Lucas said. "It's empty."

"Look like a grave that's been robbed to me," Zeke said.

"Well," Lucas said, dropping his gaze to the ground, "I guess we'll head into Dyersburg and check the hotel as long as you're going with me." There was no mistaking the failure in his voice. He looked Zeke in the eye, and both men nodded at the same time, stood up, and turned around.

Zeke didn't have a chance to answer. It was like the air had been pulled from the world. The insects went silent, and dusk fell straight away into the black of night. Except for the lone lucifer still burning in Zeke's hand. Even as the flame grew smaller, it gave off enough light to see what stood before them.

"Ain't gonna be no need for that trip, Lucas Fume. I'm here to kill you," a tall man wearing a black duster said. He had a Colt Open Top in his steady hand, pointed straight at Lucas's head.

FORTY-TWO

JOE STRAUT HELD THE GUN STEADY ON LUCAS Fume. He had expected to find his quarry riding alone. The hulking Negro had made him reconsider his actions, make sure there was no chance that either man could overtake him. There was too much at stake to not have his say.

"You just let that flame go out now, boy," Straut said to the Negro. "And stand still. Both of you. If'n I hear one blade of grass smash down toward me, or a hand slidin' for a gun, I'm pullin' the trigger without any further pleasantries, you understand?"

Neither man acknowledged him; they both just stood still like he'd told them.

The flame died away before Straut got a decent look at the men. He knew the Negro was big, but even in the dark, he looked ragged, wore out. Fume, too, for that matter. Straut had expected him to be taller.

Darkness returned to the lower river battery, and it only took a second for Straut's eyes to adjust to the men in front of him. It was a brief opportunity for the two of them to rush him. He put as much pressure on the trigger as he could without sending the firing pin on an unwanted journey.

Straut was far enough away from them so they'd have to dive at him to touch him, and he was close enough to see the whites of their eyes. "I have what you come lookin' for, Fume," Straut said. "But not on me, so's if you're thinkin' of doin' anything foolish-like, it'd be a mistake. You won't get what you come lookin' for."

"Who are you?" Fume asked. Neither man had moved a muscle after the lucifer burned out. A turn of events that Straut was glad of. He'd expected a fight from all he'd heard about Lucas Fume.

"My name's Joe Straut. I work for a man who operates mostly on the other side of the Big River, Lanford Grips. He sent me to come after you. Didn't matter whether you was dead or alive. He said he wanted your head, and I'm pretty sure he meant it. The rest of you don't matter to him."

Fume shook his head. "That name means nothing to me. I never heard of this Lanford Grips character. Why would he send you after me?"

"Ain't just me. He tried to have you killed in prison."

"I always wondered why I was getting attacked all the time. But I can't recollect a man named Grips that I offended so greatly he'd want to see me dead. I wouldn't forget a name like that."

"I never thought it was the Boss's real name," Straut said. He took a deep breath then, certain on the plan he was about to hatch, the one he'd considered the moment he heard Finney Deets's neck snap, and a little before, if the truth be told. "He travels with a woman by the name of Charlotte Brogan. A redheaded firecracker of a woman. That name mean anything to ya, Fume?"

"Barlow." Lucas seethed half a breath after Straut let Charlotte's name slip off his tongue. She was with him. The thought of it made his head swim. "Is his real name John Barlow?"

"Might be," Straut said. The Negro said nothing, just stood stiff next to Fume. They both looked like silhouettes standing before Straut, tense and ready to fight. "He aims to kill you, and me, too, as far as that goes. Now, I'm gonna tell you this real clear. So listen real careful-like. I'm gonna ease my gun to my side and take my finger off the trigger. I figure I got information that you need and want besides what was in that cache that drew you here, and I'm tellin' you plain and simple that I'll share what I know with you."

"You want to make a deal with us?" Fume asked.

"Somethin' like that," Straut replied. "I just want to stay alive, and killin' you don't seem to help that cause much, the way I see it. Either way, you live or die, I got to fend off what's comin' my way. Seems the Boss has set a team of men after me, too. Already had a dose of it, and lost the only friend I'd say I had in this world. The Boss ain't gonna stop until he gets exactly what he wants. Both of us dead. We got that in common."

"Sounds familiar," Lucas said. "Real familiar."

The campfire burned gently, low and shielded so it couldn't be easily seen from afar. Two rabbits cooked on a spit, dressed and prepared, an hour before the sun set, as an offering of Straut's seriousness about the deal he'd presented to Lucas Fume.

"Why should I trust you?" Lucas asked, sitting across from Straut.

The Negro, a man Fume had introduced as Zeke Henry, was off in the shadows, keeping watch for anything that moved. Straut had warned him of the Chinamen's tactics, since he fully expected that there'd be more of them coming after him.

Fume had asked a fair question as far as Straut was concerned. "I coulda just shot you, once't you opened up that cache. You was a sittin' duck. But here we sit, about to eat a fine meal of rabbit and some spring peas. Ain't that enough of a reason to listen to what I have to say?"

Fume had a look on his face: eyes full of anger, a nose that had been broken in more than one fight, and the same sneer of aristocracy that the Boss wore when he was about to light into a rage. But there was something calmer about Fume than there ever was about the Boss. He didn't seem like a killer, like a man who would inflict pain on a man unless he had to. Maybe that's what Straut wanted to see. He hoped he hadn't made another mistake.

"I suppose you've got a point," Fume said with an audible sigh. "He would know these places, this boss of yours. We worked them together, a long time ago if he truly is John Barlow. And now I've got every reason to believe he is."

Straut nodded. "I figure you know what he's gonna do next, too. That maybe you can outwit him. If that's what you want."

"If I prove he's still alive, I can clear my name, simple as that. It's just that she . . ." Lucas let his words trail off and looked to the ground like he was sad, searching for something he'd lost in the dark, or the past, which was one and the same to a lot of people.

Straut knew the look, and the sound of the words. He stood up, made his way over to his horse, took a newspaper from the saddlebag, and stared at it for it a second. He knew there was no going back, that he was going to have to trust Lucas Fume, if he gave him the information he'd come looking for.

"Here," Straut said, as he made his way back to Fume. "It's bait."

Lucas looked up, took the newspaper, and studied it. "She's going to be at a ball?"

"They figured you'd see it and show up if you got past me, and everythin' else they'd put in front of you."

"They figured right. But they figured I'd be alone."

"I was hopin' you'd say somethin' like that."

"It's up to Zeke if he wants to go or not. You, too, as far

as that goes. I'm still not sure that I trust what you're saying. The only other choice I have is to kill you and go after them on my own."

"You could try that. But if'n I don't go after him, he's comin' after me, one way or the other. I don't know you, Fume, but the Boss asked me to do things I just couldn't do no more. That life ain't for me. The way I see it, ridin' with a man who's out to clear his name is a far more noble way to die than runnin' like a scared rabbit. Any way that fight comes, I'm not runnin'. I can't live like that, neither. You can count on that."

Lucas laid the paper on the ground, next to his boot, and looked Straut directly in the eye. "I'm going to need to know what to expect. I figure Barlow's got the best men around him that he can buy."

"He does. More Chinese foot-fighters for sure and a crew of Irish to back them up. He's got a Chinaman next to him all the time, too. A bodyguard. Bojack Wu. Man walks like a ghost and has hands deadlier than any six-gun I ever saw. Gonna have to get through him to get to the Boss. It ain't gonna be easy."

"Figures his circle would be tight." Lucas stared down at the paper, then back to Straut. "According to this, we've got two days. It's going to be a hard ride to make it in time. It'll be close even if we don't meet any trouble along the way." He paused. "You put this in the cache?"

"No, it was already there."

"That means someone was here recently. Is that all there was?"

Straut shook his head no and walked back to the saddlebag. He grabbed two stacks of money bound together with new twine. By handing the money over to Fume, he knew he was sealing his fate, giving away another route of escape. "Looks like there's about five hundred dollars there. If I'm to guess, I'd say those Chinese left all this here, includin' the newspaper, so you would head out to St. Louis if something happened to them. They knew you'd show up here, just like I did. Grips told me where the caches were. Why wouldn't he employ them to plant the things that would spur you on? Looks like I was right. They thought they'd kill me, but it was the other way around, I killed them—but here you are."

Fume took the money and eyed Straut in a softer, curious way. "You could've been on your way with this. Made a new life for yourself."

"It ain't livin' if you're always afraid from one day to the next that the past is gonna catch up with you. No matter the miles, or the years, a man like Lanford Grips's got a long reach. Might even be able to come after me from the grave, who knows? I wasn't gonna find out. That money was left for you. And this, too," Straut said, digging into his pocket. He pulled out a single piece of paper. "Funny thing is, it's blank. Doesn't say a thing."

Fume dropped the money to his side, jumped to his feet, and snatched the paper out of Straut's nervous hand before he could say boo—or object. Fume's quickness surprised, and impressed, Straut.

"This could be more important than the money," Fume said. There was relief and hope in his voice, and if he was afraid of Straut, that fear was lost to the wind.

Fume leaned down to the fire, unfolded the paper, and held it high enough for it not to burn. In a matter of seconds, letters began to appear on the paper. Letters that made no sense to Straut. They weren't words, just a line of out-of-place letters that meant nothing to a reading man. Straut had heard of such things in the war. Messages sent in code so the other side couldn't read them.

"You know what it says?" Straut asked, watching Fume closely, leery of the magic he'd witnessed on the paper.

Fume stood and nodded his head. "It says: 'Bring her home safe.'" He looked to the ground sadly. "Her father thinks she needs rescuing. It explains a lot. It explains why I'm here."

"Miss Brogan? She never looked like no prisoner to me," Straut said.

"Maybe you weren't looking close enough. You were a prisoner yourself, and you didn't know it. You can't run far enough away from him. You just said it yourself."

"Well," Straut said, "I guess that makes sense, a code and all. I got his password pattern figured out, and I 'spect that'll help us out, too. I just need to run straight toward him. He probably ain't expectin' that."

FORTY-THREE

CHARLOTTE BROGAN SAT NEXT TO THE OPEN
window, listening to a cello player tune his instrument. The
musician was unseen, a floor below, like her a guest in the
White House Hotel. After a long stretch of note plucking,
gentle music, a Bach piece, *Cello Suite no. 1* in G Major,
wafted out into the world on a soft spring breeze. The song
most likely wouldn't be played at the ball, it was too melancholy for that, but was more than likely a favorite practice
piece for the musician. Something to calm the nerves before
the evening's performance.

Charlotte found the music comforting, and she wished
she could stay seated in her spot for the remainder of the
day, but that was impossible. Her ball dress stood on an
hourglass form just outside the wardrobe. It reminded Charlotte of her mother's statues, the marble ones in the parlor
where she and Lucas Fume had made love the first time. No
arms, no head, no legs, trapped in a permanent stance, unable to move, to think, to flee—a woman's plight that was

best left unspoken. Losing her beauty was the least of her worries at the moment.

The dress was a silk off-the-shoulder affair with a plunging neckline intended to show off her alabaster skin, firey red hair, and other, considerable, feminine assets. The color of the fabric was a subdued beige, nearly off-white, less likely to draw attention than a more garish green, which Charlotte would have preferred. Lanford Grips had discounted the notion of color. He thought she would stand out enough with her hair and corseted figure. There was no argument about the dress after that.

There had been no expense spared on the evening's presentation. The dress had been designed and made by none other than Charles Frederick Worth and had arrived by special courier earlier in the morning. A parade of boxes made their way through the lobby of the hotel and were strewn about the room in no particular fashion. It was like Christmas for a little girl who had dreamed of nothing but ball gowns and gentleman callers. Charlotte's dreams had been replaced by nightmares.

Little Ling fussed about the room, going from box to box, doing her best to pick the proper chemise, an underskirt, for the dress. She was perplexed by the abundance of choices, confused between a cotton one and a linen one. One minute she seemed certain of her decision, then the next she walked away, looking for a set of drawers to go along with the fancy dress on the form.

Like all drawers, the ones in Charlotte's closet were open-crotched, giving the wearer ease of use when the need for private matters arose. Once every button was buttoned, and every lace tied in place, it was impossible to disrobe quickly. But for Charlotte, the open crotch served another purpose, one that she hadn't shared with Little Ling just yet. There was one pair that had been altered to her instructions and that she must wear with the dress that was picked out for tonight. Luckily, Lanford, or John, was enough of a gentleman to leave the selection of undergarments to her.

Charlotte didn't pay any mind to the Celestial girl. She was still entranced by the music of Bach. It seemed to offer a calm and tranquility that had been missing from her life recently. Her stomach was already roiled, and there would be no hope for comfort once she had a corset pulled tight around her. There were days when she hated being a woman.

"Missy, you must get dressed or you be late for the carriage ride to the ball," Little Ling said, standing in the middle of the room with a linen chemise in her hand. "You don't want to be late. Mister be very unhappy, and you don't want that."

"No, Little Ling, I don't want that." Just as Charlotte stood up, the musician ended the cello suite, and regret and fear returned fully to her mind. They would remain there until the evening had ended. She was sure of it.

The sound of other instruments tuning and plucking quickly filled the air, and it was apparent that several of the night's musicians had gathered in the room below her. At least it would offer a distraction to the common comings and goings in the street outside the hotel. St. Louis was a noisy city. Especially on a beautiful spring day when there was celebration in the air. The annual Fettermans' Ball was an event that everyone in the city looked forward to in one way or another. It was a cause for commerce, for men to do business, and a time for girls of a certain age to have their coming-out, giving rise to other, smaller parties among the socially inclined.

Charlotte was wearing a simple cotton shift and was fresh from her bath. She pulled it over her head and tossed it aside, leaving her naked in the middle of the room. Little Ling didn't bat an eye at the movement. She'd been in Charlotte's company long enough to expect such things.

Charlotte's hair was dry and in place; all that remained was to tie in the ribbons that would adorn it. "There is one extra thing I must do, Little Ling, before getting dressed. But it must remain a woman's secret. Do you understand?"

"Yes, Missy, of course. I would never tell your secrets."

"I trust you, Little Ling. I trust you more than anyone else who is here with us."

Little Ling, who was dressed as she always was, in her black tunic, pants, and wood sandals, stiffened and nodded solemnly. "You no worry, now, Missy. Today is a fine day, a big party, you makey big entrance and dazzle all the men in St. Louis. I'll see to it."

"But I do worry, Little Ling," Charlotte said. "I worry every second of every day that something will happen to you. To us." She padded over to the bed, unconcerned about her nakedness, lifted up the mattress, and pulled out a knife, a thin dagger that most people called an Arkansas toothpick, and a leather sheath with dangling strips of leather.

Little Ling drew back. A curious, frightened look dropped across her full moon face. "Why you have that under your bed, Missy?"

"I must be prepared, Little Ling." Charlotte tucked the dagger into the leather, propped her right leg up on the bed frame, and strapped the sheath tightly to the inside of her thigh. "Now, get those drawers out that are folded nicely in the bottom of the wardrobe."

Little Ling shook her head no. "Missy, those not nice drawers. They have too big a hole, and a rip down the side. You need nice pretty drawers for such a pretty dress." The Chinese girl walked over to the bed and held up a perfect pair of white ruffled drawers.

"How do you think I'll get to this," Charlotte said, tapping the knife, "if I need it?"

"Why you need it?"

Charlotte sighed. "I hope I don't, Little Ling, but a woman can't be too careful. Especially on a night like this."

Little Ling dropped the good drawers back on the bed, did as she was told, and pulled out the altered ones from the wardrobe.

Charlotte smiled. There were other weapons to hide once

she was fully dressed. A Remington Model 95 double-barreled over-and-under derringer would be stuffed in her small tote, and a smaller, thinner dagger would be fitted up her sleeve. But these were her secrets. Ones not to be shared with anyone. Not even Little Ling.

The sun was starting to tilt toward the horizon as Charlotte Brogan exited the White House Hotel. She was properly dressed and outfitted for the evening in the Charles Frederick Worth dress. Everything was seen as it should be, and unseen as it shouldn't—known and unknown—in ways that she had learned from Rose Greenhow. It tugged at her heart to test Little Ling, but she couldn't be too trusting of anyone on this night. Not now. She was too close to achieving what she'd set out to do.

The doorman, a tall, thin Negro with short, wiry gray hair, closed the door of the hotel behind her. He offered no comment one way or the other about Charlotte's outfit or state of beauty. He just stared straight ahead, like there was something more interesting on the horizon.

Lanford Grips stood in wait at the carriage, next to the open door. Like her, he was sparkling clean, had his hair perfectly brushed in place, and was dressed to the nines. He wore a proper black frock coat, a top hat, and shiny new shoes that looked more like mirrors than leather. Stiff black gloves extended out of his sleeves, giving no cause for any man or woman to question his appendages. Nor was there any outward sign of weapons on his person.

Grips smiled upon seeing Charlotte. "Dear, dear Charlotte, look at you. You are a triumph. You'll be turning all of the heads in the room—eligible, and married, as well."

Charlotte stopped before the man and allowed him to give her a peck on each cheek. "I am only interested in turning the head of one man," she said, cocking her own heard curiously.

"I have no word on his whereabouts. If Lucas Fume is in the city, then he has slipped under the lines unseen and undetected."

"He was good at that."

"We all were."

"What will you do if you don't find him?" Charlotte asked, glancing up at the driver's seat. A black man she didn't know sat with the reins in his hands, staring forward, dressed perfectly in the expected black wool uniform, top hat and all. Bojack Wu sat next to the Negro in his tunic and pantaloons, stiff as a board, like he wasn't listening, but Charlotte knew he was.

"I am a betting man," Lanford Grips said. "And I have gone all in on the thought, on the very notion, that Lucas Fume will make an appearance at the ball tonight. I have risked my entire fortune on knowing him as well as I do. If he is alive and capable, he will be there."

"You're more confident than I've seen you in a while, Mr. Grips," Charlotte said with a smile, offering him her hand so she could steady her entrance into the carriage.

"Lucas Fume believes he's coming to rescue you, dear Charlotte. Only a fool would bet against that."

FORTY-FOUR

LUCAS STOOD A BLOCK AWAY, STARING DOWN
Walnut Street at the St. Louis Hotel. The stately building
was four stories high and constructed of red brick, with a
wide balcony across the front and side, accessible only from
the second floor. The first floor was host to a General Union
Railroad and Steamboat ticket office, for through points
across the United States and Canada, mostly serving the St.
Louis and Chicago railroad. The ballroom was on the top
floor.

The bright sun, a red plate on a clear blue tablecloth sky,
hung tilted toward the west, but looked like it was stuck and
couldn't commit to a proper line of descent. Lucas knew the
sun's hesitation was just an illusion. Just like the formal
attire he'd bought secondhand at a mercantile not far from
the river. Not only had the money in the cache allowed for
train passage from Tennessee for all three men, but it had
helped get them into St. Louis in a completely different way
than might have been expected. Each man rode a different

train, with a predetermined meeting point in the city set and accomplished.

Zeke was off on an errand, gathering the necessary wares for the night's excursion. Straut was out doing a little reconnaissance of his own.

Lucas stood in the shadows, two doors down from a saloon that was as quiet as a funeral parlor, watching the comings and goings at the hotel.

The St. Louis Hotel was busy with guest arrivals; a constant parade of stagecoaches and carriages up from the river paused at the front door, while wagons full of goods in wood crates were diverted to the back of the hotel by a tall, stern-looking Negro in a butler's uniform.

By the time the sun dangled barely above the horizon, the annual Fettermans' Ball would be started, and Lucas's plan would be fully implemented.

There was constant worry that John Barlow would squelch the plan. Lucas was more than aware that Barlow knew his ways, how he thought. But prison had taught Lucas some lessons that he'd lacked in the past, and then there was Zeke and Straut to consider, one being a secure source of backup, while the other remained his ace in the hole. He just hoped that when brass came to bullets Straut would not betray him. As it was, he had no choice but to trust the man.

Lucas stood at the corner for another hour, moving with the milling crowd from one side of the street to the other, trying not to draw attention to himself. Once he saw a wagonload of musicians arrive in front of the hotel, he knew it was time to leave and put the final piece of his plan in place.

The weather acted as a co-conspirator, allowing for what looked to be a perfect evening. The air was cool, but not cold, and held no humidity at all. The sunset was stunning, reaching out over the city with pulsing pink fingers, grabbing gently at the faded tablecloth sky, that looked more yellow now than blue, like it had aged considerably since Lucas had last noticed. There was no sign of the sun. It had disappeared behind the rooftops.

Lucas walked through the service entrance of the St. Louis Hotel without issue. He said, "Yellow seventeen," following Straut's instruction for using Lanford Grips's passwords. The guard looked away with a knowing nod.

Lucas was dressed in full formal attire—black frock coat, matching vest, top hat, and a cane, allowing for a feigned limp. A fresh, proper shave had left his face free of any whiskers except for the thin white mustache above his lip. The mustache had been colored with actor's *mascaro*—greasepaint would have been too obvious. A white wig poked out from underneath the top hat. Wire-frame glasses, tinted green, rested on his nose, making it difficult to see his eyes, at least from a distance. Along with the limp and an old man shuffle, Lucas hunched forward to complete the effect of being frail and aged. It was a favorite getup, one he had perfected long ago on the streets of Washington. Most times, old men were as invisible as Negroes, especially if the perception of deafness was convincingly portrayed. Acting was like riding a horse. The skills of perception and deception came back to him pretty quickly. Costumes helped complete the transition.

Piano music and the roar of gladness and reception radiated from the grand lobby of the hotel, making it sound like a distant storm from the kitchen that Lucas had made his way into.

The kitchen looked like it was in the middle of a battle, getting ready for the onslaught of guests about to descend on the hotel. There would be private parties to attend to as well as the normal plates of reliefs, small bits of food to subdue appetites, distributed during the ball. The aromas were conflicting and overwhelming, and Lucas made his way through the kitchen as quickly as he could shuffle along, along the way pocketing a fillet knife left beside a freshly cooked suckling pig. He had other weapons, and didn't really need the knife, but it might come in handy. One couldn't have too many blades on a night like this.

A hefty Negro woman stood at a soup stove, stirring a thirty-gallon pot with a small wooden oar. She stopped Lucas, eyeing him suspiciously from head to toe. "You lost, sir?" The pot was loaded with chicken giblets and vegetables to make a stock. It smelled of home, of another, less dangerous time in Lucas's life. Food always seemed to trigger memories of the past, and it was a place he refused to get mired down in. Regret and loss waited for him upstairs. No need to hurry things along.

Lucas nodded, and forced his voice down so it sounded gravelly and weak. "Oh, I am, dear one. Could you be so kind and point me in the direction of the stairs?" He trembled to give the appearance of delirium and confusion. There was no way to know if he was successful or not.

"Oh, Lawd, you can't climb no rickety stairs. They's a service lift back there, then a regular new-fangled Otis out front they just put in. Joseph run that one. He be in full flight this night. Negro's been uppity ever since he done took that job. Got him out of the kitchen some, but he still have to eat wit us. You take the back one. It won't be full of nothin' but food and music-playin' minstrels. They got airs, too. But players is players no matter the suit they wear."

Lucas nodded. "That'd be just fine, ma'am. Just fine."

He couldn't keep the memories at bay, no matter how much he tried. Lucas had ridden in the elevator at the E. V. Haughwout department store in New York, the one at Broadway and Broome, when he was a young man, a few years before the war. It was a thrill riding up and down in the car, but a little frightening. Lucas hadn't known he didn't like small, closed spaces until that day. It was a fear he'd had little choice but to conquer, but to this day, closed-in places made him uncomfortable.

The Negro woman let go of the oar she'd been stirring with and took Lucas's arm as gently as she could. "Here, you let me shows you the way. We all get old one day, if we lucky."

Lucas smiled and shuffled along beside the woman, situating the fillet knife in his pocket the best he could.

Once at the elevator, the Negro cook saw Lucas into the car and closed the wrought iron gate. "You have a good time, there now, sir." She smiled, and he watched her disappear out of sight as he lurched upward toward the fourth floor.

The noise from the grand lobby was nothing compared to the noise coming down the shaft. Music began to play, and everyone shouted and clapped in thunderous applause. Lucas hated to miss the beginning of the ball, but he hoped not to make an entrance of any kind. By coming in from the service elevator, he would not be forced to participate in the reception line. He did not want to make Harrington Fetterman's acquaintance or have to explain his presence.

The Negro guard that waited outside the elevator had been paid, but the one by the back door was white, an agent of Grips's that could not be bought—at least with the time they had. The Negro guard had been employed by Zeke and instructed to turn his head upon seeing Lucas. It was an easy arrangement and part of the plan that had fallen into place without a hitch so far.

By the time the car came to a stop at the top of the building, Lucas was beginning to sweat. He worried that the *mascaro* in his mustache was going to run down his chin. He tapped it and felt nothing. There was no mirror to check himself in—which left him with no choice but to square himself, hunch over, and shuffle out through the gate.

The guard looked away as Lucas exited, then closed the gate, and sent the car back to the kitchen.

A waltz was playing, and Lucas had come into the ballroom behind the orchestra. He stopped in the shadows amid a garden of empty instrument cases to gather himself one last time. From where he stood, he could see a flurry of movement, men and women dancing, ringed by an audience of the most influential people in St. Louis and beyond.

The opening of the West had made a lot of men wealthy.

It was a promise that had seen Lucas to prison. He had lost sight of what was really important after the war and wanted nothing but the comforts of money. Unfortunately, he had trusted John Barlow far too much in their shared greed. It wasn't a mistake he'd make again.

Lucas took a deep breath and made his way through the instrument cases. He searched the waltzing pairs for his first sight of Charlotte Brogan. It was like looking for that first swallow in spring. You didn't know the season was there for good until you saw one of the insect-eating birds swoop over a pond.

It didn't take long. Charlotte's red hair stood out like a not-so-subtle flame set to light for an eternity. She was hard to miss, standing near the main entrance of the ballroom, wearing a multilayered beige dress. The sight of her nearly took Lucas's breath away.

Charlotte was engaged in a polite conversation with a man of equal height and stature. A shiver of rage spiraled up Lucas's neck, and he tasted a harsh bit of bile at the back of his throat. He hadn't known how he'd react when he saw John Barlow again for the first time. There was no pity or ounce of forgiveness in his body. All he wanted to do was kill the man. Kill him right then and there, in front of everyone. His hand dropped to his pocket where the fillet knife rested in wait.

He had to restrain himself. That was not the immediate plan. He had to get to Charlotte and see her to safety. What came after that was out of his hands. If things worked out as Lucas hoped, then John Barlow would see the inside of a prison cell of his own in the not so distant future. Death was too good for the scoundrel.

Lucas hoped that John Barlow would rot away in prison, nibbled on by rats and harassed by men like Carl the Hammer, for the rest of his miserable life.

FORTY-FIVE

"MAY I HAVE THIS DANCE?" THE QUIVER IN
Lucas's voice was real; no acting was needed. The last time
he had stood this close to Charlotte Brogan was in a court-
room, after the guilty verdict had been read. She had turned
her back to him and walked away without saying a word.
His letters to her went unanswered, leaving him to come to
the conclusion that he was dead to her. Just as dead as John
Barlow was to him.

The orchestra had started another waltz, a slow one that
Lucas didn't know the name of. The notes hung in the air,
just like his words.

John Barlow, Lanford Grips, or whatever name he had
put on himself for this day, had been pulled into a nearby
alcove by Harrington Fetterman and a short, disheveled
man, and was involved in a deep, hushed conversation. It
was the first chance Lucas had had to make his way to Charlotte. Barlow had stuck to her like he was attached at the hip.

Lucas knew there were eyes on him, that Charlotte's

every move was being watched. But the opposite was true, too. Lucas had his own sets of eyes, and weapons, strewn about the room. He hadn't walked in without cover, or a plan of his own.

Startled by the request, Charlotte turned her focus to Lucas. She had been engaged in a conversation of her own with another woman, who wore an airy white lace-ridden dress and looked motherly in a stately kind of way. Lucas had speculated that the woman was Fetterman's wife, since they'd arrived together.

A disturbed look crossed Charlotte's face. "I beg your pardon, sir?"

Words ganged up in Lucas's throat and refused to exit. It felt like he had swallowed a rock and it had gotten stuck just below his Adam's apple. He wanted nothing more than to just stand there and take in Charlotte's presence: touch her, kiss her, grab her hand, and run out of the ballroom as fast as he could. But he knew that was impossible—at the moment.

"Would you care to dance?" Lucas asked again. He was hunched forward, making himself about half a head shorter than Charlotte and still giving off the persona of an old man. The arch allowed him to peer above his glasses and make direct eye contact with her for the first time.

Charlotte gasped, and her face flushed red instantaneously. She brought an open fan up to her face and gave it a few hard swipes. "Are you capable of such a thing, sir?"

Lucas smiled. She was going to play along and not scream for help. It had been a consideration and fear once he exposed himself to her. He didn't know what her relationship truly was with Barlow on this day. She didn't look like a prisoner. But appearances, especially appearances at a fancy ball, were deceiving. Straut had warned him that she was bait. And he had to remember that. Charlotte Brogan's allegiance could be to Barlow. For all he knew, they were lovers. It was what John Barlow had always wanted.

"I am more than capable, ma'am," Lucas answered, offering his hand. His voice was still weak.

The woman next to Charlotte smiled. "How quaint. You must indulge the gentleman, Charlotte," she said.

Charlotte returned the smile, though it was forced, and unreadable. "Of course. I must." She took his hand with obvious restraint. Every muscle in her face was tight as a drum skin.

Lucas hated to give up the cane, but it had never been a consideration in his arsenal. "Do you mind, ma'am?" he asked, offering it to the woman in the lace dress.

"Oh, no, not all." She took the cane and stepped to the side.

Lucas took Charlotte's other hand, and they stood facing each other directly. The music played on and the floor was full of couples waltzing. Any one of the dancers could have been a model for a music box figurine.

"Are you ready?" Lucas asked Charlotte. His fingers tingled, and he was overwhelmed by her touch, by her firm grasp. "There's no looking back once we go." He glanced over his shoulder to the nearest door, thirty feet to their left. It led to stairs that would take them directly down to the grand lobby. Lucas guessed that Barlow would have men there, but he did not know for sure. Most everyone was in the ballroom now, so there'd be little chance of innocents getting caught in the cross fire if it came to that.

Charlotte nodded, never looking away from Lucas's gaze.

He drew in a breath and stepped slowly, as agedly as possible, onto the dance floor one slow shuffle at a time so he wouldn't draw Barlow's attention—or anyone else's for that matter.

"Why, sir, you are a most wonderful dancer," Charlotte said at the first turn. The tension fell away from her face almost immediately.

They were twenty feet from the door, moving slowly with the measured beat of the waltz.

"I've had plenty of time to practice," Lucas answered,

then said nothing more. He just gazed up to Charlotte, still not quite able to believe he had her in his hands.

Fifteen feet to the door.

Charlotte lowered her glance, then looked to the left and the right. "You're a brave man, dancing at your age. You could fall and break a leg."

"That's the least of my worries."

Five feet—and a line of people two deep—to the door. The band played on. Lucas's back was to Barlow, and he slowed, watching Charlotte's face closely for any sign that they had been made—or that she was going to bail on him, expose him and his plan while she still had the chance.

Age had been kind to her, and she was as beautiful to him as she always had been. Maybe more so. She took his breath away, made him remember a life that was lost, but she now held the hope of escape and a fresh start.

Lucas wanted nothing more than to let all of the darkness that existed between them fall away. But that was not possible. Not until they were free. Not until he knew he could really trust her.

Lucas pressed into the ring of watchers, the hopeless and the hopeful, and pulled Charlotte off the dance floor, straight to the door.

To his relief, it was unblocked. Straut's use of Grips's passwords had already cleared the way. The exit was open—as long as there wasn't someone standing on the other side of the door with a club or a gun. Lucas opened it slowly and peered cautiously around the corner. No one was there, and he stepped through, pulling Charlotte with him. The door eased closed behind them, echoing gently down the staircase. There had not been enough hands to make sure every part of the plan was properly executed. This was the main opening, the biggest chance at being caught or confronted.

Lucas stopped at the landing, before descending and leaning against the door below. He pulled out the fully loaded Colt Single Action Army.

Charlotte let her hand slip out of Lucas's, and in a blink, they met each other in a deep, soulful kiss—that could only last five seconds, but bridged a longer span of years. She tasted like yesterday, today, and tomorrow, and Lucas felt old longings begin to stir. Her body pressed against him, and he met it. It was like walking in the front door after a long trip away.

When Lucas pulled away, Charlotte said, "What took you so long?"

The lobby was nearly empty. Music from the ball drifted down from the fourth floor, distant and undisturbed. A Negro porter stood next to an empty brass luggage dolly, polishing it with a clean white rag, and a clerk, a white man with too much pomade in his black hair, moved about behind the reservation counter, unconcerned about much of anything.

Both men looked up as Lucas and Charlotte hurried down the stairs.

Lucas had given up the ploy of presenting himself as an aged gentleman at this point. His goal now was to get out of the hotel as fast as possible, with Charlotte in tow.

The fact that they hadn't been confronted concerned him. The escape felt too easy. But he wasn't going to stop until they reached the carriage that was waiting outside the door.

Halfway across the lobby, the clerk pulled a rifle out from under the counter and aimed it directly at Lucas and Charlotte. "Stop right there, Fume."

"Keep running," Lucas muttered under his breath, then drove his hand into his pocket, grabbed the fillet knife he'd poached from the kitchen, and flung it at the clerk almost before the man could blink.

A shot fired from behind them and from the clerk's rifle at the same time. The porter had covered them, and fired again, catching the clerk first in the shoulder, then just at the throat. The shots bounced the man backward into the wall.

Lucas's knife throw completely missed its target and fell to the ground.

The clerk's shot missed, whizzing between Lucas and Charlotte as they kept running. It wasn't like either of them had never been shot at before. The worst thing you could do was stop your momentum.

They reached the door and pushed through it without so much as a look over their shoulders.

The empty carriage stood just at the bottom of the steps. The door on the hotel side was standing wide open. Zeke Henry sat in the driver's seat wearing a proper driver's uniform, with a Winchester across his lap and a big smile on his face.

FORTY-SIX

TWO SHOTS CRACKED THROUGH THE AIR; sudden thunder on a clear evening. The sky was pink, roiling to red, as if sundown had washed the ceiling of the world with blood. The shots hit the dirt behind Lucas and Charlotte. The thuds and reports slowed them, caused Lucas to consider pulling Charlotte to the ground, but he kept running toward the carriage. He tightened his grip on her hand, intent on dragging her to safety. Running full out in her getup was impossible, but she was trying to escape as hard as she could.

The smile on Zeke's face disappeared, and he leaned to the side of the driver's seat. He was an easy target, a sitting duck. Making himself smaller was another impossibility.

"Don't look back." Out of the corner of his eye Lucas could see fear on Charlotte's face. He tried not to show her any of his own.

In a blink, Lucas and Charlotte were five feet from the carriage. Another shot rang out from behind them, and

Lucas cringed. His heart stopped. In that second, he was waiting to die. But the bullet didn't hit him or Charlotte, or anywhere near them.

When Lucas looked up again, preparing to dive into the carriage and pull Charlotte in with him, there was a man standing in between him and the destination. A Chinese man. One second the way was clear, then the next there was a man in traditional garb standing there.

Lucas came to a screeching stop.

"Bojack Wu," Charlotte whispered.

The name registered with Lucas only because Joe Straut had warned him of the man, and his skills. Consideration had been given to the foot-fighter's possible presence, but not at this moment.

Suddenly, the world went quiet. There was no distant music filtering out of the hotel, no commerce crowding the street. Only moments earlier, it was like the circus had come to St. Louis. Now the tent seemed to have fallen, and everyone in the crowd was holding his or her breath—or had run inside and was peering out the window. Even the horses in front of the carriage stood still as statues.

"Well, look at the wonderful couple, reunited and still trying to run off together."

The voice came from behind Lucas. It sent shivers up his back. Charlotte slipped her hand out of Lucas's, turned to her side, and looked up. Lucas followed suit, stopping so he could still see Bojack Wu in his peripheral vision.

Lucas stiffened, and settled himself. He was ready to die to save Charlotte, if it came to that. "I've been waiting for this moment for a long time, John. Or should I say Mr. Grips?"

Barlow was standing in the center of the second-floor balcony, surrounded by five angry Irishmen, all with their guns drawn on Lucas and Charlotte. "Call me what you want. It doesn't matter. What matters is that you're finally here. Now, be good boys and girls, and rid yourself of your weapons. We don't want any gunplay in front of the respectable citizenry of this great city, do we? You're surrounded, Lucas. Your circle of protection, if you want to call it that, has been disbanded. I'm a little surprised that you would rely on an untethered band of Negroes to see you out of town. But I guess your resources are sparse."

"I got here, didn't I?" Lucas said.

"You got here because *I wanted you* to get here," Barlow said. His lip turned up in a sneer. "On second thought, don't move a muscle. I'll be right down." He turned to a bulky Irishman wearing a dirty felt flop hat and said, "If they so much as cough, shoot them both in the head."

The man nodded and readjusted his aim at Charlotte.

Lucas didn't take his eyes off the balcony until Barlow disappeared. Beyond Bojack Wu, who stood expressionless, waiting like a cat to pounce, Zeke sat in the driver's seat. There was a fresh bullet in the side board, meant to get Lucas's attention, but at the moment, Zeke was safe and unharmed.

Lucas knew Barlow was serious and did as he was told, trying to process it at the same time. It was Barlow who had broken him out of prison, bought off some guard most likely, who had planned the whole escape. Lucas had thought it was Charlotte's father who arranged the escape. Especially after reading the note in the cache, with the money. He had thought he was rescuing Charlotte, that she was Barlow's captive. Now, he didn't what know what was going on.

Barlow walked out the door of the hotel alone and stopped just at the edge of the boardwalk. "You look a little confused, Lucas. You, too, dear Charlotte. Your ploy was so simple, you'd think I was a fool."

"Oh no," Charlotte said, "I never mistook you for a fool, John. I can call you John, can't I? I just took you for the petty, evil man that you are, and that you've always been."

Barlow shrugged. "No matter. Call me what you will. You can't hurt me anymore, Charlotte. I recovered from your rejection long ago. Besides, I answer to almost anything these days. But thank you for helping me bring Lucas here.

It's so good to see you two together again. It's just like old times, isn't it?"

"Why am I here, John?" Lucas asked through clenched teeth.

"Lucas, Lucas, Lucas, you always thought it was about you, didn't you? A charmer of women, the whole world at your fingertips, a great hero of the war. You could have had everything you wanted, but you refused to do business the way it needed to be done."

"I was not going to give you the profits of what was mine and my family's," Lucas said.

Barlow sighed dramatically. "It is yours no longer. It is Charlotte's. Or it will be once you're dead. And then it will be mine. Then I will have everything I have always wanted." Barlow stared coldly at Charlotte.

"I could never love a snake," Charlotte replied.

"Easier to love a dead man I suppose, but it is not your love that I want. Not now." Barlow glared back at her, then crossed his gloves in front of his body. He wore no guns or other apparent weapons. "You brought me what I'm truly after, Lucas. You are not the prize. You are only the lowly deliveryman. The man set to kill you in prison was the opportunity created for Zeke to rescue you. The business side of this transaction is just the icing on the cake." He smiled then and cast his gaze upward to Zeke. "Loyalty has always been your downfall. It is Mr. Henry who interests me. Not you. Not really. You proved difficult to kill. Not that I was surprised. After you escaped from Libertyville, I figured out that you would bring me what I wanted most. You're predictable, Lucas. Always have been. You went straight to the cache, and here you are, rescuing Charlotte."

Lucas knew better than to move an inch, but he had to restrain himself from lunging forward at Barlow, or turning to Zeke and screaming at him to run. "Your sister," Lucas said, woefully, with a deep gasp. It came to him then, why he and Zeke had been put together.

"You're quick," Barlow said. "Yes, Lucas, my sister. The one that lives every day and doesn't know where or who she is. I wanted to look her killer in the face myself. Justice wasn't done when they sent him to prison instead of hanging him, and I want to see it done for myself, just like I want to see you die, so I can know for sure that the deed is done."

"What you want is vengeance," Charlotte said. "It's always been what you have wanted. Retribution for a perceived wrong. Your sister is not dead. And it was your father who beat her senseless, not this man. Everybody knows that but is too afraid of him to say so." Charlotte pointed upward at Zeke, whose face was covered in fearful perspiration.

"My father is a powerful man and incapable of such things, Charlotte. You know he would never harm one of his own. He buried one daughter, a dear nun, and now another is near mental death every day. Justice is demanded," Barlow said.

"Incapable? I know what he's capable of—and you, too. Any man who would have his hands cut off to send another man to prison is a madman," Charlotte sneered. "It is hard to tell what your father could do, senator or not. That hardly makes him a saint."

Barlow shrugged. "We all make sacrifices for the cause, Charlotte."

"There is no cause, John. Not anymore. The war is over," Lucas interjected. He gazed at Charlotte. He had no idea what she had just been talking about, until he glanced at Barlow's stiff gloved hands. "You greedy, sick bastard." It was a pair of hands that had sent him to prison. "I always said you'd do anything to be the wealthiest man alive, but I never thought you'd go this far."

Barlow laughed loudly.

Zeke shifted in his seat, drawing Lucas's attention. "I loved her, and she loved me. Ain't no justice needed for that."

"Shut up, boy. You shut up right now. You hear me? I don't want to have you killed here and now. I want you to suffer long and hard, just like my sister has, but I could easily lose my temper and give the sign for you to be shot right now, you keep goin' on. You understand, or do I have to have the beatin' start now?"

"That's your plan? Kill us and torture Zeke?" Lucas asked.

"Something like that," Barlow answered. "But not until the paperwork is complete."

"Paperwork?" Lucas asked.

"Yes, the paperwork. Dear Charlotte is the beneficiary of your father's estate upon your death, and she's going to sign it over to me. Aren't you, Charlotte?"

"I'm sorry, Lucas," Charlotte muttered. "I didn't mean for it to turn out this way. Once I knew he was alive, I was caught up in his web, and it was too late to break free of him. I knew he would bring you here. He had to, and I had to stay alive to see a chance of escaping. Both of us. I wanted us both to be free of him . . . forever."

"Shut up, Charlotte!" Barlow screamed. "Shut up now, and come to me so you don't get hurt."

"I will never come to you," Charlotte said, as she slipped her hand inside her dress.

Sweat dripped down Lucas's nose. The sky overhead was red with anger, and the street had remained vacant, silent. He could see Zeke's shadow, sitting still in the driver's seat, unmoving—as if he had surrendered and was ready to die.

Almost like a warning, or a signal from Libertyville, a flock of pigeons took to the sky, in a great flutter from the roof of the dry goods store across the street from the St. Louis Hotel.

Bojack Wu flinched; a reaction to Charlotte's movement and the sudden appearance of the birds.

Lucas knew it was time to act, even though it might be too late. He didn't know what Charlotte would do—they hadn't had time to discuss his plan. She didn't know what was coming next. She didn't know that Joe Straut and another gang of men, mostly Negroes, had penetrated Barlow's circle because Straut knew the pattern of passwords. He would just walk through like he was one of Barlow's men, and no one would know the difference.

Gunshots erupted. The Irishmen on the second-floor balcony were caught unaware by ten Negroes, all holding rifles on them with instructions to shoot over their heads. Lucas wanted as little bloodshed as possible.

The Irishmen were ordered to lay down their weapons. The command echoed downward, and a look of panic crossed Barlow's face.

Charlotte didn't seem to be fazed by the gunshots. There was a focused, angry look on her face as she pulled a knife out from her dress, reared back, and prepared to launch it toward Barlow.

She never had the chance.

Bojack Wu countered her intention with a knife throw of his own. Barlow's valet, the man who acted as his hands, produced a machete from underneath his tunic and threw it silently, with pinpoint accuracy, slicing into Charlotte Brogan exactly between the shoulder blades. It sounded like the slap of a sharp axe piercing soft wood.

Charlotte was caught by surprise, the air taken out of her throat as she tumbled forward and fell to the ground in a heap of fancy silk and blood.

Without regard for his own life, Lucas spun, reached inside his coat, pulled his gun, and emptied all six bullets into Bojack Wu's body before the Chinaman had time to react.

A surprised look came to Bojack Wu's face as he collapsed to the ground. Death came before his head hit the earth.

John Barlow screamed like a mother hen witnessing the death of her child. He turned to run, to make a break for it—and came face-to-face with Joe Straut and his Open Top Colt, set and ready to fire.

"You move an inch, and you're a dead man, Mr. John

Barlow," Straut said. "I always wondered what your real name was. Now I know."

"Don't kill him," Lucas ordered, seeing the rage in Straut's face.

Straut nodded, but Barlow didn't comply. He started to run past Straut. "You always were a coward, and a second-rate sergeant," Barlow said.

Straut spun the Colt and smashed the grip upside Barlow's head, sending him straight to the ground. "That's for Finney Deets. He was a good man and didn't deserve what you had done to him. You're going to jail for a long, long time."

More of Straut's Negro recruits made their way into the street, bringing Barlow's men with them, hands up, surrendering.

Lucas looked up at the driver's seat, to Zeke, who sat there unscathed, his rifle pointed at Barlow. "You best get out of here, Zeke. Now's the time to go. You're still an escaped convict. This doesn't change that."

"But you be free now," Zeke said.

"Yes, I'll be free. But you have to go. You linger too long, and there won't be anything I can do to help you," Lucas said. He held Zeke's gaze for a long second, then turned his attention to Charlotte.

Her eyes were open, and a thin smile was pasted on her pale face. "I should have killed him a long time ago," Charlotte said, as Lucas eased her head into his lap.

"Then I would have had to break you out of prison," he said, trying to laugh, but not able to find it in himself.

"I'm sorry," Charlotte said. Her voice was weak and her eyes were starting to dim.

"No, no, you have nothing to be sorry for."

"I was afraid of losing everything. Afraid I'd drown with gold around my neck," Charlotte said. "I didn't love you enough to break free of him . . ."

"Be calm. There'll be a doctor any second."

"It won't do any good, Lucas. I waited too long."

"You can't die. I just found you again," Lucas said, as a tear filled his eye and dropped to the ground. "We can see the world together, just like we always dreamed of doing. Just you and me. No hidden agenda, no spy games, just for the fun of it, just because it's there for us to see. We still haven't walked the streets of Paris."

"Good-bye, Lucas," Charlotte whispered, then began to cough. "I knew you'd come for me. I always knew you would."

"But I couldn't save you," Lucas said, as Charlotte drifted away, and died in his arms. "I couldn't save you."

FORTY-SEVEN

TWO BURLY TEAMSTERS UNLOADED THE COF-
fin from their wagon and carried it on their shoulders to the
waiting train.

Little Ling stood solemnly next to the open door of the
boxcar, her head down, as the men secured the coffin in
place. She was a wearing a long white silk dress. Her black
hair was free of the pigtail, and she looked more like a
daughter of wealth instead of a wayward Chinese girl more
accustomed to emptying chamber pots than traveling alone
on a train.

Lucas held back until the men walked away. He approached
slowly, trying not to look at the coffin. "Hello, Little Ling, it
looks like you're ready to go."

Little Ling nodded. "Yes, Mr. Lucas, I am ready to see
Missy home now."

"I appreciate it. I'm sure Charlotte would want to be
buried next to her mother at Harper's Belle, instead of here
where she had nothing but bad memories."

"Yes, I think so, too." Little Ling paused. "What about you, Mr. Lucas?"

"I hope to not be buried for a long time to come." He tried to smile, but he still hadn't found a reason to.

"No, no, I sorry. What happens to you now?"

"I'm free to go. I might have to come back for Barlow's trial, but that will be weeks if not months from now. I need to figure out how to be free again. Stand on my own two feet, as they say."

"You no go back to Tennessee?"

"No, there's nothing for me there now. My family's all gone, and I have rid myself of all that tied me to the business I once had there. Mr. Fetterman and his lawyer made me a fair deal. There is nothing in this world tying me down or holding me there now."

"I'm sorry Missy couldn't see this day now," Little Ling said.

"She's free now, too," Lucas said. "All of us are. Well, most all of us. You have a safe trip. And you know how to get ahold of me if you ever need anything?"

Little Ling nodded. "I'll be fine, Mr. Lucas. I think once I see Missy home that it might be time to see home myself. It has been a long time since I set foot in the Valley of the Sleeping Dragon. I have decided that is where I want to die."

"Let's hope that doesn't come for a long, long time," Lucas said. "You have a safe journey now. And thank you. Thank you for looking after Miss Charlotte for me."

He turned then to go, and came face-to-face with Joe Straut. "I figured you'd be off, too, since you're cleared of any wrongdoing yourself."

Joe Straut forced a smile. "Those three folks were already dead, killed by the Chinese. All Deets and I did was put them under the bridge instead of dispose of them how Mr. Grips wanted us to. My only crime was not tellin' anyone, but how things worked out here set me free of that. I just had to write a statement for the trial sayin' as much. I'm not sure where to go now. Cities make me nervous. But it seems to me a fella can get lost in a city as much as he can alone in the mountains."

"I suppose so," Lucas said.

"What about you?" Straut asked.

"I'm riding on. Not everything is taken care of. Not sure that it ever will be."

"Zeke?"

"Yes, Zeke."

"He's a good man. Don't seem the kind to do what they say he did."

"He'd be happy to hear you say that," Lucas said. He extended his hand, and they shook heartily. "Thanks for all you did. I owe you my life."

"Well, sir," Joe Straut said, "that there's a kind thing to say, but I couldn't keep that woman out of the way of Bojack Wu's blade. Have to carry that with me for the rest of my days, I 'spect." He stared at the coffin, but Lucas didn't follow his gaze.

"None of us could save her, Straut. I'd been trying all my life."

The sun had dropped below the horizon, and the sunset had lit the sky ablaze with color. Pinks, yellows, and a little red reaching out to the east. Spring was in full force. The road was lined with purple and white violets, and the dogwoods bloomed white. The air was fragrant and fresh with possibilities. But none of that mattered to Lucas Fume as he rode as fast as he could west of the big river. He searched diligently for the silhouette of a big man, on a horse, waiting for him.

Finally, just as the gray sky was about to turn black, Lucas spied Zeke, standing on the side of the road, next to his horse.

"Been here long?" Lucas asked, sidling up to the Negro.

"A little whiles," Zeke answered. He was dressed in new clothes from head to toe, including a new wool Stetson that fit his head like it had always been there. "You sure you wants to ride with me, Mistuh Lucas? Law's gonna be on my tail, and you associatin' with me can't lead to nothin' but trouble."

"Well, Zeke Henry," Lucas said, settled into the new saddle on his bay gelding, "if you don't want to ride alone, it sure it would be my honor to ride alongside you. I think there's more out west waiting for us than just trouble."

Zeke smiled so broadly it almost lit up the coming darkness. He took a deep breath, climbed up on his horse, settled in, and pulled up next to Lucas.

"Now, let's go see what all the fuss is about, and have us an adventure or two," Lucas said, urging his horse to get a move on.

"If you say so, Mistuh Lucas. If you say so."

They both broke into a short trot then. Neither man bothered to look back as they urged their horses to run.

Lucas and Zeke rode as fast as they could, for as long as they could, before the darkness of night forced them to stop.

ABOUT THE AUTHOR

Larry D. Sweazy (larrydsweazy.com) is a two-time
WWA Spur Award winner; a two-time, back-to-back
winner of the Will Rogers Medallion Award; a winner
of the inaugural Elmer Kelton Book Award; and a
Best Books of Indiana award winner. He was also
nominated for a Short Mystery Fiction Society
(SMFS) Derringer Award in 2007. Larry has published more than fifty nonfiction articles and short
stories and is also the author of the Josiah Wolfe,
Texas Ranger, western series (published by Berkley)
and a modern-day thriller, *The Devil's Bones* (published by Five Star).

He lives in Indiana with his wife, Rose, two dogs,
and a cat.

Don't miss the best
Westerns from Berkley

LYLE BRANDT
PETER BRANDVOLD
JACK BALLAS
J. LEE BUTTS
JORY SHERMAN
DUSTY RICHARDS

M10G0610

Penguin Group (USA) Online

What will you be reading tomorrow?

Patricia Cornwell, Nora Roberts, Catherine Coulter,
Ken Follett, John Sandford, Clive Cussler,
Tom Clancy, Laurell K. Hamilton, Charlaine Harris,
J. R. Ward, W.E.B. Griffin, William Gibson,
Robin Cook, Brian Jacques, Stephen King,
Dean Koontz, Eric Jerome Dickey, Terry McMillan,
Sue Monk Kidd, Amy Tan, Jayne Ann Krentz,
Daniel Silva, Kate Jacobs . . .

You'll find them all at
penguin.com

*Read excerpts and newsletters,
find tour schedules and reading group guides,
and enter contests.*

Subscribe to Penguin Group (USA) newsletters
and get an exclusive inside look
at exciting new titles and the authors you love
long before everyone else does.

PENGUIN GROUP (USA)
penguin.com

M224G0909